MW01060083

ICE CREAM FOR FREAKS

A novel by

DeJon

Q-Boro Books
WWW.QBOROBOOKS.COM

Published by Q-Boro Books

Copyright © 2005 by DeJon

ISBN: 0-9753066-93

First Printing August 2005
10 9 8 7 6 5 4 3
Library of Congress Control Number: 2005904824

This is a work of fiction. It is not meant to depict, portray or represent any particular real persons. All the characters, incidents and dialogues are the products of the author's imagination and are not to be construed as real. Any references or similarities to actual events, entities, real people, living or dead, or to real locales are intended to give the novel a sense of reality. Any similarity in other names, characters, entities, places and incidents is entirely coincidental.

Cover Copyright © 2005 by Q-BORO BOOKS all rights reserved
Cover Layout & Design – Sublime Visuals
Proofreader – Melissa Forbes

Q-Boro Books
Jamaica, Queens NY 11431
WWW.QBOROBOOKS.COM
(For store orders, author information and contact information, please visit our website.)

Printed in Canada

Dedications

I dedicate this book to my grandmother, Mrs. Sallie Mariah Hammond, who passed away on January 18, 2004 at a young age of 78. Her final resting place was Westminster, South Carolina at Pleasant Hill Baptist Church cemetery. I'm sorry that she didn't live to see my first work materialize but I believe that she somehow knows.

I would like to thank my mother Charlotte G. Patterson, who taught me a love of books and encouraged my passion for writing. She always taught me at a very young age to pursue any goals and aspirations I set my mind to.

My pops, James who repeatedly told me, "When you make moves you make sure you do it strong."

I would like to dedicate this book to my son DeJonn Marcus, 6, and my daughter Julisa Asia, 3.

I also would like to give crazy props to all my people who know what time it is from the get-go. I don't have to mention any names, because you know who you are. Peace!

Last but not least, I would like to dedicate this book to my brother James, and my sisters LaShondra, Shalondon, and Shannon.

And a crazy shout out to Mark Anthony, who recognized the realness and the potential of *Ice Cream For Freaks.*

Linda, don't think I forgot about you (smile).

(CHAPTER ONE)

"Yo, you know what time it iz," Ice whispered. He said it with enough cold-hearted venom to cause the unsuspecting victim to have a chill run down his back even though it was a warm, muggy night. The victim, whose street name happened to be Preme, short for Supreme, momentarily thought maybe it was somebody from his click trying to test his style to see if he would fold like an envelope. But Preme's worst fears were confirmed when he felt the cold steel barrel of a gun pressed tightly behind his ear. Big Preme, as he was called by people who feared and respected him, first thought that if word got out that he got taken like a chump, especially in his own stomping grounds, it would be a wrap. He would lose respect, his comfortable rep, and his self-esteem. Never mind the fact that he had a pair of newborn beautiful twin daughters. To Preme, his reputation came first before anything else. He had to take a chance, no matter how slim, and try to flip the script back on this would be stick-up kid.

Ice, being a vet to the streets and his art form, sensed a slight hesitation on Preme's part. Ice had heard stories of overly cocky stick-up kids having the tables flipped on them by their victims because of their sloppy ways. In more than one case, the guy getting bagged couldn't accept the fact that someone had the audacity to try to come off, especially if he thought of himself as wild, or he had an ill crew backing him. Usually the guy holding the heat thought that a gun was all it took to catch wreck, but sometimes this proved to be a fatal miscalculation.

Ice quickly swung his chrome three pound seven (.357) Smith and Wesson gat into the side of Preme's head. The blow was hard enough to form a lumpy speed knot, but wasn't thrown with enough force to knock him out. Ice didn't want this bitch ass nigga to fall out on the street in public like this so that he would end up having to go through Preme's pockets, taking a chance of someone peeping his get down. As soon as Preme heard "pap" and felt the stinging sensation on the side of his head, all his thoughts went blank except to give this guy whatever he wanted.

"Okay, okay. You got it, man. Just take it," Preme stuttered as he slid off his thirty-six inch platinum chain with the iced out Jesus headpiece attached.

"Don't think that I didn't peep da bracelet," Ice spoke hoarsely. "I hope you're not trying to play me," Ice added.

"No, I forgot I had it on," Preme replied, his eyes dancing wildly for any sign of help. Preme realized for the first time how shook he was when his shaking hands couldn't unclasp the triple lock on his matching diamond platinum bracelet. It seemed like it was taking forever for him to get the piece off, and any second he knew he was going to get another taste of Ice's gun for taking so long. He finally slipped his precious "Jacob the Jeweler" shines into Ice's palm.

"Now turn your motherfucking pockets out bitch ass nigga," Ice demanded, irritated that he was taking so long to wrap up his business. "What? Only a couple hundred dollars and a bullshit played out Sprint phone!" Ice said. "I knew you was a fronting ass wannabe baller. I should push your wig back on G.P. (General Principle)," Ice growled.

Preme's whole body was trembling now and all he could force his mouth to say was "I.. I... I," in a dry whiney voice. Even more irritating than only having come off with minor money, was this supposed gangster acting like a female being caught on her period without a pad. Ice gave his victim two quick short hits on the bridge of his nose with the butt of his gun. Preme fell to his knees holding his smashed nose while curling up like a cheese doodle. As Ice calmly walked away, he had to take one last look at the man who had stood two inches over him only minutes ago, and now was balled up like a newborn baby. The scene brought a little smirk to Ice's face as he turned the corner.

(CHAPTER TWO)

Ice parlayed down a dark side street walking normally just in case his vic happened to call the police or flag down a blue and white who happened to be passing by. You could never tell in the hood. He had seen it too many times, when a so-called gangster had his back against the wall or the beef they cooked up got too sizzling hot to handle. They would be the first ones to run to the police screaming for help to cool things down. Ice hated and despised those type of wannabe thugs with a passion. Be a man and handle your own. "Fuck the police" was Ice's motto.

Anybody taking a glance at Ice's six-foot, slim figure with the baby face, would never consider him or see him as one of the illest gunslingers around. Ice loved people to judge him on face value alone, especially the guys. That's why his so-called pretty boy looks always gave him the advantage in most situations.

Ice, government tag (name) Nathaniel Wilson, was twenty, but he could easily pass for sixteen or seventeen, mostly because of his hairless face. He only had a pencil-thin mustache that never seemed to thicken. Nathaniel had always been tall and extra slim for his age. He had a complexion that his jealous schoolmates called piss colored. He also had what was coined in the ghetto as "good hair" and "pretty eyes" because of their light color. The color conscious hood rat females were always quick to point out those specific features when first meeting him. Nathaniel really didn't care about what genetics gave him, but he didn't mind either. Later in life his looks would give him as much pussy and valuables as he wanted. Valuables being Ice's first choice, and hood rats being the second, because they were always plentiful and overly impressed in the hood. M.O.B. was a saying Ice always quoted. "Money over bitches," he always reminded his boys.

Ice turned down 122nd Avenue, two blocks away from where his triple black Acura 3.5 RL whip was parked. He had to admit that he rode clean with the twenty-five percent limo tints keeping him on the low low. He had twenty-inch Hartage rims with low profile tires. The chrome rims were sparkling under the moonlight. Ice deactivated the alarm system and climbed into his baby. The first thing he did was turn on his sound system. DJ Clue's newest mixed CD flooded the interior of the Acura.

Even though it was a hot and sticky night in Queens, New York, Ice wore a light green and black army camouflage suit with a matching du-rag to conceal his face. He wore his black Timberland boots with the strings loosely laced up. He took off his jacket and threw it on the crisp black leather seat in the back. Ice was left wearing a white wife beater. He then took his newest shines and placed them in a black velvet pouch. He then put the pouch, along with his gat, under the passenger seat in a hidden compartment. Ice had built a simple hiding place under the seat by cutting out a square hole and covering the space with another piece of metal with a hidden latch. He pulled back the floorboard carpet covering his stash.

After getting situated, Ice began heading toward the bootleg, after hour's spot for a bottle before heading home. It was a long and unexciting day. Ice wanted some Hennessy to even things out. Fifteen minutes later he pulled up to an old nondescript corner house which had a tall, rusted, metal fence around it. Ice walked toward the back fence and pushed a button that he had to stick his hand through the gate to reach. The house was once a respectable average-looking house in Queens until the new owners took over and turned it into a bootleg liquor spot for when the regular liquor stores were closed. There was always some kind of dice or card game going on in the smoke filled, back room.

A couple of seconds later a middle aged woman came strolling out the back door. "Oh, Ice. Where you been hiding at? I haven't seen you for a minute," she replied smiling and revealing one too many cups of coffee stained teeth.

"You know me, Miss Teal. I'm here and there trying to maintain. You know how the game goes when you're trying to do your thang," Ice responded, smiling back with his most sincere smile.

"So, Ice, what will you have tonight?" Miss Teal asked.

"I feel like dat Hen-Rock," Ice said while handing her a twenty. She came back with a pint of Hennessy and a plastic cup.

Ice got into his car, poured himself a shot, and lit up a Newport. He turned up the music so he could finish listening to the CD. The car clock read one forty-five, so it was about that time.

(CHAPTER THREE)

The first thing that Preme heard was a barking sound. He instantly looked up, fearing that maybe his attacker had come back. He was relieved to see an old woman holding a dog leash, which was attached to a small dog who appeared to be a cross between a poodle and a sewer rat.

"Are you alright?" The elderly woman asked. Preme slowly rose to his feet looking around to see if anyone had witnessed his humiliating situation. "Child, did you fall down and hurt yourself? You want me to call the ambulance?" The woman replied with an overly amount of concern in her voice.

Preme suddenly realized a slight trickle of blood was easing from his nose down to his shirt. Already embarrassed enough, Preme replied, "I'm good." Not wanting to look her in the face any longer, he quickly rose to his feet and headed back toward his apartment building. As Preme walked away, he could hear the old lady say, "Dem children sure are wild nowadays." He reached the door to his lobby and fumbled for his keys. Preme was hoping and praying that he didn't run into anyone he knew or didn't know. There was no way he could explain the way he looked at the moment. Anyone in the street knew if a person was always seen rocking their shines, and all of a sudden that person was bare, it could mean one or two possible scenarios. You started smoking and had to pawn your shit, or you got robbed.

Preme finally reached his third floor apartment and entered. His girlfriend, Mia, was sitting on the couch watching B.E.T. and trying to get in the last puff of her Philly roach. Mia was a shapely woman in her twenties with an olive-skinned complexion. When first looking at her, she reminded you of an Egyptian goddess of royalty. She had her long jet-black hair pulled neatly back in a ponytail accentuating her flawless bone structure even more. She had on a pair of Preme's boxer shorts with an oversized white T-shirt rolled up in a knot in the back showing off her diamond studded cat belly pendent in her navel.

Mia first words were, "Baby, where's the food? You know how hungry I get when I smoke weed." Then it hit her slow moving mind when she saw blood droplets on his shirt and his jewelry was missing. She vividly remembered him taking it off the glass coffee table before leaving. Preme would always tell her, "Jewelry always sets off the right gear even more."

"Oh shit, Preme. What happened? Why are your pants all wet?" Mia asked. Once again Mia's thought process was a step behind when she saw Preme look down at the front of his jeans and the shocked look on his face. His expression said it all. He had gotten himself into a little street drama and pissed on himself. Mia wished that she could have taken back what she blurted out and at least acted like she didn't notice that one particular degrading fact.

"Bitch, shut da fuck up and bring me da phone in the bathroom."

Mia knew this was the time to keep her mouth shut and follow the instructions. His manhood was on the line and she didn't want him proving it to her tonight. After a hot shower and placing all his clothes in a black trash bag, Preme started dialing Half a Dread.

"Yo, Dread, get you and your cuz over here right now," Preme said. "What! Fuck dem ally cat bitches," Preme shouted into the receiver before hanging up.

Forty-five minutes later the doorbell rang. Preme, now dressed in a pair of fresh Phat Farm jeans and a matching hoodie, looked through the peephole, while holding a black Desert Eagle gun at his side.

"What's going on?" Half a Dread asked as Preme swung open the door. He got the nickname Half a Dread because of how he kept his dreads. The sides of his head were completely shaved and the top of his head held cinnamon colored dreads that hung down to his shoulders. He kept his dreads wrapped in a red, black, and green silk headscarf. He always wore a different fish net tank top shirt revealing a bony frame with stab and bullet wounds. He wore a heavy, thick, Italian gold link chain attached to a medallion. The medallion was a solid gold replica of an Uzi machine gun. His deep, dark skin made the gold seem even shinier. He wore baggy jeans that always seemed to be way too big for him, even by hip-hop standards. Dread's outfit was completed with brown Reebok sandals showing his ashy feet. At first glance you might think that he was out kicking flour somewhere.

Standing next to Half a Dread was his cousin Rico. Rico was a short and stocky man, standing five feet, five inches tall with a small afro. He also was dark skinned, though not as black as Dread. Rico's facial expressions never gave anyone any idea of what he was thinking or planning to do. He was a quiet person by nature, which some people automatically mistook for him not being too bright. But Rico was just the opposite, always studying and observing, paying close attention to small details.

Both men stepped into the apartment and took a quick look around. Preme's residence was spacious and laid out with a cream-colored imported leather sofa with matching love seats. There was a sixty-two inch flat screen TV next to a fully stocked mini bar. Located on the opposite side of the living room was a hundred and twenty gallon aquarium tank specially and expertly mounted on the wall with a solid refined oak base for extra support. The tank was neatly decorated with colorful assorted underwater decorations. The soft blue fluorescent light showed off a pair of stunning Japanese fighting fish. A couple of feet away from Preme's prized possessions stood a state of the art sound system with surround sound hooked up throughout the apartment.

"You gonna have to take your footwear off by the door before you go any farther in my place," Preme said. He wanted his cream-colored plush carpet to remain free of any foreign substances. This was the first time Dread and Rico were in Preme's apartment. He usually met them downstairs, so Rico figured it must be serious if he let them up in his place.

Meanwhile Mia was in the back bedroom pretending to be asleep, not wanting to be around Preme when he was in one of his "I don't give a fuck" moods. A minute later all three men were at the mini bar, each preparing their own drinks.

Preme spoke once everyone was situated. "I'm gonna get straight to the motherfucking point. Some kid had the nerve to try to get paid off of me. Can you believe that shit? Me! Big Preme," he boasted. Can you imagine? He must have been on buck naked (P.C.P.) or something. He then realized at the last moment who I was and bounced, without anything except knowing dat he fucked up."

Preme took a deep breath and continued. "I want this piece of shit found and brought to me."

Dread spoke up after taking a long sip of his hundred proof white label drink. "Did you peep who he was, or what he looked like?"

"Nah, he had something covering his face and scurried away in the shadows like a motherfucking cockroach does when the lights come on." Preme now stood up and said, "The streets are always talking like a bitch. Find out what you need to find out real quick and there's an extra bonus in it for the both of you."

Half a Dread finished the last of his strong drink and gave Preme some dap before heading toward the front door. Dread was just a street soldier who took orders without asking too many questions. He really didn't care about details as long as he got dat paper. Rico, on the other hand, was hanging onto Preme's every word and studying his movements. Something didn't seem quite right with Preme's story, but he couldn't place his finger on it. Rico planned to find out the real deal later.

After the duo left, Preme double locked his door and put a steel bar behind it before heading to bed. Preme was glad they were gone before they realized how shook he was. If Dread and Rico knew what really jumped off, they would definitely lose respect for him. Also, they might try to play him sooner or later. Preme knew he had to get whoever did this to him as quickly as possible. He knew from experience that he had to find his attacker and have him wearing a toe tag before he started flapping his gums.

(CHAPTER FOUR)

Ice turned down the music as he circled his block twice. It was a regular habit of his to make sure no one was laying in the cut waiting for him. Ice lived in a semi-quiet neighborhood in Queens called the Heights. When he was sure that everything was okay, he pulled into the driveway of a modest looking house with a neatly trimmed lawn. Ice retrieved his newest shines, his ratchet, and his Hennessy, and turned on his car alarm. He walked toward the back of the house, where he had his own private entrance. Ice turned on the light switch in the hallway and stepped into his basement apartment.

His grandparents lived a quiet life upstairs and he shared the bills in exchange for privacy. Ice considered his place all right for someone living by himself. He had a thirty-two inch Panasonic TV with a DVD player, VCR, and a cable box sitting on top. He had an average dark green sofa with a single matching recliner. He had hardwood floors, which he cleaned on a regular basis. Above the sofa was a glass encased framed picture of Tupac on stage at a concert somewhere. On top of the photograph were the words "Only God Can Judge Me." Next to the kitchen was a small dinette set with four chairs around it. On the wooden table sat a chessboard with glass pieces already set up. Right across from that was his bedroom. Ice knew his set up was all right because so far no chicken heads had complained. Ice flopped down on his sofa and kicked off his Tims. He then pressed play on his VCR. Tupac's first movie role, "Juice," appeared on the screen. Ice sat back sipping on his favorite drink while enjoying the movie.

Half an hour later, and feeling a little tipsy, Ice started thinking about his mother. He remembered growing up in a regular household with both of his parents, and his older sister, now a Chicago housing cop. He remembered him and his sister repeatedly hearing his mother debase, humiliate, and mentally abuse their father to a point where he just picked up and left one night. On any given day and time both siblings could hear their mother say, "You fucking wimp, how could you let your supervisor make you work on your day off, when you know you had work to do on the house?" Or, "You spineless maggot, how you let him take your parking space?" Or, "You're not a man. A real man can keep his wife satisfied." The remarks were as endless as the venom they held.

Little Nathaniel vividly recalled one evening when his mother sat him down after his father left. She said, "Nat, I never want you to be like your no good dad. He let society and every white person trample on his manhood. That's why he left, because he couldn't stand to look at what he had become, an empty eggshell of a man. When you're weak, it spreads like cancer affecting everyone around you. Mrs. Wilson wasn't having that," his mother replied speaking about herself in the third person.

Mrs. Wilson then sat close to her only son and said, "From now on, I'm going to call you Ice. I want you to respect and protect what is yours at all costs. Any male or female standing in the way of you getting yours, have no feeling for them because they don't give a damn about you. I want your heart to be like a block of ice with no emotions, like a real black man should be."

Later on Nathaniel, now known as Ice, started running with a crew of kids who called themselves B.M.W, (Brooklyn Most Wanted). Even though Nathaniel was from Queens, he preferred to go to school and hang out in Brooklyn. B.M.W. harassed girls on the train, boosted anything of value, smoked weed, and every thing else a crew of wild teenagers with no parental control would do in N.Y.C., known as the "Rotten Apple." Some of the guys' older family members were into armed robberies. The older brothers and cousins would often say, "Fuck dat snatching chains and shit. Dis is where the real dough's at." Ice finally convinced one of the older guys to let him roll with them on one of their juxxes.

From then on, Ice was hooked with the thrill of easy money and the feel of power he felt with a gat in his hand. Ice loved the way his victims' eyes bulged out of their heads when they saw the gun pointed in their grill. The older guys saw that Ice was a natural and put him on to their many different tactics dealing with various situations. Eventually Ice decided to do his own thing and go solo. Some of the guys crumbled under pressure and started snitching on each other. "I could never drop a dime on myself," Ice would jokingly say, but he meant it from the heart. Ice took some of the street craft he learned from the older guys, added shit on his own, and got down for his crown.

(CHAPTER FIVE)

Ring, ring, ring, ring. Ice sleepily reached for the cordless phone. "Who da fuck is dis?" Ice wondered who could be calling so early.

"Wake up sleepy head. Dis is Shareese," the voice came back from the other end.

"Wuz up, baby girl. What time is it?" Ice asked.

"It's nine. I'm at da train station. You still want me to drop by and do your hair?" she asked.

"Yeah, yeah, come around the back. I'll see you in a half. Peace!"

Ice turned on the TV, watching nothing in particular, just to have some background sounds. He lit up a Newport while he straightened up a little bit. Thirty-five minutes later, he heard a faint knock on the back door.

"Damn, your eyes are mad red. Did you just break day or something?" Shareese asked while smiling.

In stepped a pretty girl, standing five feet, seven inches with a caramel skin tone. She had the eyes of a young woman who was still trying to find her place in the world, but wasn't as naive as she looked. Her older brothers were constantly putting her onto the way guys tried to game females just to get the panties, or use them for whatever they needed at the time.

Ice and Shareese both gave each other hugs like old friends normally do. Ice had liked Shareese ever since he met her during freshman year in high school. She was a little different from most girls he was used to dealing with. For one, she wasn't overly impressed with his light-skinned complexion and green eyes. They clicked more like brother and sister than anything else. They used to hang out at one of the many rooftops in B.K. They would tell each other what they wanted for their futures. Shareese wanted to be a fashion designer and famous hair stylist. Ice wanted to make it to the NBA.

One night while up on the rooftop, puffing trees and talking as usual, they both seemed to just look at each other as if to say, "It's about dat time." Ice laid his brand new Polo jacket and rocked her as best as a virgin could. He always thought that she had a little more experience than him, until the awkward movements of their bodies revealed the truth. It was her first time as well. The second time around went smoothly once they got their rhythm down pat. The both tried to go at it as boyfriend and girlfriend, but that lasted only three months. They decided it would be best to remain friends. Since then Ice and Shareese both had their share of boyfriends and girlfriends, but they still did their thing on Pebble Beach every now and then. They shared a common bond, and made a vow that no one could ever break it.

"So wuz up, Ice? Dat chicken head must have put it on you proper like to have you looking tore up from the floor up," Shareese said jokingly while giving Ice a playful shot to the stomach.

"Nah, it wuzn't nothing like that. I wuz just taking care of bizz, getting my pockets up," Ice answered. "Yo, baby girl, you want something to drink or eat?" He asked.

"I'm straight. I stopped by Mickey Dee's and had a little sum-tin. I'll take a loosie though," she replied while reaching for the pack of cigarettes on the table. After sharing a Newport, Shareese took off her DKNY backpack and proceeded to braid Ice's wild 'fro. She sat on the couch while he sat comfortably between her legs.

"So wuz up with that nigga you were rolling with from uptown? He still getting paper or what?" Ice asked her.

"That fake ass nigga was pulling mad stunts. My home girl Nickie put me on. It turns out dat da truck that he was trying to floss with wasn't even paid for. He wuz talking about how he had shit on lock, when he was really a go-to boy for dem other dudes from the other side of town." Shareese rolled her eye's as she continued, "Dat cornball even had the nerve to try to get me to cop him some rims."

"I hope you didn't give that bitch nigga any of the nappy dug-out," Ice said with a huge grin on his face while squeezing her knee.

"Hell no. I just let him eat my pussy and he couldn't even do dat. I should have bagged some of his jewelry before I cut his wack ass off," she replied while laughing up a storm.

A couple of hours later, after Shareese finished his braids, Ice stood up and went into the bedroom, while Shareese stretched her tired legs. "You sure know how to get down on the hair tip," Ice yelled from the bedroom while looking at himself in the mirror.

"What you said?" Shareese asked as she entered the room. He had a king size bed with two matching oak nightstands on both sides. Both stands had every current hip-hop magazine spread crazily about. His closet door was slightly open and she could see mad gear. Some clothes still had the tags on them, and some still had plastic over them like they had just came back from the cleaners. Outside of the closet were crazy flavors of

Timberland boots and all types of kicks. By now Ice had come out the bathroom wearing only his boxer shorts.

"I see you still got those six packs." Sharese smiled admiringly while sitting on the edge of the bed going through a *Source* magazine.

"You know I gots to keep my physical up," Ice said as he sat down next to her on the bed.

"I see dat's not the only thing dat's a little up," Shareese said as she squeezed his semi hard dick through his boxer shorts.

"I see you looking mad good in those jeans," Ice shot back while patting her ass.

"I just joined this new gym around the way. I got a little toned up. Wanna see?" Shareese asked. Without even waiting for his answer, which she already knew anyway, Shareese wiggled out of her tight Blue Falcon jeans. She was wearing a satin midnight black thong and had "baby girl" tattooed on her back, a nickname Ice had given her a while back. She wore a gold ankle bracelet that he had given her on one of her birthdays.

"I know I must be doing something right at da gym," Shareese said with a wicked smile on her face. "Look at you," she said while trying to pose like a runway model. Ice noticed his dick nearly busting out his shorts.

"Come here," he ordered. She walked over slowly, still smiling, and sat on his lap. He then slid his hand under her belly tank top shirt and gently squeezed her nipples, which became instantly hard. Shareese closed her eyes and put her head back against him. In one swift motion, Ice reached inside an open nightstand drawer and pulled out an extra large magnum condom. He pushed play on his CD player as he brought his hand back into the mix of things. R. Kelly's voice filled the room, and by the time he reached the second verse, Ice had his swollen organ inside Shareese's hotbox, while bouncing her up and down like a beach ball.

A while later Ice said, "Fuck dis shit," and lifted Shareese up by her small waist. He then laid her on her belly while he rammed her from the back. Ice stood up while Shareese was half on and half off the edge of the bed. All you could hear was Shareese moaning. R. Kelly's voice could hardly be heard over the noise. Ice finished his business proper like, while Shareese looked like she needed an oxygen mask. Moments later they were in a steaming hot shower splashing water on each other.

While Shareese was putting on her baby blue Tims, Ice was at the closet trying to decide what to wear. He chose an off-white Rocawear jumpsuit with a light gray line down the sleeves and legs. He threw on a crisp, brand new pair of low top classic Air Force Ones. Ice had three more fresh pairs of the exact same kind of shoe still in the box. Ice always said, "You can never have too many Air Forces as long as they are sparkling clean. Nothing fucks up your outfits as much as busted ass kicks."

"So where you're off to? You want me to drop you off somewhere?" Ice asked.

"I'm good. Just call me a cab. I gotta go check my home girl out," Shareese answered.

"Do I know her?" Ice asked.

"Nah, I've been knowing her for about six months now. We talking about opening up a beauty salon together. She know some business man who's gonna invest with us to get us started. She's mad cool," Shareese added.

"You met the dude yet?" Ice responded back.

"Not yet, but she always yapping about how he's feeling our business plan, and how much dough he got," she said. *Beep, beep.* The cab was outside honking his horn.

"Ice, I'm out," Shareese said while grabbing her bag.

"Hold up. Let me bless you with a little cab fare," Ice replied. Ice went to his closet and came back with a roll of twenties. "Here you go, baby girl," he said holding the money out.

Shareese stuffed the money in her bag and gave Ice a peck on the cheek before bouncing.

"Tell your brother to give me a shout out," Ice yelled out as the cab was pulling away from the curve. He proceeded to go back inside his house.

(CHAPTER SIX)

Rico drove while Half a Dread sat back on the passenger side puffing on a vanilla skunk weed. "Dis is some good shit," Dread yelled while trying to talk over the music. They were blasting an underground reggae tape with Uglyman battling some unknown gritty, raw, up-and-coming artist. Their sound system was so loud, it had the windows in the old burgundy Maxima vibrating. Anyone passing by on the sidewalk could easily hear the music. By looking at the old car, they knew right away that the sound system cost more than the car by at least double.

"Turn right here and park behind dat van," Dread ordered, but not in a demanding way.

Even though it was only noon, the block was busy with people coming and going. Most were involved with doing various legal and illegal activities, trying to get ahead any way they could. Rico, being the person that he was, quickly surveyed the area. Dread turned down the music while Rico slid the Maxima into a parking space. Dread pulled out a heavy .45 and checked the clip. He made sure everything was in working order. His cousin did the same thing with his gat before stepping out the vehicle. They spotted a dice game going on, on the side of a twenty-four hour Laundromat half a block down.

There were six young guys rolling c-low. As the men approached the game, a stocky well-built guy wearing a du-rag was yelling, "Fuck dat shit. Dem rocks hit his foot. You gots to roll over."

A chubby but taller guy who had just rolled a four, five, six (c-low) responded, "Nah nigga, it's a done deal. You got a dove (twenty dollars) for me, so what's up?" He asked while stepping a foot closer.

Dread, pressed for time and bored of the petty argument over chump change, spoke so everyone could hear him. "Any one of you guys seen Rahmel?" Everyone in the circle automatically looked at Dread, then at Rico, and back at Dread.

The chubby guy looked at Dread cautiously and said, "Look here, Ras, first off you interrupting my money flow. Second, who da fuck is you, rolling up on the set like you da motherfucking police or sumthin."

Rico had already peeped another guy inching his way over by a steel garbage can already overflowing with trash. He knew from being in the street for so long, that they had their burner stashed there. Right before the guy could get to his hiding place, Rico pulled out his seventeen shot nine from under his shirt and hit the guy in the middle of his forehead with the gat. *Whap!* Everyone's heads turned toward the unsuspecting sound except for Dread. He already knew what was up. Before the group of young dice players could take flight, Dread snatched out his .45 and backed down everyone else against the wall. Before the stunned guy could regain his balance again, Rico hit him on the top of his head with the gun. *Whap!* The unconscious guy fell on his back while still holding onto the garbage can.

"Right there, cuz," Dread said, pointing to a half-opened, wrinkled-up Burger King bag. Rico then snatched a small, silver .380 automatic out of the bag and placed it in his pocket.

Dread grabbed the loud mouthed chubby kid by the throat and said, "Now, rude boy, once again, have you seen Rahmel around?"

"I wasn't trying to start no beef. I just didn't know who you two wuz," the chubby kid replied while sweating profusely. Dread looked at the nervous kid and then kneed him in the nuts with a strong rock hard knee from all his years of playing soccer. The kid dropped like a sack of potatoes while holding his beginning-to-swell, smashed privates.

Dread then grabbed the closest guy to him and said, "Now, bahtee boy, do I have to repeat myself?"

"Da only Rahmel I know is Rahmel that pushes dat black and red Decanta 1000 bike," he answered praying he didn't get the same treatment his friend got.

"Dat's the one," Dread replied, looking pissed by the minute.

"Last time I saw him, I mean, his bike, it was parked in front of dat pool-hall on 175th Street," he weakly answered.

"Dat's all we wanted to know. Now who got some ganja?" Dread asked with a huge smile plastered on his face. The stocky guy who lost his money on the dice roll reached in his sock and pulled out a dime bag. Rico grabbed it from his hand, sniffed the product, and threw it back at him saying, "Dat's dat feeble shit from Pac-man's spot." Dread then ordered the remaining guys who were standing to start walking. The guys bounced with a quickness, their hurried movements saying, "Fuck their fallen friends.

Ten minutes later, Rico pulled up in front of a rundown pool hall that doubled as an illegal numbers operation. Just like the kid said, there was a banging, shiny, black and red Decanta parked on the sidewalk. They both walked through the door and saw Rahmel right away. He was leaning on an empty pool table with a red-boned girl between his legs. The girl had on a pink wraparound tennis skirt with a matching belly shirt that showed off her flat, smooth stomach. The skirt she wore was so short, if she were to try to tie her Nikes, you would know that she was a hairy person by nature. As Rico and Dread came within reach of Rahmel, they noticed that the young girl was no way as attractive as her well-formed body. She had unhealthy looking skin with tiny red bumps and a slightly big nose. Her lips were a little large, but that particular feature was welcomed in the ghetto, especially by the freaks.

Rahmel noticed the pair of guys walking toward him and said, "What's up," while giving Dread some dap. He nodded to Rico out of respect for Dread. It was something about Dread's cousin he wasn't feeling. Rahmel thought Rico had the tendency to always stare too much at everyone and everything. Rahmel became instantly on point because of the pair's reputation for being violent. You could never be too careful when it came to these two.

"So, Dread, what brings you around?" Rahmel smiled, trying to lighten up the mood.

"You, playboy," Dread responded while looking directly at the girl's muscle toned inner thighs, and lusting openly. Rahmel could tell by the look on Rico's face that he wanted the female to break out so they could have some privacy.

On cue Rahmel said, "Peaches, take my helmet and go stand by my bike. I'll be out in a minute." Without saying a word, she took the helmet and started to walk away, shaking her fat ass more than usual for Dread's sake. Rico, on the other hand, was not impressed. He thought, *dat hood rat is probably burning.* Once Peaches was out of earshot, Dread spoke.

"Listen, you know Big Preme?" Rahmel nodded, still on point wondering what he had to do with him. "Well, some rude cat try to get at Preme. Nothing went down, but we need to find out who dis guy is, you know what I'm saying. Talk to some of your bitches on the low-low and see if they heard anyone talking about scheming on Preme or trying to set him up. You let me know what's up and I'll look out for you about dat thing we spoke about a while back."

"You know I'm going to look out for you, we go way back," Rahmel responded.

"We gotta roll out," Dread shouted back giving Rahmel some dap. Rahmel watched them walk away, knowing that they were both holding. He said to himself that next time he was going to be strapped when he ran into the pair. You can never predict the outcome when it came to Half a Dread and his cousin.

When Rico and Dread reached the street, Peaches was leaning on Rahmel's bike talking on her cell phone. When she saw Dread looking, she spread her legs open just a little bit giving him a small sample. Dread smiled and hit Rico in the ribs with his elbow. As soon as they were back in the Maxima Dread said, "Next time I bump into dat bitch, I'm going to rock her where she stands."

Rico adjusted his gat and started the car up. Before turning the music up Dread lit up the rest of his blunt and said, "Yo, cuz, let's get something to eat. I'm hungrier den a motherfucker."

(CHAPTER SEVEN)

Oh shit, Ice said to himself. He ran back into his house while he left his car running in the driveway. He then went straight to his closet and pried loose a couple of wooden panels that were located in the far left corner. Ice grabbed a metal locked box, pressed in a combination, and took out a stainless steel Rolex flooded with crystal clear diamonds. He slipped it on, knowing his outfit was now complete.

It was mad sunny out, so Ice decided to have his whip detailed. After his car was gleaming under the sun, he decided to get something to eat. He pulled up a moment later in front of a Golden Dragon takeout Chinese restaurant. There was a sign next to the name that said "Best In Town." *They all say the same thing*, Ice thought. Ice was parked directly in front of the restaurant, which was located in a "No Standing Zone."

"Ice, what's going on?" A a voice that caught him off guard asked. Ice turned his head and saw a young guy about fifteen on a pedal bike.

"Nothing," Ice responded. "Trying to get mine like the next man."

"I see you definitely getting yours," the young man replied, peeping the Rolex's diamonds, which caused blinding rainbow reflections in the sunlight.

Rizz, the young guy, had met Ice through his older sister, when Ice used to stop at their house on a Ninja 600, flashing his shines, to see her. Ever since then, Rizz always looked up to Ice like an idol. Rizz wore a black T-shirt with "Thug for Life" printed across the front, and a pair of baggy black jeans. His sneakers had seen better days and he wasn't much better off with his haircut. Ice still liked the kid. He was always throwing advice about street life Rizz's way. Rizz always hung on Ice's every word, absorbing everything. Ice thought the kid had potential to do his thing.

"So, Rizz, what you been rocking wit lately?" Ice asked.

"I've been slinging some crill's (crack). I be getting off here and there. The Jakes got the block on lock after dem Blood's sprayed shit and made it mad hot," Rizz replied. "I'm just riding around catching fiends before they reach the block," he added.

Ice spotted a police car riding by real slowly and checking him out trying to decide whether to fuck with him for parking illegally. They kept going so Ice said, "Go get me a small shrimp fried rice, and a Pepsi in a bottle. And get whatever you want," Ice added while handing Rizz a twenty. Rizz ran inside the Chinese takeout to place the order. He came back outside to finish kicking it with Ice, who was now outside leaning on the passenger side door smoking a Newport.

"So, Ice, when you going to let me get paper like you, so I can ball out?" Rizz asked.

"In due time, in due time. I'm working on something right now. I'm gonna try to put you on," Ice answered, giving him a pound to let him know he was real about what he had said. Ice continued to speak as Rizz listened intently. "When I put you on, you got to remember one thing. Always be a man and stand up for yourself no matter what the pressure. If you ain't a motherfucking man in the street, you might as well hang it up, cuz. Even a crackhead won't respect you or your hustle no more. Shit is real out here!"

The Chinese man started signaling that their order was ready, so Rizz went in to get their food. He gave Ice what he ordered, and Ice waved the change away when Rizz tried to give it to him. Ice hopped in his car while the young boy stood outside by the driver's side door. Ice then scribbled his math down on a piece of torn paper bag.

"Check it out, tell your sister to call me on my celly. If I don't pick up, then tell her to leave a message. You hold it down," he said while giving Rizz five. Ice turned up the CD player blasting Wu-Tang's "Cash Rules Everything Around Me." Ice needed this particular song to motivate him the rest of the day. He then sped off while Rizz peddled away, looking for more fiends to stack his pockets.

Ring, ring. Ice answered his cell phone. "Hello, who's dis?" He asked.

"Ice, dis is Cherry," came a high-pitched female voice.

"Cherry, who?" he asked, going through his memory bank.

"You know I met you on Jamaica Avenue in front of dat new sneaker store last week."

Ice waited a few moments before answering. "Oh yeah, shorty big butt," he said, referring to her natural big ass. She then giggled a little too much.

"So when are we going to hook up?" She asked.

"Shorty, I'm in da mix of things right now. Hit me up later on." Ice then pressed the end button on the cellular phone before she could respond. Ice knew she was just another ghetto bed bug, who was on his dick for his looks. *She wasn't all dat in the grill piece, but had the ill banging body*, Ice thought. He smiled knowing he was going to tear shorty up real soon and then make up excuses about why he couldn't see her, like all the rest.

Ice parked his Acura on a quiet side street and ate his food. After his quick meal, he smoked a loosie and sped off again. Soon he was knocking on a door on the south side of Queens. A male voice yelled through the door, "Who's there?"

"This is Detective Jenkins. I'm here for a Mr. Robert Lewis. I just want to ask him a couple of questions pertaining to a case I'm working on," Ice replied in a professional manner, trying to hold in his laughter. There was some frantic shuffling from behind the door, so Ice decided to end this little game.

"Yo, Rob, dis is Ice. Get from under the sofa and open the motherfucking door," he yelled while cracking up. The heavy wooden door cracked open a bit with a cheap chain attached to the door and the frame. The door swung open and a dark brown complexioned man with a cock diesel physique spoke.

"Nigga, I knew it wuz you. I'd recognize dat soft voice anywhere."

"Stop fronting. You wuz shaking like Las Vegas dice behind the door. I bet you was already halfway out the back door," Ice shot back.

Both men started laughing and play boxing. "So, how you know I was home?" Rob asked.,

"Nigga you know da streets are always talking," Ice responded.

Rob had just finished doing a two-year bid upstate on attempted robbery charges. Him and Ice used to wild out with B.M.W.s back in the days. Rob's mother had to move out of the projects in Brooklyn because the Housing Authority's rules stated that anyone convicted of a felony couldn't live on the premises, so now Rob resided in south side Queens.

"So Ice, you rolling hard, outshining the sun," Rob said while looking over at the triple black Acura.

"Yeah, it's a little something to get around from point A to B. Nigga, get your swole ass in, so we can roll out," Ice said.

Minutes later they were in Ice's whip driving slowly down the Avenue. Rob had his window rolled down hollering at a couple of girls walking by saying, "Shorty, you want to do something strange for some change? Sumthin funny for some money?"

Ice laughed, saying, "Dat lame shit played out years ago."

Moments later they pulled up in front of a liquor store. Ice came back with a bottle of Hennessy and a couple of plastic cups filled with ice. Rob filled both cups while Ice hopped on the B.Q.E. (Brooklyn, Queens Expressway). They hit a couple of stores in Brooklyn copping Tim's, the newest kicks out, some throwback jerseys, and various other gear you could never have too much of.

"Good looking out. You know a nigga be fucked up in da game when first coming home," Rob stated sincerely.

"Come on, you know how we get down. I remember plenty times you breaking me off. Remember when you came off with dem leathers and hit me off," Ice said. Rob smiled and Ice knew the embarrassing moment had passed.

After they finished shopping, Rob wanted to chill in B.K. so he could check some of his peoples he hadn't seen for a while. Ice gave Rob his cell number and told him to hit him up later. He then gave Rob the rest of the Hen-Rock and jumped back on the highway. An hour later Ice pulled up in a sixteen dollar an hour underground garage, located by 34th Street in Manhattan. He walked about three blocks before he came to a small but expensive looking jewelry store. He stood by the front door and a second later a pocked-face, chubby white man in a neat gray Armani suit buzzed him in.

"What's up, my man? Long time, no see," the man behind the counter said with the widest, fakest grin he could muster. Ice shook the man's sweaty hand and wiped it on the glass jewelry display counter while pretending to look at some platinum chains.

"So, Ice, you got some Ice for me today?" The man asked while laughing at his own corny joke.

The owner of the jewelry store, Nick Castastine, only sold and bought top-notch jewelry with no questions asked. Ice met him a year ago through some wannabe pimp who was in the Feds right now for taking underage girls across state lines to work for him. Nick never really trusted Ice, but his greed soon won over after he brought in some high quality jewelry to sell for a low price.

Ice took out the velvet bag and laid the platinum chain with matching bracelet on the counter. Nick told Ice to give him a minute while he went into the back behind a black curtain. Nick returned and bluntly said, "I'll give you four thousand for everything."

"Don't try to play me," Ice said while looking Nick straight in the face. Dat shit is worth five times dat amount."

"Business is slow. What can I say?" Nick replied, holding his hands up.

"I suppose business is so bad that they about to repossess dat big ass Benz out front you rolling in," Ice remarked.

"Come on bro'," Nick replied while trying to sound hip. "Everyone's got to eat," he added.

"I feel you. Now, what about my ring? Is it ready?" Ice asked, now irritated that he had to do business with this man. Nick quickly returned with a ring in a black box. Ice took the ring and looked it over carefully. It was a heavy platinum pinky ring with the letters I.C.E. laced out with high quality clear diamonds. He tried it on. Impressed, Ice said, "So how much do I owe you now?"

Nick responded, "With what you brought me today, let's just call it even with the four grand."

"Dat sounds good. Peace," Ice replied while holding his new ring up to the light. Nick went once again in the back room and came back with a small stack of fifties and twenty dollar bills. Ice expertly counted the money and zipped it up in his front pockets.

"Bro' come back real soon," Nick said while getting buzzed out. Walking back to the garage Ice thought, *I'm gonna get dat rich cracker one day.* He sat back in his car, smoking a Newport doing eighty heading back to Queens blasting his music.

(CHAPTER EIGHT)

Preme sat on his couch in his silk Japanese house robe listening to some R&B. The phone went off and Preme answered it with a, "Yeah!" Half a Dread was on the other line. "So what new?" Preme asked curious to know of any new updates.

"Me and Rico are looking on a couple of angles. We'll hit you back when we get something more solid."

"You do that," Preme responded back.

After the brief phone call Preme strapped on an extra large Kevlar bulletproof vest over his oversized white T-shirt. He then threw on a dark blue five hundred dollar Diesel jeans suit with a pair of spotless tan Timberland high top boots. One thing about Preme was that he never took unnecessary risks or chances. He knew from the heart that he wasn't built for the ruthless dope game. He was constantly thinking about switching his hustle to pimping. He just knew the flesh game would go well for him because he had chicks that would do anything for him, or so he thought. Before heading out the door, he took a hit of coke and slid his Glock in his jean jacket.

Preme let Mia push his whip, and he had a forest green rented Pathfinder for himself. Why take any chances riding around in his cars, until he found out exactly what the deal was in the streets? Preme glanced around quickly before getting into his vehicle. Soon he was on the Southern State Parkway. An hour later he pulled up to a house in a quiet neighborhood with tree-lined streets. He rang the doorbell and waited. No one came so she pushed the button again. The door finally opened and a pretty, light-skinned, overweight woman said, "Derrick, what took you so long? I'm glad you found time away from your busy schedule," she spat with an attitude. Preme took a deep breath, exhaled, and stepped inside the lavishly furnished house. He automatically heard his newborn daughters crying.

"Keisha, the twins are crying," he stated.

"I know, I know," she replied back while heading toward the noise. Preme sat down while Keisha was in the babies' room trying to calm them down.

Preme wished he wasn't here. He started thinking back to when he first met Keisha at the bank. When he first laid eyes on her and peeped her nonchalant style, he said to himself that she was definitely wifey material. Right after that day he always made sure that he had her as his teller. Keisha always seemed to have on an up-to-date, stylish, business suit that blended in perfectly with her model-type figure. Her makeup and hair were always flawlessly done. They always had good-natured smart remarks to say to each other.

A month later she agreed to go to the movies with him as friends. Soon after, he began to spoil Keisha, taking her to the nicest restaurants, on shopping sprees at Sak's Fifth Avenue and Prada, plus giving her anything else she wanted. They were planning a trip to the Bahamas when she informed him that she was pregnant. That's when everything changed. First of all, Preme didn't have any kids at that moment in his life, but he was willing to have a high class woman like Keisha as his baby's mother. Then she quit her job right before she was due for a much-earned promotion. And then she wanted to move in with him.

One of Preme's main attractions to Keisha was that she was a very independent female who always paved her own way. Then the straw that broke the camel's back was when she started putting on weight at an extremely rapid rate. Preme knew that it was natural for a woman to put on a little weight during pregnancy, but damn this was too much. She also stopped wearing her sexy business outfits he liked so much. Keisha claimed that now they were uncomfortable now so she resorted to wearing baggy sweatpants and tank tops. And her gobbling down of buckets of fried chicken and huge trays of lasagna didn't help their already slipping relationship either. He wanted her to have an abortion, but she stood fast on so-called religious reasons. Preme always believed it was so that she could have an easy, carefree life. Preme never thought he would get trapped off ghetto style like so many other guys he knew. Having a seed with a girl that was living foul, was despised, or who a man was no longer attracted to, was a no in any guy's rule book.

"Derrick, would you like something to drink or eat?" Keisha voice rang out, snapping him back to the present.

"Nah, I'm straight," he answered back. He then dug in his pockets and handed her eight hundred dollars. Keisha took the money, counted it, and then screwed her face up.

"Is dis all you gonna give your daughters?" She asked. Preme knew she really meant "me," but threw in "daughters" to soften him up.

"Dat's all I'm working wit right now," Preme answered.

"Oh, it's like da? You probably throwing your money away on dem bum ass bitches," Keisha shot out. She continued while stepping closer to Preme. "I know dats why you moved me away out here, so you can have your coke up orgy parties on the low-

low. Yeah, I know about you and that wack ass bitch you're running around wit," she spat.

Keisha was now breathing heavily from her spitfire verbal exchange. Preme looked at her and thought, *you got the nerve to call someone wack, you fat piece of shit.* Preme then got up and started walking toward the front door.

"Oh, I'm sorry, Derrick. I didn't mean it. You know I've been under mad stress with the twins and everything else," Keisha said softly while blocking his path. "You haven't even seen your daughters yet," she added for good measure. Preme turned around and went into the children's bedroom with Keisha following close behind him. The twins' room was hooked up with everything imaginable that newborn babies might have. They were both sleeping in a very expensive Eddie Bauer crib. Preme gently touched their small heads and started to walk back toward the front door. Keisha stood in his way.

"You don't have to go so soon do you?" Keisha asked in her famous voice that had always gotten what she wanted before. "Why can't we spend a little time together?" She was practically begging. She opened her robe slightly, revealing her cleavage and trying to persuade him to stay. Preme looked at her in disgust. There was nothing that was more of a turn off than a fat chick wearing a stained housecoat and trying to be sexy. Keisha caught the look and embarrassingly closed her robe.

"Keisha, I gotta roll out," Preme said as he stepped out onto the sidewalk.

"Yeah, okay," she shot back and then slammed the door, waking the twins up. Preme hopped into the Pathfinder with relief, glad to be heading back to the city. Preme's cell phone vibrated so he answered it.

"Yeah, I'm on my way. No, just hold tight. See you later." He ended his call and put on some music to relax.

(CHAPTER NINE)

Shareese paid the cab driver and then jumped out in front of a small apartment building. She was glad to be out that stuffy car. It smelled like corn chips and unwashed feet. To make matters worse, the Haitian cab driver kept trying to strike up a conversation with her. When he couldn't take the obvious hints, she flatly said, "Listen, I tried to be nice, but you couldn't get the polite hints. I'm not in da mood for small talk, especially from a geek like you. Now drive this raggedly piece of shit and we'll get along fine. After that the driver kept his mouth shut, but he briefly kept looking at her in his rearview mirror.

Shareese reached her destination, which was a first floor apartment. Before she could knock, the door swung open and a guy rushed out. They both startled each other.

"Is Trina in?" Shareese asked.

"Yeah, go right in," the man responded as he headed out toward the front doors. Shareese walked into the apartment.

"Girl, where the hell are you?" Shareese asked.

"I'm in the bathroom. I'll be right out in a minute," shouted a female voice.

Shareese closed the door and sat down on a cluttered couch. *Damn, she could at least clean up every once in a while,* Shareese thought. The small apartment was littered with beauty products, half filled wine bottles, clothes thrown about, and at least a dozen fashion magazines.

A short while later a tall, white woman wearing a red towel with another towel neatly wrapped around her head, emerged from the bathroom. Even though Trina wore a loosely fitted towel, you could easily tell by her feminine assets that she could hold her own against any well-stacked black woman. Her well defined ass and melon sized breasts caused men of all races to try and get with her. Her thick, shapely legs told the story of a used-to-be runner.

"Girl, what took you so long?" Trina asked while plopping down on the sofa preparing to do her toenails.

"I had to make a stop and braid Ice's hair," Shareese said with a smile. The smile made Trina look over at Shareese more closely.

"Yeah girl, I recognize dat glow anywhere. He put it on you. You wasn't braiding no hair! Your sore ass just couldn't walk," Trina yelled out, and then broke out in a laugh.

"You know how me and Ice do. When I don't have a regular fuck partner, he blesses me every now and then with no commitments. Dat's how far back we go," Shareese responded back with a devilish grin.

"Well anyway, I hear Ice dis and Ice dat, so when am I going to meet dis mysterious guy who got you walking pigeon toed?" Trina asked.

"Fuck you, bitch. You need to swing your ass a little more so dat business man of yours would come up wit dat dough he's been promising us a lot quicker," Shareese replied in a joking manner.

"You always talk about how Ice always have major paper, so why don't he invest in our beauty salon? What does he do anyway?" Trina asked curiously.

"Let's put it dis way, he's like Robin Hood. He takes from the rich and gives to the needy. And the needy is him needing to stack dat dough," Shareese replied slickly.

"Dat's what I'm talking about," Trina shot back and they both gave each other high fives.

"So when are we all getting together to discuss our business deal with your friend?" Shareese asked Trina.

"Dat's why I'm getting all ready now," Trina answered while blow drying her dyed black hair. "He's suppose to scoop me up a little later on. We'll all hook up when we find da time," Trina said.

"I feel you," Shareese responded. Both females joked and kidded each other for over an hour while Trina was preparing herself for her friend. Shareese then told her girlfriend that she had to bounce, so Trina called her a cab. They both walked to the lobby doors and gave each other hugs.

"Call me," they both sang out as the cab driver approached. Shareese hopped in the cab and waved to her good friend and soon-to-be business partner. Trina walked back to her apartment to wait for the arrival of her male friend.

[CHAPTER TEN]

Ice made it back to Queens feeling nice from the Hennessy he and Rob had earlier. He wolfed down a couple of slices of pizza and then headed to the barbershop. He got a razor sharp shape up to make his freshly done braids stand out even more. While walking back to his whip, Ice spotted a definite dime piece walking toward him. She had on a Burberry dress with matching open toe Versace high heel shoes. You could tell that she had just come from getting her hair done because she looked as if she was stepping out of a fashion magazine. The beauty salon on the same block was a dead giveaway also. She didn't wear any jewelry except for a pair of diamond-studded earrings, but still she had the same enticing effect.

When they approached each other, Ice smiled and said "How you doing?"

He knew that his looks and that simple comment would be enough to instantly stop any girl in her tracks. To his surprise, she ignored him and kept going, not missing a beat. Ice thought that either she didn't get a good look at his style, or she was one of those females who wanna put up a front for a minute to keep their egos up.

Ice turned around and jogged up to her. He lightly touched her on the shoulder and said in his most charming voice, "Excuse me, Miss. I was just saying hi, maybe hoping I could get to know you and we could take it from there." She didn't even bother to respond and kept it moving. "Miss you can't be in that big of a hurry. Slow down so you don't break one of dem fine ass legs," Ice said, still smiling and trying to get a reaction out of her. She stopped and looked directly at Ice with cold eyes.

"What are you going to do? Follow me up and down the street like a dog in heat?" she asked with a heavy Trinidadian accent. "I suggest you tighten up your game before trying to approach a real lady." With that, she kept walking even more gracefully than before.

"What are you, anti social or sumtin?" Ice yelled at her. Never in his life had any girl played him out like he was a nobody or something. *Enough about her*, he thought as he headed home.

Ice made it home, took a long shower, and fell out. *Ring, ring, ring, ring.* "Who da fuck is dis?" Ice said after answering his cell phone, vexed that someone had broken his sleep.

"Who da fuck you think it sound like," shot back a voice on the other line.

"Oh, Rob, what's up? Where you at?" Ice asked.

"I'm still in B.K. I should be heading out your way a little later. You gonna scoop me up at the train station?" Rob asked.

"Yeah, hit me up in a couple of hours. I'm trying to rest up some," Ice responded.

"Peace, one love," Rob said, and the phone went dead. Ice then dozed back off to sleep.

Some time later Ice woke up and smoked a Newport. He turned on the TV and some old black and white gangster movie was playing. He admired those types of movies. The gangsters always took care of business, and if shit got too thick, they never went to the police. They just took their girls to their secret hideout until things died down a little.

A while later Ice put on some baggy blue jeans, some fresh Tims, and splashed on a little Essence cologne before putting on his new Ecko racing jacket. While smoking his third Newport, Rob called him and told him he was at the train station on Parson's Boulevard. A half hour later Rob was getting in Ice's Acura and giving him some dap. Rob was wearing some of his new gear that he had copped earlier. He had on a throwback jersey with some long jean shorts and a pair of new Lebron James sneakers. Ice drove fast while blasting his music as usual. He soon parked on a fairly isolated street. As they were getting out Rob asked where they were headed.

"You'll see," came the response. They ended up in front of Jezebel's (the local strip club). There were all types of vehicles parked in the parking lot adjoining the establishment. Some were fifty thousand dollar luxury cars, and others were five thousand dollar blue-collar workers' vehicles.

"Why are we parked way around the corner?" Rob asked when he noticed that there were still more spaces in the parking lot.

"If shit was to jump off, we won't be caught up in the mix when dudes be trying to bounce from dat tiny ass lot," Ice responded.

"I feel you. You still the same old Ice, always on point," Rob stated.

When they reached the front door, a fat bouncer with a pit bull thickness type of neck was throwing a little white man wearing glasses out the front door. The mid-forties white man was trying to explain his case.

"Sir, I was getting a table dance and the dancer was going in my pockets trying to take my money. I wasn't doing anything.

All I asked was what she was doing, and the next thing I know I'm getting jumped on by her and her girlfriends."

The man was nervously talking a mile a minute. Ice noticed the front of the white man's shirt was soaking wet, probably caused by a stripper throwing a drink at him. The huge bouncer still had him by the collar shaking him around.

"She said you tried to lick her ass," the bouncer said. "Get your freak, perverted ass outta here before I fuck you up for real." The bouncer then threw him up against a parked car. The ex-customer started yelling saying he was going to sue everyone, from the owner of the club to the Mayor who allowed such a dump to exist in the first place.

Ice and Rob made it inside and sat a table in a corner. The place was always jumping on Friday nights. As usual, Jezebel's was packed, with various activities going on. In the far corner someone was selling bootleg CDs along with X-rated DVDs. All shapes, sizes, and colors of women were walking around, talking, smiling, and giving seductive lap dances. No matter what the women were doing, they were after the same goal: "Money!"

There was a small crowd around the center stage. A very thick, dark complexioned woman was on stage with her leg behind head. She was slowly pushing a large white egg in her vagina with a look of ecstasy on her face. The crowds of guys were going crazy throwing dollar bills at her. Once the egg was fully inside, she pushed it back out. Some guys offered money for the egg, others offered money for her. She grabbed her pile of money and headed backstage. During all the commotion, somehow the egg mysteriously vanished.

A pretty, medium sized waitress with full lips approached Ice and Rob. She was wearing an all black one-piece leather skirt outfit with see through pumps. Her red painted nails and toes were neatly done.

"What are you fellows having tonight?" The waitress asked. Rob was too busy staring at her chest to respond.

"Get my boy a chilled bottle of Moet and I'll have a Thug Passion," Ice said.

"I'll be right back," she said, smiling her brightest smile knowing that when a customer ordered Moet at the club, it usually came with a hefty tip. She also noticed the Rolex and the sick ring on Ice's pinky. She didn't pay Rob much attention because he looked like a tagalong. The waitress came back with an ice-filled bucket with a bottle of Moet sticking out and accompanied by two champagne glasses. She came back a second later bringing Ice's Thug Passion drink.

"Here you fellows go. I hope you enjoy the rest of the evening," she said, looking directly at Ice. Ice paid the bill and gave her a twenty dollar tip. The waitress's eyes were glued to Ice's knot as he counted the money. She lingered around hoping that Ice would try to talk to her. She was more than willing to break out for the rest of the night with him, hoping to come off on some of his dough. When Ice resumed his conversation with his partner, the waitress started slowly walking away.

"Oh Miss, can I ask you a question?" Ice asked. When she turned around a flicker of hope flashed across her face. "Have you seen Jade around tonight?" Ice asked. The waitress's face then transformed into a mask of pure envy.

"Yeah, she finished doing a set about forty-five minutes ago. She should be in the back," the waitress answered, trying to hide her disappointment.

"Then can you tell her that Ice is out here?" The waitress walked away toward another table thinking, *dat stuck up whore Jade is probably doing freak shows for him and his whole crew on the low.*

Meanwhile Rob was wilding out drinking glass after glass of Moet and saying he wanted to dig out every girl he saw. Ice had drunk half of his drink when a very slim brown-skinned dancer with extremely large breasts came over and sat down on Ice's lap.

"You want a dance, player?" She asked while taking her top off. Ice looked at her like, *what da fuck!* He then gently lifted her off of him.

"First of all, you look like a man with those big ass gorilla hands," Ice said. "Second, those nasty ass stretch marks is turning me da fuck off. Dat shit reminds me of a hot dog dat's been in the microwave too long. Now, beat it!"

Rob was busy cracking up and beating his hands on the table spilling champagne. The dancer was too embarrassed to spit back anything mainly because she knew it was true. She acted as if the music was too loud for her to have heard Ice's comments. She walked away unconsciously rubbing her stomach.

"Dat bitch have some nerve working up in here. I should complain to the fucking manager or someone," Ice said jokingly.

"You bugged out. Why you had to get gully on shorty like dat,?" Rob said, all the while still laughing.

A couple of minutes later an above-average looking dancer walked over to their table. You could definitely tell she was of Spanish origin by her jet-black hair with dyed blond streaks in it that hung to the center of her back. Her Aztec features secured that fact. She had emerald green eyes and a well-proportioned body that was screaming to be released from her one-piece, light blue, cat-like outfit. Her nipples pressed against the thin fabric looked like she was smuggling two small grapes. When she spoke, a silver tongue ring glittered in the light.

"Ice, I thought you wuz going to drop by tomorrow night," she said while giving him a passionate hug.

"You know how I do. I like to surprise a motherfucka every now and then," Ice replied. "Anyway, dis is my man, Rob. Rob, dis is my peoples, Jade." Ice ordered another bottle of Moet, a Thug Passion, and an Apple Martini for Jade.

"Yo, Rob, check it out. You see those two females over by the bar? They been peeping our style since we set foot. Here's a hundred and I'll meet you in the V.I.P. room in a little while."

The V.I.P. room was just a small room with a soft leather sofa and a thin curtain separating the entrance. Rob took the money and the bottle of Moet, and headed toward the direction of the bar.

"So Jade, everything been good with you? How's little man?" Ice asked referring to her two-year-old son. "Everything's on the up-and-up. Juan is doing fine, getting bigger by the minute," she answered back. Jade then leaned forward and whispered, "So you took care of dat?"

"No doubt. Shit went smooth, but it wasn't no cash though," Ice replied.

"I'm telling you that motherfucker always rocking mad chips," Jade responded, surprised at the news.

"I guess I just caught him at the wrong time, but I still came off with a little sumtin," Ice said with a smile. Jade's green eyes lit up after hearing that. Ice handed her a gee, which she quickly stuffed in her pocketbook.

Ice had met Jade about three months ago when he was leaving Jezebel's one night. Some drunk guy was harassing her in the parking lot talking about, "Nah, bitch. I bought you mad drinks and now your stinking ass is gonna try to play me? Fuck dat shit," he screamed while grabbing her arm.

Ice appeared out of nowhere and said, "Rhonda, I thought you was going to be home an hour ago. Mom's been worried about you."

Playing along, Jade responded, "I'm trying to, but dis ass hole thinks I owe him sumtin."

"Excuse me, can you let go of my sister's arm so we can head home?" Ice asked.

"Listen, punk," the drunk man started to say. But before he could finish his sentence Ice pulled out a .44 Colt Python with a walnut grip, and he pistol whipped the surprised man to the pavement. Ice then relieved the man of his gold chain and Cartier watch, which were the real reasons he jumped into the mix of things. He then drove Jade home, only speaking to her when asking for directions.

A week later he ran into Jade inside of Jezebel's and they struck up a friendship. Jade knew from his vibe that he was a natural stick-up kid, and he pulled that stunt for his own benefit. Jade started telling him which customers had dough and who could also be easy marks. She supplied Ice with all sorts of information to make the take-down all that smoother, and Ice would break her off every now and then. Ice could come off with forty gees, and give her only two. Jade didn't care. She wasn't putting her neck on the line. She didn't think she was doing such a big thing telling him what those stupid motherfuckers told her over a bottle of champagne trying to impress her. They all got what they deserved, she reasoned.

"So how's dat other thing you were working on?" Ice asked, finishing the last of his drink.

"Dis chick who dances at dis other club is supposed to hit me off with some more info on him. He's fucking her, and she's begging to eat my pussy. I'm just stringing her along until I get mine," Jade said with a smirk on her face. "Well, Ice, I gotta go change and bounce. My moms can't watch little man all night." She gave Ice a peck on the cheek and promised to call him tomorrow with the rest of the information on their move.

"Put your hands together for Tabatha," the DJ yelled through the microphone. The DJ was playing Jay-Z's, "Big Pimping." A dancer came out wearing a french maid outfit, with black fishnet stockings and a duster to complete the effect. Tabatha took her get-up off piece by piece and slid up and down the pole like a pro. She definitely gave the crowd what they came for. She bent over and made her butt cheeks move up and down one at a time, showing her skills. Ice had to give the girl her props, so he gave her all the singles he had. Rob then came over smiling.

"Man, you missed a good time. Dem bitches were off the chain. I told shorty about you and they all want to hook up after shit closes down. What's up? You wit it or what?" Rob asked excitingly.

"Nah, playboy. I got shit to do. You do your thing," Ice replied. The club closed down at four a.m. Ice and Rob pulled out in front of Jezebel's.

"There she go," Rob yelled while pointing at a short built light-skinned girl with a snatch back hairstyle. She was wearing baggy jeans and a tight belly shirt, and she was carrying a backpack.

"Slow down, nigga. She can't see you through these tints," Ice said. Rob rolled down his window so the girl could see him, and waved her over. She quickly hopped in the backseat.

"Dis is my partner, Ice," Rob said.

"Hi, I'm Spank," the dancer responded and reached over to lightly shake Ice's hand. *She held on a little too long*, Ice thought. He knew what time it wuz. Fifteen minutes later they arrived at the weed spot and Rob jumped out to get a couple of dime bags. Soon as Rob left, shorty redbone spoke up.

"Yo, I'm not really feeling your friend. You think we could drop him off and we could do something together?" She asked, giving Ice the "come fuck me" look.

"Shorty, I know you're hotter den a firecracker, but I got shit to do right now." Ice knew the game and how females got down. He was her type because he had a ride and was flossing with the shines. Spank had tried to correct her mistake by trying to get with Ice, after she saw that he was the one really rolling. She pocketed his number just as Rob was getting back in the car. Ice drove while Rob was busy rolling up a Philly blunt. Ice dropped the new couple off at a cheap hotel. As Spank walked away, she shook her ass as if to say to Ice, "Yeah, nigga, dis what you coulda rocked."

Meanwhile, Ice was thinking, *shorty definitely ill, I should had dropped dat nigga off, and broke dat bitch back, fuck it, dat nigga just came home I'mma let him live.* Ice headed back to the Heights, circled the block twice, and called it a night

(CHAPTER ELEVEN)

Dread and his cousin Rico were sitting at a table in their apartment snacking on baked chicken and fried fish smothered in roasted onions.

"Cuz, let me get half of dat fish," Dread asked Rico. Rico cut the fish in half with a plastic knife and gave Dread the smaller portion. Fifteen minutes later Dread looked at Rico and told him that it was about dat time. They both grabbed their guns, sticking them in their waistbands, and headed out the door. Rico drove while Dread opened up a couple of Irish Mosses for them to wash down the grub.

They arrived at a quiet park located in a residential neighborhood. They chose this particular park because of its many surrounding trees, giving it an undercover flava. Both men walked in and sat on a bench over by the swings. The only other people in the park were a teenage couple who were laughing and smoking weed. The park closed down at night, but people still snuck in and left only when the police van rolled in to threaten trespassers with arrest.

"Where da fuck is she?" Rico asked, wanting to take care of business and bounce. Rico knew there was nothing worse than getting bagged by the jakes just to catch a case on a humble.

"Relax, she be here in a minute," Dread replied while starting to split a blunt down the middle.

Just as soon as he finished rolling the blunt up, two dark figures appeared and started walking toward the men. Both men automatically became on point, putting their hands on their gats. When the duo saw that one of the people was the person they were expecting, they relaxed a little bit, but not much because there was an extra person walking with the girl they were meeting.

"Dread, you got dat like I asked?" The woman asked once she was in talking distance.

Dread, visibly angry, shouted, "Listen here, you crackhead bitch. I told you to come alone and you bring dis bumbaclod stranger in my presence. Den you come asking me questions." By this time Rico had already stood up and was standing off to the side waiting for shit to jump off, knowing she had crossed the line with his cousin.

"No," the woman said. "I didn't mean anything, Dread. You know how I get sometimes. Dis iz my cousin Dave. He's alright. I swear on my mother's grave." Her words were weakly and unconvincingly spoken.

Dat's one thing about dope fiends, Rico thought. *Everytime they bring a new person around, and when they questioned on it, it's always the case that the stranger is their cousin or a close friend who can be trusted.* Rico then ordered the shabby looking man to go and stand at the other end of the park. The man walked away slowly, disappointed because he wanted to be a snitch on the payroll from guys that pay well, from what he'd been told.

Once the man was far enough away, Dread continued, "So, what da fuck you got for me?" He demanded. The thin, frail woman, who looked well over forty but was actually twenty-nine, smiled with dope fiend breath contaminating the surrounding air.

"Well," she said. "There are three known stick-up boys who I heard don't give a fuck even about their own mothers from the Shadyville area. One is on lock-down, the other got gutted by his girl up in the Bronx."

"Who's the third one?" Dread asked, not giving a fuck about the other two.

"His name is Ice, and from what I hear, he's a pretty boy out to prove himself," the crack head replied, smiling because she knew she had information that was of worth.

"Fuck all dat other silly shit," Dread shouted and grabbed her by her moldy sweat hood. "What's his real name? Where does he rest at? What kind of whip does he push?" Dread took the blunt from Rico and took a long drag while waiting for his answers.

"Nobody knows too much about him except that he's a sneaky little fuck who gets gully."

"We'll see," Dread responded. Dread then reached inside his jeans and pulled out a clear plastic bag. The bag contained eight jumbo crack rocks. The woman hungrily took the bag and looked at its contents.

"You keep me informed, and I'll keep looking out for you. And next time come by your motherfucking self, or you won't be walking out dis park," Dread replied.

"Okay, okay," she answered back, not caring about what threats the man made as long as she got her dope. She wanted to leave as quickly as possible to go smoke up. At the last minute the female crack fiend changed her direction, heading toward the other exit opposite her friend, saying to herself, "It's not really enough for the both of us."

While Rico was driving away, Dread called Preme on his cell phone. He didn't pick up so he left a message about his newest info. After putting out the roach, Dread said, "Rico, let's go and try to hunt down some pum pum."

(CHAPTER TWELVE)

Preme made a call on his cell phone. When someone on the other end picked up he said, "I'm out in front, so leave the door unlocked." Preme hung up and proceeded to get out of his whip and walk toward the apartment building. A minute later he was inside Trina's apartment grabbing her white ghetto ass.

"Preme, you brought my nose candy like you promised?" Trina asked in her sexiest voice.

"You know how we do," he answered back. They headed back to Trina's bedroom where she pulled out a medium sized flat mirror. Preme then took out a six-inch glass valve filled with a powdery substance and poured its contents onto the mirror. He then rolled up a twenty-dollar bill and took a hit of his grade A coke.

"I needed dat shit," he replied while starting to take his jacket and Kevlar vest off. Trina came back from the bathroom with a straight edged razor, and proceeded to cut the coke in single straight lines. She took the rolled up twenty and sniffed two lines with the quickness.

"Yeah daddy, dat's what I'm talking about.

"I feel you. I needed to relieve some stress, too," Preme replied.

"Your babies' mother is still flipping da fuck out?" Trina asked.

"Yeah, yeah. I was doing like ninety on the Southern State trying to get as far away from her nagging ass as possible," Preme responded with a loud laugh. Trina got up, killed the lights, and lit up a couple of rose scented candles. Twenty minutes later, and a couple of more hits of nose candy, and Preme was spread eagle on Trina's dark purple satin sheets while she rode him like a mad Russian.

"Yeah, bitch, do your thang," Preme said between heavy grunts. Everytime Trina bounced back down it sounded as if a group of people were clapping. *Pap, pap, pap.* Trina had already cum three times, but the coke had her wilding out like there was no tomorrow. Preme grabbed her by her waist so hard that it left fingerprints. He busted off and Trina fell on top of him panting and still wanting more.

A half hour later, while talking bullshit to each other, Preme checked his cell phone and realized he had an urgent message. He put in his code and listened to the message. The message said: "Preme, dis is Dread. From what we know so far it's some rude boy named Ice who might have got down like dat. We think he's the one."

The message blew Preme's high, causing him to stare off momentarily into space. Trina caught the far off look.

"What's wrong, baby? You got troubles?" Trina asked.

"Nothing I can't solve," he responded back with confidence. "Some cat called Ice wanted to bring the drama to me on a robbery tip, so now we got to see who really gets ill." Preme replied with a devilish grin.

"Dat's the second time I heard dat name Ice today," Trina replied.

Preme sat up and quickly said, "Yeah, from who?"

"Oh, you remember my friend Shareese who I told you about? Dat's da one who's suppose to cop dat beauty salon with me."

"Keep going," Preme said with interest.

"Well earlier today, before coming to see me, she was with a guy who calls himself Ice. From what I hear, she's been dealing with him for a while."

"Have you seen dis guy? How does he get down?" Preme asked.

"I haven't seen him yet, but Shareese told me he get his paper by rocking motherfuckers to sleep," she answered while starting to feel like she was being interrogated.

"Iz dat so," Preme said while Trina started putting two and two together.

"You think he's da one you got beef with?" Trina asked.

"Dat's what you going to help me find out," Preme answered back, looking her over carefully. "What have you told dis Shareese about me?" Preme asked, getting hyped up.

"I just told her how you get mad paper and you gonna help us out on getting our shit started," Trina replied a little nervously, hoping Preme didn't think she was involved in whatever was going on.

"I want to meet dis friend of yours right away. Give her a call and set something up for tomorrow evening," Preme barked. Preme sniffed up a line while Trina dialed Shareese's number. *Ring, ring, ring..*

"Hello," a sleepy voice answered.

"Shareese, dis is Trina. I'm sorry for calling so late, but I spoke to my friend about our business deal today. He wants all of us to meet tomorrow so we can discuss the financial part. Trina noticed a pause and quickly added, "It has to be tomorrow because he'll be out of town for a minute, and plus I think he might hit us off with dat dough."

"Word up," Shareese responded with excitement and now fully awake.

To be on the safe side Trina threw in, "I think it's already a done deal. All he says is he wants to meet you face to face. Be at my place at six," Trina said while trying to sound sincere.

"I'll be there girl," Shareese said, smiling from ear to ear.

"Don't forget. Six at my place. I got to go now," Trina said, praying that her phone conversation had cooled Preme's suspicious nature toward her. "I'll see you tomorrow Shareese. Bye."

They both hung up. Preme was hanging onto every word to try to peep anything shady on Trina's part.

"You did good," Preme said while still studying her. He then called Dread and filled him in on the situation. Preme laid back down on the bed a little more relaxed and said, "Now come over here and give daddy some brains." Like a good girl, Trina obeyed.

(CHAPTER THIRTEEN)

Ice woke up to a fresh Newport and Nas doing his thing on Hot 97. He took a cold shower while the music blared throughout his apartment, preparing him for the day. He had to take a long ride to Brick Town (New Jersey) to see his man Santos. After his shower, he dressed quickly and double checked his .357 to make sure it was fully loaded. He then tucked his gun in his waistband before heading upstairs to see how his grandparents were doing.

"Oh, Nathaniel, it's so good to see you," his grand mother said while giving him a long sturdy hug.

"I'm glad to see you too, Grandma. And you too, Grandpa," Ice replied back with genuine sincerity.

"Child, you come and go so fast we hardly get a chance to see you," his grandmother said while looking him over.

"Have you spoken to your mother or your sister?" His grandfather asked.

"Yes. They're doing just fine. I'm going to call mom again later on today."

"That's good," his grandmother interrupted, happy to see her only grandson. "You look so thin. Let me heat you something to eat. I made Alabama collard greens with smoked neck bones, homemade cornbread, and macaroni with your favorite cheese."

"Oh, Grandma, I'm sorry I can't right now," Ice replied with a sad puppy dog look. "I have to go way over to New Jersey and help fix a friend's car." Ice had told his grandparents that he fixed cars and did other odd jobs so that he could afford college courses when he got enrolled. He walked over to his grandfather, handing him four hundred dollars.

"Nat, you paid the rent already," his grandfather replied puzzled.

"I'm just giving you something extra. You both have been so helpful to me," Ice responded. He then shook his grandfather's hand and kissed his grandmother on the cheek.

"Come up anytime, Nathaniel," his grandmother yelled as Ice walked outside toward the driveway.

He climbed in his car and adjusted his du-rag in the rearview mirror to make sure his shit looked proper. He then drove off toward the liquor store. He wanted something light, so he purchased a small bottle of blue Alizé. Ice didn't want to get bent with something stronger because he had to be on point for where he was going.

A couple of blocks from the liquor store, he stopped at a red light and took a long swig of his cold Alizé. He happened to look over at the whip next to him as people in the hood normally do, and he peeped a brand new platinum-colored Range Rover sitting on twenty-fours. *Oh shit!* Ice said to himself. *Dat's dat dime piece shorty by the barbershop who flipped on me.*

The driver whom Ice was referring to, was wearing Gucci shades and talking to another female passenger. *Even with dem shades on I still recognized her star qualities*, Ice thought to himself. He started honking his horn trying to get the woman's attention. When she looked over, Ice gave his best smile and then told her to pull over. The driver looked at her friend, said something, and they both looked over at Ice and broke out in a laugh. She then rolled up her window and sped off.

"What!" Ice couldn't believe what had just happened. "She played me out like a cornball, and for a second time in front of another bitch," Ice thought out loud. "We're going to meet again one day and things are going to be different," Ice promised himself.

He hopped on the Vernazano Bridge, finishing his bottle before he even knew it. Ice had reached his destination in good time, but he had to walk a full block because there were no parking spaces. He made it to a small, two-family house. He rang the bottom bell.

"Ice, my main man. You're right on time as always," a short Hispanic man shouted with a New York Rican accent as he answered the door.

"You know I gotta take care of mines," Ice replied while giving Santos some dap. They both walked inside, passing through the living room where five little kids were playing Playstation, laughing, and enjoying themselves. They headed to the kitchen where a big pot was boiling.

"You want something to drink or smoke?" Santos asked.

"I'm straight," Ice answered back.

"Okay, my man. I'll be back in a minute," Santos replied before walking off toward another room. Ice sat down at a small table and patted his gat to make sure he still had it on him. Santos returned with a small book bag. He pulled out two black automatic handguns.Ice grabbed one of the guns.

"So dis is the new P-90 I've been hearing so much about?" Ice asked, acting very impressed.

"Yeah, it took me a month to get it, and it shoots armor piercing bullets," Santos replied while placing a box of hollow point bullets on the table.

After five minutes of examining his new toy, Ice started studying the other gun (the P-40).

"Yeah, dats the P-90's little cousin," Santos said with a smile, knowing he was satisfying a good customer. After making sure everything was in working order, Ice pulled out his dough and began counting out twenty-six hundred dollars for Santos.

After they finished their business transaction, Ice said, "I think I'll have dat drink now." Santos went to an old cabinet above the sink and pulled out a half-filled bottle of top shelf Tequila. Ice had two shots and told Santos he had to bounce. Santos gave him five and told Ice to let him know what else he needed in advance. Ice put the backpack in his trunk under the spare tire and sped off. He was feeling good that he had some firepower. He was dying to test it on some fronting motherfucker. He lit up his last Newport and headed back to Queens.

(CHAPTER FOURTEEN)

Shareese rode in the back of the cab thinking to herself how lucky she was. Her plans of opening up a beauty salon since she was a little girl were beginning to materialize. She did her hair and bought a Dolce & Gabbana dress with the leftover money that Ice had given her. While walking out the door her mother asked her who she was going to see looking so nice. She didn't mention Trina's name because everytime her name came up, her mother would preach that something just wasn't right about her. To avoid all that drama, Shareese just told her mom that she was going to see Ice, whom her mother adored. After daydreaming about how she was going to fix up her shop and where everything was going to be laid out, the cab pulled up in front of Trina's building. When Shareese knocked on the door, she was smiling from ear to ear. But when Trina opened the door, Shareese thought she had a funny look on her face.

"What's up, girl," Shareese asked, getting no response. She looked at Trina more closely to see if anything was wrong, and that's when she noticed there were other people in the apartment also. Shareese saw Half a Dread and Rico, and knew right away that they weren't Americans. Dread had his hair down and was wearing one of his endless supplies of fishnet tank tops and sandals. Rico was dressed in all black looking directly at her. The third man was dressed ordinary, wearing expensive jewelry and looking dead serious like the other two. Their stares made her feel uncomfortable, so she said, "Hi, I'm Shareese."

When no one responded Trina nervously stepped a little closer and said, "Dis is the business man I've been telling you about. His name is Supreme, and those are some of his business partners," she said while pointing toward the other men.

Already being from the streets, Shareese knew that the situation was more than it seemed. She decided to play along to see what was really up. Preme smiled a fake smile.

"Shareese, take a seat and relax so we can talk," Preme said, Shareese did as she was told. Studying everyone's faces would help her to detect anything that might reveal what was really going on. Dread and his cousin stood in the middle of the room, while Trina stood close to Preme.

"So Shareese, I hear you have a boyfriend named Ice. So tell me a little about him," Preme asked coldly. Right away Shareese knew what time it was. She thought these guys got into some kind of beef with Ice and somehow they found out that her and Ice knew each other. Shareese decided to downplay everything until she knew more about what was going down.

"Ice is not really my boyfriend. He's just a guy I knew from school," Shareese innocently replied.

"You still didn't tell me how he gets down," Preme said, growing more impatient by the second.

"I don't know. I think he might sell weed or something," Shareese answered. Preme shot a look at Trina.

"You said he be robbing motherfuckers, dat's why you had dat knot he gave you," Trina quickly said. Shareese gave Trina a cold stare, her eyes saying, "so you flipping the script on me?" Trina held her former friend's stare. Without warning, Preme backhanded Shareese so hard she fell forward onto the glass coffee table, causing a slight hairline crack down the middle of the table. Rico had a smile on his face, wanting to get in the mix of things.

"Get da fuck up, bitch," Preme growled. Shareese slowly rose to her feet and sat shakily back down at the end of the couch. Preme then said very quietly, "Now keep it real wit me and we won't have to go there anymore. Do you understand?" Shareese shook her head up and down while holding her bruised face. "I wanna know where your boyfriend rests at right now," Preme demanded.

"He lives somewhere in the Heights. I'm not sure where because he always picks me up from the train station. Trina knew that she was lying because she vividly remembered Shareese telling her that she braided Ice's hair at his place.

Trina, thinking only of her own well-being, shouted out, "Dat bitch is lying. She told me dat she was at his place kicking it with him yesterday."

Without hesitation, Preme punched Shareese in her jaw, knocking her back down to the floor and stunning her. Her dress rose up, revealing white panties. Dread stared, which brought a lustful smile to his face.

"Dis bitch is gonna show us exactly where dis cat rest at. Get her on her feet. We out," Preme ordered. Dread rushed over and snatched the still dazed Shareese to her feet while grabbing a handful of her ass.

Ten minutes later they were all in Dread's tinted window van, except Trina. Preme told her to wait until he got back. Dread drove while Preme and Rico sat with Shareese in the back. Shareese's mind was racing a mile a minute. Her only thought was getting away safely. She heard stories of girls dealing with thugged out niggas. On occasions, their girlfriends got murdered because the guys they had drama with couldn't get to them. Shareeese never thought in a million years that she would find herself in this type of heart stopping situation. They drove up and down a couple of blocks.

"Where da fuck does dis nigga live at?" Preme asked.

"I think da next block," Shareese responded. She pointed to a stranger's house and said, "Dat's da house, but I don't see his car." Just at that moment a fat lady walked out of the door holding two small children's hands.

Dread said, "Preme, she's trying to play you. Dat motherfucker don't live here." Preme punched her in the mouth, knocking out her two front teeth and causing Shareese to stagger to the side of the van by the window. Shareese knew these men meant to kill her sooner or later, so in her panic-stricken mind, she pushed Rico aside with all her strength and managed to open the sliding door halfway. She then started yelling at the top of her lungs.

"Help! Help! They trying to kill me. Call the police, call the police." Rico was caught off guard momentarily but reacted quickly by grabbing Shareese by the throat and squeezing with all his might while Preme yanked the door shut. The fat lady had reached the sidewalk and looked toward the van because of all the commotion.

"Drive dis piece of shit," Preme shouted over at Dread. Dread sped off while Rico choked the battered girl into unconsciousness. Dread drove to one of Preme's rundown crack houses. Rico had his Tech-9 pointed at the still unconscious Shareese. When the group reached their destination, Rico slapped her awake while Preme looked out to make sure no one was around. They all quickly rushed the terrified female around to the back entrance. They took her to the cold, damp basement where all the doors and windows were secured. Preme then turned on a radio while the other men sat Shareese down, tying her hands and feet to the chair.

Shareese regained her senses and realized that she was now in some kind of basement with her hands tied behind her back.

"Please, let me go. I won't tell anyone. Just let me go. I promise," Shareese pleaded. The kidnappers laughed out loud because they had heard that before. Shareese then looked down at the blood on her dress, which caused her to begin crying and begging even more.

"Shut dat bitch da fuck up," Preme shouted. Dread gave her two sharp slaps to the face, swelling one of her eyes. Preme settled at the table in the corner and pulled out a small bag containing coke. He poured some of the drugs onto a plate and took a strong hit. "Now, do what you do best," he said to his hired men.

Shareese started crying uncontrollably just as Rico was coming back from the bathroom carrying a medium sized glass bottle of ammonia. Dread thought to himself, *dat motherfucker is always coming up with some new shit.*

"Yo cuz! Hold her head backwards," Rico said.

Dread grabbed a handful of Shareese's hair and yanked her head backwards. Rico then poured almost half of the ammonia up the victim's nose. Ten seconds later Dread let go of her head. Ammonia mixed with blood and snot flowed from Shareese's burning nasal passages. She started gasping for air, shaking her head wildly from side to side like a pit bull.

"Now, where does dis rude boy really live at?" Dread asked, getting a closer look at the girl's wet dress, which made her nipples more visible.

"He lives at 118 Avenue. I, I think in a yellow house."

"You think?" Dread acted like he was outraged and ripped off her dress, leaving her in only her panties. Rico didn't really care what went down as long as he got that info.

"I'll take you back. Please, I won't try anything. Give me another chance. Please don't hurt me again," she screamed.

"We tried it your way before, and now you'll try it our way," Rico replied with a smirk. He then went back to the dirty bathroom and came back with a silver curling iron that was being heated up. Rico had purposely set the temperature at maximum for full effect. When Shareese saw the curling iron in the mad man's hands, her eyes grew wide beyond their limits, causing her to shout out Ice's address and what kind of car he drove. Dread slapped her again with his ring hand, causing a deep cut on the side of her head.

To Dread's surprise and pleasure, his cousin said, "We're going to make sure you're telling us the truth," and he ripped off her panties. When Dread saw Shareese's neatly trimmed pubic hairs, he wanted her right there on the spot. But business always came first. Shareese started a hopeless struggle as the possessed Rico leaned closer with his torture tool.

Preme, who had just taken another hit of coke, said, "You two are bugged the fuck out."

Shareese looked at Preme and said, "I told dem everything I know. Please let me go. I won't tell. Fuck dat nigga. It's his fault he fucked with you. I don't have nothing to do wit anything," Shareese shouted through bloody lips.

Preme ignored her pleas and threw his feet up to finish watching the show. In one swift motion Rico shoved the hot, burning curling iron up in Shareese's vagina. The shocked female let out an ear-shattering scream, causing her whole body to tremble. Her eyes then rolled into the back of her head before she passed out.

"Damn cuz, you should have let me hit dat first before you went and fried da poom-poom," Dread said, disappointed.

Preme stood up and replied, "Yo, let's finish up and go get dis fucker."

Rico, satisfied with his victim's answers, cocked his gat back and shot Shareese through the right eye. Splooosssh! The eye disintegrated upon contact with the bullet. Both men rolled the body up, along with her clothing, in an old moldy bedspread and placed it in the van.

"Yo, do what you gotta do!" Preme stated. As Dread drove off, Preme called Trina and told her to come and pick him up. While he waited, he did a couple more lines of his product.

(CHAPTER FIFTEEN)

Ice drove at a normal speed thinking, *damn my pockets are hurting right now.* He decided to head over to Jade's place to see if she had any more info on the next guy they were scheming on. Ice wished she had a cell phone because he didn't want to bounce over to her place for nothing. *She's probably out shopping, spending time with her son, or doing whatever she do in her free time,* he thought.

Halfway to Jade's house, Cherry hit him up on his cell phone.

"Ice, you gonna come pick me up today?" She asked, sounding horny.

"You know the Armory on the corner by the Indian store?" He asked.

"Yeah," she responded.

"Well be there at around ten. If I'm a little late, don't go anywhere. I'll be there," Ice said while making a sharp turn.

"Okay," Cherry said. Before she could prolong the conversation, Ice pushed the end button on his cell phone.

A little while later, Ice was ringing Jade's doorbell. One thing he noticed about her house was that it was always so quiet and peaceful. The other girls he knew who stripped, or performed adult shows as they put it, always had various activities going on around their residences. The other dancers had guys pulling up in all types of vehicles, with no regard for the time. Every so often petty beef jumped off when certain customers bumped into each other at a promiscuous dancer's house. Fights broke out when that particular female misled the guy, making him think he was the one (so to speak). Ice thought, *how lame could some of these guys be. First of all you fronted with your little bankroll to get her attention, and then when she steps up to someone with bigger pockets, you get jealous and start shooting up shit. When would these clowns realize that those type of women were after only one goal: the nigga wit the fattest knot and what he could do for her.*

Jade never let anyone know where she lived, not even her fellow dancers. When she did accept a ride from a customer who was sweating her, she always let them drop her off a block away from her place. When she saw the frustrated driver was far enough, she would then walk to her real destination. Ice knew how most women in that situation feel about strangers knowing where they lived. When Jade tried that trick with him, he pulled off, waited a few minutes, and came back around the corner just in time to see her putting the key into the lock. Ice then yelled, "I caught you," which made her break into a laugh.

Ice heard a little bark, which he knew to be Snowball, her white poodle. He heard a soft click and knew someone had opened the peephole device. Jade opened the door wearing a simple, no frills, pink sweat suit. You could still make out her thick, shapely figure even though the clothes she wore were baggy. She gave him a hug, and grabbed his arm, pulling him inside.

Jade's house looked just like any other house in a middle-class neighborhood. She had average furniture. A simple polished coffee table, and a variety of family portraits, plastered the walls. Snowball started sniffing around Ice's feet, wagging her tail.

"Go on, get in the kitchen and eat your dinner," Jade playfully shouted. "You want anything to drink since I'm going to the kitchen?" She asked.

"Nah, I had some wicked shit earlier," he answered back. Jade came back carrying a wine glass filled with the mixed drink, Sex On The Beach. She sat down next to Ice.

"So, what's up?" She asked.

"I just dropped by to see what the deal wuz wit dat move we've been talking about." Ice inquired.

"Shorty said she gonna stop by Jezebel's tonight and have a couple of drinks wit me while filling me in," Jade answered with confidence. "Da way shorty was kicking it, da kid has crazy cheddar and da only reason he's still flowing is because he's living off da strength of some real motherfuckers," she added.

"Fuck dat nigga and whoever else he's down wit," Ice responded back, eager to get at this guy. "So what you was doing before I came over?" Ice asked.

"I just put Juan to sleep waiting for moms to come watch him so I can start getting ready for work," Jade replied while finishing the last of her drink. They talked for about a half hour before Ice said he had to bounce and take care of something.

"I'll call you later on about dat," Jade shouted as Ice was getting into his car.

A while later Ice pulled up in front of the Armory, and sure enough Cherry was leaning on a mailbox waiting for him. He beeped the horn and rolled the window down to let her know it was him. She smiled and hopped into the passenger side with a quickness. He rolled the tinted window up because he didn't want to be seen riding around with this hood rat bum chick. Cherry had on a green Boston Celtics team dress with white lettering. Ice had noticed the same team dress in the window on Jamaica

Avenue for ten dollars. Ice thought, *her body was definitely banging in that tight, short ass skirt.*

As soon as she got into the vehicle, she started to adjust the radio station. Ice decided he had to check her quick. He knew this was a ghetto girl's way of testing the guy when first meeting them.

"Yo shorty, don't no one fuck wit my sounds unless they ask first," Ice said coldly, letting her know what time it was.

"My bad," she responded, and then added, "Dis is an ill whip," trying to change the subject.

"It's alright," Ice nonchalantly responded. He knew automatically what type of chick Cherry was. She was the common ghetto bird who didn't have two nickels to rub together, always looking for a good time. They just wanted to hang out with guys who had access to a car, weed, or liquor money to get them straight. After that, if the guy had a little game (not much), he could get some pussy. The only guys they smoked and ate off, and didn't give up the panties to, were the extremely lame ones.

Ice double-parked in front of the weed spot, which was a regular looking bodega. Inside was dusty and had old, outdated junk foods that one would dare to buy. A person would go to the back of the store where they would be confronted with bulletproof glass. Ice handed her a ten-dollar bill and some singles, and told her to hurry up. As Cherry was climbing out, Ice knew right away that she wasn't wearing any underwear, because a dress that tight would have shown some sort of panty line.

Cherry came back, and right away she began splitting the Philly with her house keys before he even had a chance to pull off. Ice didn't want to take this scallywag to his apartment because he didn't know how she got down and who she knew. He didn't want to take her to a hotel because he was low on funds and plus he didn't think she was worth it. So Ice decided to hop on the Belt Parkway and just ride around blasting a DJ Clue CD.

They rode in silence until they both got their first strong pull in. Ice turned the music down and asked her, "So, what's your status apparatus?"

"I like fucking wit real dudes who's bout it, bout it," she answered in between puffs. Ice noticed the weed relaxing her body movements more and more, causing the already short skirt to rise higher and show more of her perfectly sculptured thighs. *Dis bitch has a crazy ill body, if only I could do something about her grill piece*, Ice thought.

"So why they call you Cherry?" He asked, knowing that wasn't her real name.

She gave Ice a look and said, "What do you think?"

"You tell me," Ice said. She then moved her dress up a couple of inches, showing him her hairy bush. Ice, being well acquainted with hood rat protocol, reached over and put his hand dead center on the kitty cat. Cherry smiled, and he slid his middle finger inside her semi-wet vagina. She then threw the roach out the window and spread both her pussy lips apart, revealing pinkish-red inner pussy.

"Dats why they call me Cherry," she replied, thinking, *I got dis nigga open. I'm going to get some of dat paper.*

Ice automatically started thinking about a place to fuck this freak. Before anything else could jump off, his cell phone went off. He removed his hand and answered it. It was Jade. Ice spoke carefully, trying to keep the conversation a mystery to Cherry or whatever her name was.

"Yeah, word up! I'm listening. Tonight? No problem. I'm on it. Peace." Ice then hung up.

"Who was dat?" Cherry asked. *Here we go again*, Ice thought. *Fucking chicken head trying to test me again.*

"Check dis out, shorty. You just met me and you're all in my business. I suggest you slow down," Ice said while looking her dead in her eyes. Before she could reply, Ice finished, "Yo! I got shit to do. Where you want me to drop you off at? He wanted to hit shorty, but he wanted and needed dough even more.

Cherry looked over, rolled her eyes, and said, "You can drop me near the Ave."

"Good enough," Ice responded. They rode in silence. Ice was deep in thought about his money plan, and Cherry was thinking on how she was going to get some money from Ice before he dropped her off.

As they approached the Ave, Cherry said, "Can you give me some money for a hotel, so we could have a place to chill later on? Ice thought to himself, *dat's a new one.*

"I'm cool, shorty," he replied as they reached the Ave. Cherry got out and leaned forward on the passenger side window, showing her cleavage. *Dis is gonna be her last attempt of trying to get some of my cheddar*, Ice thought.

"Yo, Cherry I'm gonna call you," Ice said before she could throw some more weak game at him, and knowing damn well he didn't have her number. "Okay," she said not wanting to push the issue. Ice rolled up his window and raced off. Cherry began walking down the block swinging her hips and hoping to attract a guy in a ride.

(CHAPTER SIXTEEN)

Dread drove his cargo van, and what was left of Shareese's once beautiful body.

"Dat bitch sure could yell," Dread said, directing the statement to Rico. Rico just nodded his head up and down.

"I still wish you would have told me first before you rammed dat thing up in her." "I'm sure if she would have seen my mandingo swinging toward her face, she woulda gave up everything including da poom-poom," Dread replied while cracking a smile. He talked about nothing for ten minutes before he saw police lights flashing for him to pull over.

Dread pulled over slowly and whispered, "As soon as dis cop walks over, I'm gonna put two in him and keep it moving.

"Relax, and let's play it by ear. He's probably a rookie," his cousin replied. Even as he was telling Dread to cool out, he still took out his own gun and held it down against his leg.

A white cop with dirty blond hair walked up to the driver's side window, while his partner, a pudgy black officer, stood off by the passenger's side.

"Yes, officer?" Dread asked in his best "please don't fuck with me voice."

"Sir, are you in a hurry for some reason?" The cop asked the driver. Both men in the van tensed up, ready for any type of threatening words on the officer's part.

"No, why do you ask?" Dread answered, tightening his finger on the trigger.

"You have a real low tire in the back of your vehicle. It must be a slow leak. You're going to be riding on your rims real soon," the cop said.

"Thank you, officer. I appreciate it. I was headed back home already," Dread responded back.

"You gentlemen have a nice evening," the officer said. As the killers were driving off, Dread said, "Dat cracker must have gotten some head last night or something."

"Yeah, he lucky he did, because he almost had his shit pushed back." Both men then laughed.

"Let's get your bad-luck bitch out of here and to her new home," Rico said, not wanting any more surprises.

Moments later the men arrived by the train tracks and threw Shareese's body among the trash. They then drove back to their apartment to switch rides back to Rico's Maxima. Both men were now riding clean so they decided to pick up some skunk weed.

"Yo, cuz. Ain't dat a black Acura with twenty-inch Hartage rims in front of da spot?" Dread asked Rico.

They drove slowly by the weed spot as Dread looked more carefully and replied, "Hell, yeah." Just at that moment Cherry was getting out of Ice's car to purchase their weed.

"Oh shit! Dat's that red-boned bitch dat was fucking with Rahmel up in da pool hall the other day."

"I remember that ugly face and dat fat ass," Dread shouted, getting hyped up. "Dat's gotta be dat bodtee boy Ice pushing dat whip," Dread added. Rico was at the corner by now, so he turned the corner so they could go around the block.

"Cuz, you pull up right alongside of him so I can get busy," Dread replied while holding his gun in his lap. When they got back around the block, the black Acura was gone. The men in the Maxima drove around the area for fifteen minutes before going back to pick up their weed

While they were smoking and riding, Dread asked Rico, "Do you think Rahmel got something to do wit dat jump off with Supreme?"

"Yeah, why else would one of Rahmel's ho's be riding around wit dat Ice cat. I say we kick it to Rahmel first to see what's really up," Dread said.

"Fuck dat shit. Our guns gonna do da talking," Rico spat out.

"Yeah, fuck it. Dat motherfucker is already convicted and found guilty on all accounts," Dread added while taking a long pull of the skunk weed.

"Dat bitch is gonna get it, too," Rico replied.

"I feel you, but let me do my thing first before you fuck up the poom-poom," Dread said. Both men laughed, still puffing on their blunt.

[CHAPTER SEVENTEEN]

Ice was straight now that he received the phone call that he had been waiting for. He raced home and threw on his desert storm camouflage outfit with the sand color North Face boots. He then put his newest toy (P-90) in his waistband and stuffed a couple of sets of handcuffs and duct tape in his jacket before heading out the door. Jade had informed him that the Dominican guy they planned on getting would be at a certain location only for tonight. Jade gave him the address.

"No matter what dat nigga tell you, he's definitely holding," Jade told Ice.

On his way to his mission, Ice stopped and picked up a double deuce of Heineken. Ice sipped his cold brew as he listened to a Funkmaster Flex mix CD, getting into the mood. He arrived at the apartment building just as he tossed his empty Heineken bottle out the window. He drove around the surrounding area to see if he could peep anything out of the ordinary. When he was sure everything was normal for a Saturday night, he parked his whip and started walking toward entrance of the building. He noticed security cameras pointed at the entrance, but he didn't care. He never came to this part of the neighborhood anyway. He spotted a lady carrying a couple of shopping bags and offered to help her in order to gain entry. The woman felt very flattered that someone with Ice's looks would pay attention to her. She was single and Haagen Dazs had destroyed her figure, not to mention her social life. Once they got inside Ice asked her what apartment the superintendent stayed in, because he just moved in and his sink was stopped up. She told him the apartment number. Before she could tell Ice her apartment number, he politely said thank you and walked off.

Damn, the lady thought as she watched Ice walk away. Ice made his way to the super's door. *Knock, knock, knock.*

"Who the hell is it this late at night?" Ice heard a voice from behind the door.

"I'm sorry to disturb you, sir, but my toilet keeps overflowing and it's making me a little sick," Ice responded through the closed door. The door swung open and an older man in a tattered housecoat stood in the doorway. The man looked Ice up and down suspiciously.

"Who are you?" He asked. "I don't recognize you. What apartment did you say you stayed in?" Ice threw a number off the top of his head.

"4C," he answered.

"I know who lives in 4C. That's Mrs. Waterbuam. Who the fuck are you?" The man asked, trying to intimidate Ice by his stare. Ice pulled out his gun and shoved it into the man's potbelly.

"Get back inside," Ice ordered. The man slowly backed up with his mouth wide open as Ice backed him up into the man's apartment. Once inside, Ice kicked the door shut and took a quick look around to make sure the man was alone.

"I don't have any money," the man stuttered.

"It is about the money, but not yours," Ice replied. "Now go sit your ass on dat raggedy chair." The man did as he was told with his hands still in the air.

"Now listen," Ice said. "I want you to put on your overalls and tool belt, and whatever else you motherfuckers need, and come wit me. Put your hands down. Dis ain't no motherfucking western," Ice said.

The man quickly dressed in a pair of dingy blue jeans and grabbed a rusted toolbox. Both men rode the elevator to the fifth and last floor.

"Now you tell whoever answers the door that you have to get inside. Now if you don't convince dem, I'm going to put a bullet in dat big ass head of yours," Ice stated coldly. They reached the apartment with the super sweating profusely as he knocked on the door. Ice stood off to the side pointing his gun at the man's kidneys. Now he had a black du-rag covering his face and he looked very much the part of a bank robber from the old west. The super knocked once again and a male voice called from behind the door.

"Yeah, what you want?"

"Hello, I'm the super of the building and there's a gas leak coming from an apartment on this floor. I have to check every apartment," the super said, trying to remain calm under the circumstances.

"Why you coming so late? Come back in the morning," the male voice responded back.

"I can't, because the reading on my gas monitor is at dangerous level, and it could result in an explosion," the super answered while glancing over at Ice and the gun that was pointing at him.

"How long will it take?" The voice asked.

"Five minutes, that's all," came the response. There was some slight noise from behind the door as if some latches were being opened. The door swung open. All the guy got to say was "hurry da fuck..." before Ice pushed the super into him, knocking them both off balance and onto the floor.

Ice shut the door and asked the confused man, "Who else is in the apartment?"

"Nobody. Just me," the guy answered looking at the extremely large gun pointing at his head.

Ice then pulled out his handcuffs and extra strong duct tape. He then ordered the super to handcuff and duct tape the guy to a chair, while still holding them at gunpoint. Once he made sure the guy was tied up pretty tight, he proceeded to secure the super in the same manner.

"Whatever is going on between the two of you is your business. I have nothing to do with nothing," the super said, stating his case.

"Keep your mouth shut and you might make it through dis," Ice replied.

"Yo, I got a couple of gees in my coat pocket," the guy said in a heavy Dominican accent. Ice walked over to the expensive lambskin jacket and pulled out a huge knot of money from an inside pocket. He stuffed the money in his own pockets.

"Don't you all go nowhere," Ice told them. Ice walked slowly throughout the apartment. When he reached the bedroom, he thought he heard a faint noise. He stopped in the middle of the floor and just listened, trying to detect where the noise had originated from. He then went over to the closet, which had sliding doors, and carefully opened them.

"I know you're in there. Come out or I'm going to start blasting," Ice stated, meaning every word he said. He waited for a second and said, "I'm going to count to three and then it's on." He raised his gun and counted.

When he got to two, he heard a female's voice say, "All right. I'm coming out. Please don't shoot." A woman slowly emerged from the darkened corner. Ice, being on point, noticed something by her foot so he tightened his finger on the trigger and told the girl to hold up. He then told her to kick whatever was on the floor over to him. She did as she was told. The object on the floor turned out to be a stun gun. Once he had the weapon in his hand, he told her to come out in the light.

Oh, shit! Dis got to be the smallest world in da universe, Ice thought. Standing in front of him wearing a see-through nightie, and smelling like fresh crushed berries, was the female in the silver Range Rover who had dissed him earlier that day. Ice played it off like he had never seen her before.

"Get in the fucking living room," he said. She quickly walked toward the living room where the other two men where tied up. Ice watched her swaying hips thinking, *Damn, dis bitch is definitely a star.*

Once Ice had the girl tied up like the men, he waked over to the Dominican guy and said, "I thought you said you were the only one here?" Before the guy could respond, Ice smacked him in the face with his gun.

"Ahhh!" the guy yelled out as his eyes grew wide with fear.

Ice then said, "I'm going to ask you a question, and all I want is a simple answer." Ice stood directly over the man and said, "Where the shit at?" Ice didn't want to spend time searching the apartment because that took time, and anything unexpected could happen.

"What you talking about?" The Dominican guy asked, playing dumb. Ice took out the stun gun and turned it on. The dangerous blue light crackled across the two metal points. Ice had never used a stun gun, but he was eager to test its effects on someone. Without hesitation he pressed the device into the man's neck. The man screamed and fell backwards, drooling from the mouth.

Ice put the chair upright and waited a minute before saying, "Now where's the motherfuckin shit at?"

"I don't know what you're talking about. I gave you all the money I have." Ice took the stun gun and put it to the man's crotch.

"Okay tough guy," Ice said. "I'm going to fry your nuts in three seconds and den we're going to see how long your bitch stay with you."

"It's behind the fridge. It's behind the fridge," the man said, knowing he could always replace the drugs.

Ice smiled and walked toward the kitchen. He moved the refrigerator and snatched up a black duffle bag. He unzipped it and saw four neatly wrapped bundles in clear plastic containing a crystal white powdery substance. Just by looking at the color and texture Ice knew it to be some top notch cocaine. He never fucked with drugs, because he considered it a hassle to get rid of. When he did come up with some product, he usually sold it real cheap.

Ice walked back to where everyone was tied up. By now the Dominican guy had regained his composure and was grilling Ice.

Ice looked back at him and said, "Now nigga, dis is for giving me a hard time." He walked over and pressed the stun gun against the man's privates. The man screamed, started shaking, pissed on himself, and passed out.

"You didn't have to do dat foul shit. You got what you wanted," the female shouted. Ice turned toward the girl and thought, *I don't believe dis shit, dis bitch is still trying to play me.* He then walked over and stood over her thinking about what to do. The girl caught the brutal look in Ice's eyes and wished she had kept her mouth shut. Ice then took his gun and hit the super in the back of the head, knocking him unconscious.

"Okay bitch, now we're alone. Well, almost alone," Ice said, smiling. He then went into the kitchen and returned with a knife. He cut the now terrified woman from the chair and re-taped her hands together.

"I think your boyfriend has another stash in the bedroom. If there's nothing back there, then I'm out," Ice said. The girl walked with Ice toward the bedroom to let him search the room, eager to have him on his way. Once they were in the bedroom, she spotted the hungry, lustful look in Ice's eyes and she knew he wanted more than an extra stash. She tried to run to the door, but was yanked to the floor by her hair.

"Bitch, if you try dat again I'm going to make your face look like a jigsaw puzzle." Ice growled while holding the knife to her cheek. Ice then ripped her nightgown off, revealing as damn near perfect of a body one could have.

"I'm on my period," she shouted out, hoping that it would turn off the would-be rapist.

"Is dat so?" Ice replied, not believing her. With his free hand, he pulled down her panties. He saw a Kotex attached to her underwear with a spot of blood on it. Ice stared for a second, and she breathed a sigh of relief when she saw the look on Ice's face.

"You lucky, bitch, but not that lucky," Ice said in a heavy voice. She had no idea what he meant until he ordered her to turn onto her belly. Right away she knew his intentions were to sodomize her.

"Listen, I know where there's a lot of money at. I could take you there right now. It's at least three hundred thousand dollars," she said, hoping that his greed would overcome his rapist motives. Ice was beyond thinking about money right now. This female had treated him like a nobody twice, and plus her body was turning him on like an unthinkable animal.

"Bitch, I said get on your stomach," Ice demanded.

"Please, please. I know exactly where the money is at." She refused to budge an inch. Ice pulled out the stun gun.

"Now are you going to do what I told you, or is shit going to get real up in here?" Ice said.

"I know dis guy who has mad weight," she fearfully said in her Trinidadian accent. Ice shocked one of her breasts, causing her to scream and curl up into a crying ball. He then went to the bed and grabbed a pillow.

"Now bitch, what it's going to be?" He asked.

"Okay. Please just don't hurt me anymore," she responded back with snot and tears running down her face.

Ice took off his pants and knelt down toward the floor. For some reason this pretty woman crying and begging had Ice fully hard. He slipped the pillow under her stomach and inserted his throbbing penis into her dry rectum. She let out a little scream when he tried to enter her. He realized that he wasn't making any progress, so he went to the kitchen and came back with a small can of Crisco oil he had noticed earlier. When he reached the bedroom, the girl had crawled into a corner with the pillow covering her body. Ice grabbed her by the hair and forced her to the bed. By now she was crying hysterically, so he slapped her, which caused her to cry even more.

Let me get this over with, Ice thought as he rubbed a good amount of Crisco oil on his dick. He positioned the now in-shock female and eased himself into the girl's sacred body cavity. She tried in vain to wiggle away, but he held her tightly by the hips. He pounded away at her insides for about three minutes before he felt himself explode inside her. When Ice withdrew, she farted, and a light stream of feces ran down her leg.

"You nasty, ho," Ice shouted as he hopped up from the bed. He then noticed that the girl was looking at him funny. That's when he realized the sweat had caused his du-rag to slide down around his neck showing his face. Ice wiped himself off on the sheet thinking, *shorty is too traumatized to remember me.*

When he was fully dressed he looked at the girl with disgust and said, "Bitch, you ain't all dat. You're just another hood rat who came up lucky." She looked at Ice with murderous eyes, remembering both times she had run into him. Ice grabbed the dope and was out.

Twenty minutes later, when she knew that the rapist was long gone, she cleaned herself up and put on some clothes. She picked up the knife off the floor and slowly walked toward the living room. She heard a slight moan coming from Carlos and she cut him loose. She helped him over to the couch while looking over at the super. He was still unconscious with a line of dried blood running down the back of his neck.

"Mia, are you alright?" Carlos asked, looking around to make sure his attacker was long gone.

"Dat motherfucker violated me. I swear on my mother's grave he's going to be six feet deep before the week's out," Mia shouted. "I've seen him around the neighborhood before. He must have been following me all along," she added. She then reached for the phone.

"Who you calling?" Carlos asked.

"Who else? Supreme," she answered.

Carlos grabbed the phone and said, "What da fuck are you doing? You can't tell Supreme or nobody what went down here tonight. Think about it. How you going to explain to Preme what you were doing in dis apartment with a nigga in the middle of da night?" Carlos asked.

Mia knew he was a hundred percent right. If Preme were to find out about her creeping around, it would be a wrap for her. Mia ran to the bathroom crying, knowing that the guy who raped her in the worst way would be getting off. Carlos didn't give a fuck about Preme, but Preme might bring drama, and drama was always bad for business. Carlos then made a phone call to his peoples to help him get rid of the old man's body.

(CHAPTER EIGHTEEN)

Trina was relaxing in her apartment, sipping on Chardonnay, and watching TV. She flipped from channel to channel not finding anything that really interested her. All night and day she wondered what they had done with Shareese. She tried to hint to Preme about what happened, but he just brushed it off and changed the subject. They probably just slapped her around a couple more times and put the fear of God in her.

The phone rang and she chit-chatted with one of her girlfriends for a while. Her attention was drawn back to the television set. Trina jumped up and spilled her drink when she saw a picture of Shareese flash across the screen. The newscaster continued her report.

"A Miss Shareese Jackson, age twenty, was found nude and beaten to death earlier this morning by a man walking his dog. Her badly beaten body was found partially hidden in a weeded area among the debris." Then the news channel showed two medical examiners carrying a black body bag toward the city coroner's van, with residents milling around. They would have something to gossip about for a couple of weeks to break the boredom of their bleak lives.

The anchorwoman appeared back on saying, "If anyone has information about this homicide, please contact your local prescient. All calls are kept confidential."

Trina just sat there with her mouth wide open and staring at the screen even though they were talking about the weather now. She snapped out of her trance and poured herself a full glass of champagne, wishing she had some cocaine. She was thinking about what to say if Shareese's mother were to contact her. She settled on saying she hadn't seen or heard from Shareese in a week. That's it. She would stick to her story and no one would ever be the wiser.

"Shareese shouldn't have been fucking wit the wrong motherfucker. She's from the streets. She knows what time it is. She just caught a bad decision," Trina rationalized. She desperately wanted to call Preme and get high, but for some reason she didn't want to be around him. The phone rang and Trina nearly jumped out her skin. She just knew it was the police calling to ask her some questions.

"Hello," she answered with trepidation.

"Trina what's up? There's money to be made," the voice on the other end said. Trina knew right away who it was.

"You know I'm wit dat," Trine said. "What time you planning on breezing by?"

"I'll be there in a couple of hours, so be ready. You're never fucking ready when I come through," the male caller stated.

"I promise you, I'll be ready. I need some air. Oh, bring some of dat thang," she quickly added.

"Peace, I'm out," the guy said as the phone went dead.

Trina was feeling better now that it wasn't the cops, and also that Born was bringing her some coke. *His shit wasn't as banging as Preme's, but it was better than nothing*, she thought. She took a long hot shower and started preparing herself for tonight.

Trina was thinking that she wanted to get away from Queens for a while when she heard someone knocking on the door. Her first thought was that it was a couple of detectives in some cheap suits to bring her down to the station. She breathed a sign of relief when she looked through the peephole and saw that it was Born. She opened the door.

"Damn, baby, you're gonna spoil the tricks tonight," Born said while looking her up and down. Trina was wearing a short Genevani dress with a split on the side and matching three-hundred-dollar pumps. She grabbed her purse and told Born that she was ready.

As soon as they were in Born's candy apple red Lincoln Navigator Trina asked, "So, you bought it?"

"Slow down and relax. You know I got you," he answered. Born jumped on the Belt Parkway heading toward Brooklyn. He then pulled out a small plastic bag and handed it to Trina. She took the bag and dug one of her long painted fingernails into the product. Once she snorted a couple of times, she asked Born did he want a hit.

"You know I don't fuck around, but do you," he answered back. *More for me*, Trina thought as she took another hit.

They got off their exit and drove down Pennsylvania Avenue. They hit the strip to see who was out and if the customers were feeling generous tonight. Born knew which guys would pay plenty to fuck a pretty white girl with a ghetto laid-out body. He set Trina up with high paying customers, and she in turn got thirty percent of what he charged them (or so she thought).

The strip was pumping, but it wasn't yet at full force. When the clubs and bars let out, the guys would hit the blocks to find a girl to fulfill their needs. On weekends the majority of customers were the guys who struck out in the clubs and bars. Drinking and lusting after women they couldn't have made them extremely horny. There were about six girls on the strip getting their hustle on, and there two cars with guys in them trying to select the best dates for themselves. A beginning-to-turn-chubby brown-skinned female in her late teens, wearing a cheap leopard skin printed mini skirt, was cursing out some guy in a hooptee.

"You clown ass trick motherfucker. Take dat twenty dollars and shove it up your ass. Or better yet, take that money and get your teeth cleaned," the girl spat at the driver.

"Fuck you, you nickel and dime ho. I was trying to help you out, so you can wash dat stink ass rat hole you call a pussy out," the driver yelled back while laughing. The angry girl reached down to grab an empty beer bottle while the guy sped off still taunting her. The bottle struck the back of his bumper.

"Fuck dat wild silly shit. That kind of drama brings attention," Born said, not directing his comment at anyone in particular.

"What time they supposed to be here?" Trina asked.

"I got a couple of fellows rolling through ready to spend dat cheddar. These cats ain't cheap, so do your thang and we could hang out later on," Born answered while rubbing her thigh. "Oh yeah, I almost forgot," he added, "these dudes love blow, so you can get dis pack off for me."

Born then reached under the seat and pulled out a small plastic Ziplock bag filled with coke. As soon as Trina saw the bag her first thought was, *Nah, dem niggas ain't gonna sniff all dis shit. I'm gonna bag some of this for later on.* She took the bag and stuffed it down in her pocketbook. Born pulled over and parked by White Castle.

"Damn, baby, slow da fuck up," Born shouted at Trina. She had pulled out a small bag and started getting her party on again. "Let's at least wait until dem niggas get here. I don't want you smashed the fuck out," Born said.

"Don't worry, I got dis," Trina replied. At that moment while checking Trina he didn't notice the blue and white police car creeping behind them. The police car hit its flashing lights, catching both occupants in the SUV off guard.

"Put dat shit away," Born growled at Trina. She did as she was told just as both policemen walked over to their ride. The cop shined his flashlight in Born's face and then at Trina.

"Sir, you know you can't park here. Can I have your license, proof of insurance, and registration?" The officer asked.

"No problem, officer," Born calmly replied as he reached into his glove compartment for his information.

Feeling good and bold Trina said, "Why da fuck you messing with us for? You see a nice car and automatically you think something's up?

The second officer said, "Miss, can you lower your voice and calm down?"

"Chill out," Born added. The first cop came over and told Born everything was okay with his license and information. He told him he was going to let him off with just a warning.

"I appreciate it," Born replied, trying to be as polite as possible knowing that he was riding dirty.

"Come on and let us go before they try to fuck with us some more," Trina said.

The second officer opened the passenger side door and said, "Miss, can you please exit the vehicle?"

"Why? What da fuck did I do?" Trina asked.

"Miss, could you please exit the vehicle," the officer repeated again, this time in a sterner voice.

"Okay. Fuck," Trina whispered as she complied. She leaned against the SUV's fender while the first officer asked Born to do the same. The first officer watched Born while the second officer searched the Navigator. He found Trina's bag under the passenger seat.

"Miss, is this your pocketbook?" The officer asked.

"Yeah, why?" Trina replied.

"Do I have your consent to check it?" The officer asked.

"No you may not," Trina rudely responded.

"Well then you can wait one or two hours until the canine unit arrives," the officer responded with a smirk.

"Okay, go ahead," Trina said, knowing that her bag was full of makeup and other stuff, so the cop might miss the stash. Born shot her a look, but she didn't notice. Her mind was only concerned with getting on with business. The cop placed the handbag on the hood of the SUV and began going through the contents. As soon as the officer found the plastic bag with the powdery substance he held it so his partner could see it.

"So what do we have here?" The officer asked?

"What you got there, Tom?" The first officer asked while still watching Born very carefully.

"It looks like cocaine," his partner responded, smiling and knowing the arrest was going to look good on his record.

"I never saw dat shit before," Trina shouted, getting excited.

"Oh yeah? It was in your bag along with your I.D.," the officer added. He then told Trina to turn around while he placed handcuffs on her. The other police cars arrived shortly thereafter. The first police officer began to joke.

"Damn, this is a lot of coke," the first officer said. "I think we got a couple of drug kingpin's here."

"I told you dat shit ain't mine," Trina shouted.

"You're going away for a long time, Miss. This is way more than for just personal use."

"Dat's not mine. It's his," Trina yelled, looking at Born. "He told me to hold it as soon as you pulled up."

"I don't know what she's talking about or what's in dat bag," Born calmly stated.

"Sir, do you admit that you gave her this bag to hold?" The second officer asked, knowing the answer already.

"Hell, no!" Born quickly added.

"So you gonna let me go down like dat, Born," Trina said while giving him the sad, puppy dog look. Another officer had given the powdery substance a street drug test. He held up a glass cylinder shaking it to reveal a light blue color.

"It tests positive for cocaine all right," he said.

The cop who put the handcuffs on Trina said, "Miss, you're under arrest for cocaine possession."

"You're free to go sir," he said, directing his statement to Born. Born threw his car in drive and was out. They placed Trina in the back of the patrol car while she kept crying and saying it was his over and over again. When they arrived at the precinct, the arresting officer took her to the desk sergeant to log in her property.

"Officer, I need to speak to detective Chad O`Brian from the 113th precinct," Trina told the desk sergeant.

"Settle down, Miss. We have plenty of competent detectives right here," he said, leaning over to get a good, lustful look at Trina's body. After fingerprinting Trina and taking her picture, they then took her to a holding cell. The cell wasn't as crowded as Trina was used to. A couple of women were discussing their cases.

"They don't have nothing on me. They found the pipe in the bushes," one dope fiend stated.

"Just cop out to ninety days in the drug treatment program," another woman added her two cents in.

Trina had no intention on getting involved in conversations with crackheads, so she stood by the bars waiting for an officer to pass by. When one did, she said, "Excuse me, I need to speak to a detective about an important case."

He looked at Trina with boredom and replied, "I'll see what I can do," and walked off. Trina settled on a wooden bench trying to ignore her new roommates. One hour later a man with a cheap gray suit appeared at the front of the bars.

"Someone wants to speak to a detective about some pertinent information," he stated. Instantly everyone in the holding cell became quiet as Trina walked over to the bars.

"Yes, dat's me," Trina answered.

"What you got for me?" He asked.

"I really need to speak to detective Chad O`Brian from the 113th precinct," Trina said, talking real low knowing everyone was trying to listen in.

"What's your name?" The detective asked.

"I'm Laura Davenport, but you can mention Trina and he'll know who I am."

"Okay, I'll see what I can do," he said and walked off. Trina found a spot in the corner while the other women eyed her suspiciously as she dozed off.

"Miss Laura Davenport, Miss Laura Davenport." She woke up to the sounds of someone calling her name. Waking up, she thought that she had been bailed out, but realized she hadn't even seen the judge yet.

"Dat's me," she replied wiping the sleep out her eyes.

The officer opened the door and said, "Come with me." Trina straightened her dress and followed the officer into a small room.

"Sit tight and someone will be with you momentarily," the officer said before locking the doors. It seemed like forever to Trina before the door opened and a man walked in carrying a folder.

Trina's face produced a smile and she said, "What took you so long?" The man, whose name was Chad O`Brian, worked as part of a narcotic task force out of the 113th Precinct.

"I just can't drop everything and come running every time you get yourself in a jam," the officer stated. Trina began speaking rapidly.

"Dis motherfucker slid some drugs in my bag and when the cop pulled up he said it was mine. I swear to God I didn't know anything about it. Can you see what you can do, maybe get him to say it was his or something?" Trina said while breathing hard.

O`Brian knew right off the bat that she was lying through her teeth. He knew Trina was a cokehead since he busted her two years ago with a small quantity. That time they came to a mutual agreement with her giving him a blow job in exchange for him not taking her in. They fucked and snorted together every now and then.

"Trina, Trina, Trina. It looks like you hit the big time," he responded.

"What you talking about?" Trina asked.

"Well, with the quantity the arresting officer caught you with, they upgraded your charges to transporting. Second, this is election time and the courts are being tough on crime, especially drug related offenses," O`Brian said while looking in the folder.

"I told you it wasn't mine. It was some guy's I barely knew," Trina threw in.

"That's beside the point. The drugs were found on you. Unless he admits they were his, you're stuck with the charges."

"Can we work something out?" Trina replied in a soft tone touching O`Brian's hand. O`Brian smiled at the prospect of banging Trina again. Lately his wife claimed she'd been having migraines and wanted to just put an ice pack over her head and go to sleep. His tight blue jeans showed a small outline of him getting aroused.

He broke Trina's spell and said, "You can't fuck or suck your way out of this one. The only thing I can advise you to do is to cop a plea instead of going to trial. The judge is surely going to throw the book at you with your record. I gotta go," O`Brian said while standing and preparing to leave. Trina's quick thinking, desperate mind acted.

"Wait! I have an ill case I know about," Trina said.

"Keep talking," he said while standing over Trina.

"Do I walk if I give you what you need?" Trina added.

"I don't know. With what they got on you, it's got to be big," the Detective stated.

"You know dat black female Shareese Jackson, whose body was found dead in Queens dis morning?"

"Yeah. A couple of friends of mine are working on the case. A real dirt bag of a crime. What you know about it?" He asked curiously.

"So I walk or what?" Trina asked, knowing she had his full attention.

"Trina, stop playing fucking games and spit it out," the detective yelled out.

"Well, she was murdered by her boyfriend who goes by the street name of Ice," Trina said.

"What's her boyfriend's real name and where does he live at?" Detective O`Brian asked, pulling out his little notebook.

"I know he lives somewhere in the Heights," Trina said.

"If that's his girl then why did he sexually assault and kill her?" He asked.

"I don't know all the details, but I heard she told about a robbery he pulled and he just flipped da fuck out."

Detective Chad O`Brian had been around long enough to know that Trina wasn't telling the whole story, or had left out key parts because the events didn't add up. It was worth checking out, though, because from what he heard there weren't any real leads until now.

"Okay, Miss Davenport. Give me a little time to check things out. I'll talk to my captain and the D.A. to see about getting you out on some reasonable bail."

Trina breathed a sigh of relief, knowing she was going to beat her case. She was then escorted to the holding cell to play the waiting game like everyone else.

(CHAPTER NINETEEN)

Carlos called a couple of his boys to help him clean up the situation that had went down. He kept the conversation very brief, not knowing who could be listening in. He was feeling stressed that a dead man was up in his apartment tied up. He wasn't stressed due to the fact that a human life was lost, since it was attributed to something that he had no part in. He had just finished cutting away the unfortunate man's bonds and was about to drag him onto the side of the sofa when he heard three thunderous knocks on the front door. Carlos froze immediately, knowing only one type of people knock on doors like that, the N.Y.P.D.

Carlos quietly slid the chain and slightly cracked the door. Sure enough, standing on the other side were two policemen looking deadly serious.

"Yes, may I help you officers?" He said, trying to sound as respectful as possible.

"Sir, we got a call of some disturbance coming from this apartment. Are you alone or is there someone else with you?" The officer asked while trying to peek inside the apartment.

"No, I'm here by myself. Dat must have been the T.V. dat someone heard," Carlos replied with a weak smile. He knew from past experience that if the police received a call for disturbance and found out that a female was in the vicinity, they would want to talk to her separately to see if she was all right. Under the circumstances that would have been a dummy move on his part.

"Sir, do you mind if we come in and take a quick look around?" The second police officer asked with a stern face. Before Carlos could respond, Mia called out his name in her still frightened voice. Carlos caught the "I knew you was a lying sack of shit," look in both of the cops faces and slammed the door shut. He proceeded to run to the bedroom where he had some more coke stashed.

Hopefully him and Mia together could convince the police that they all were victims of a home invasion and the super just got in it the worst. They had visible bruises, but there was no way he could explain the drugs they were sure to find when homicide did a thorough search of the premises. He planned to grab his stash and flush it down the toilet. He knew the police would keep knocking with the threat of kicking in the door.

Fuck da door. All I'm worried about is dis twenty-year bid for coke, Carlos thought. He ran past the startled and confused Mia into the back bedroom. He barely reached his hiding place when he heard the familiar crash and heavy footsteps coming toward him.

"Oh, shit," Carlos heard one of the policemen shout and he knew that they had seen the body. He knew he didn't have time to retrieve his drugs, much less get rid of them, so he decided to rush the cops, hoping to get away from the scene that he had no way of explaining.

Carlos ran smack into the first officer losing his balance and falling on top of him. The officer's gun slid toward Carlos's foot as both men twisted and grappled for the upper hand. His partner had his weapon drawn shouting, "Jim, he's going for your gun!" The partner took nervous aim at Carlos's back. He let off three quick shots. The third one hit Carlos just below the shoulder blade. Carlos felt the searing hot white pain and was overcome with a burst of adrenaline. He made it just as far as the hallway when the next bullet tore into his back, shattering his spine and lodging in his liver. Mia just stood there in shock, staring in disbelief at what had just happened. One officer grabbed her arm as the other officer went to check on his handiwork.

Twenty minutes later the blood bath scene was crawling with detectives, regular uniformed officers, and a couple of departmental photographers. One detective had Mia sitting on the couch handcuffed, shooting question after question at her and hoping to catch as many discrepancies as possible in her story.

"So you said you were beaten and raped by an unknown intruder who beat your boyfriend and killed the maintenance worker?" He asked while staring intently at her facial expressions.

"I told you just like I told everybody else what happened," she answered in a aggravated tone.

"So the so-called home invader brutally raped you and you didn't call 911 after he left because you said you were so distraught?" He asked in a non-believing voice.

"Yes, yes, yes. Just leave me the fuck alone. You killed my friend in front of me and then you treat me as if I did something wrong," Mia shouted. The paramedics came over and started asking her where she was feeling pain, if there was any dizziness or nausea, and a whole other host of possible health related problems. Homicide Detective Martinez then instructed a rookie police officer to escort the paramedics to the hospital while the doctor fully examined Mia to see if she was indeed raped.

The police led Mia out of the apartment still handcuffed with E.M.S. following close behind. The hallway was equally filled with police, mostly just standing around talking. Mia's jaw dropped when she saw Carlos lying on his back with his hands behind him, apparently handcuffed after his murder. His face held a death mask of surprise and disappointment that his young life was cut short in such an unreasonable fashion. Dark blood trickled out the side of his mouth and ears as a couple of cops stood close by smoking cigarettes. They were laughing and being jovial as they considered the recently deceased Carlos as no more than trash who needed to be taken out before it started to stink. Mia closed her eyes, wishing that everything was just a drug-induced nightmare.

At the hospital the doctor wrote in his official report that Mia had some sort of slight trauma to her rectum, but he wouldn't confirm that she had indeed been raped. The unsympathetic doctor repeatedly asked her unnecessary and humiliating questions while the officer stood close by behind the thin curtain snickering.

"So was this the first time you had anal intercourse? If not, what was so different about this one that you consider it rape? Why would he want to penetrate your rectum instead of your vagina as you put it?" The doctor asked while taking his latex gloves off.

Mia was then taken to a police station where Detective Martinez continued his abusive questions in the most degrading way possible. After a couple of hours of relentless non-stop harassment, he informed Mia that the District Attorney would want to talk to her in the morning and they would make their decision on how they would want to proceed with her. They then placed her in a holding cell with other women, where she sat close by the phone praying to get in contact with Supreme. She decided to wait until she spoke with the D.A. before making up a lie to tell Preme how everything went down.

(CHAPTER TWENTY)

Rico and Half a Dread were up early to take care of business. After they spotted the black Acura with the unmistakable Hartage rims last night, they went to the address that was provided for them by Shareese. The house was extremely quiet with no sort of activity, plus they didn't spot the car. The hit men sat in their car listening to music and smoking weed, laying in wait for their intended victim for over two hours. When they were sure it was a waste of time, they hit the streets in search of better luck.

The duo rode around the neighborhood in hopes of spotting Rahmel on his bike. They didn't want to step up the pressure on people who might know Rahmel's whereabouts because they would surely put him on point. Some people around the way had love for him and would tell him some crazy Jamaicans were asking about him.

"Dat motherfucker probably know what time it is," Dread replied while puffing on the ganja. He probably bounced outta town or something. Let's head to dat new titty bar, Foxy Sista, across town," Dread stated to his cousin.

"It's the middle of the day. You think it's gonna be bitches up in dat piece?" Rico asked, feeling bored also.

"You know dem hos love paper no matter what time it is. Let's roll out," Dread added. He directed Rico toward the location of the club. They reached their destination and made it inside with no problem because during the day there was only one bouncer on duty and he didn't search anyone. The place was almost empty except for a couple of dancers at the bar talking bullshit to each other on how they got this guy or that guy for his paper. There was one dancer on stage not putting her all into the act, because there wasn't much of a crowd except a few blue collar workers who were holding their dollars like their life depended on it.

Dread and Rico walked toward the back where the pool table was. They played pool for a couple of hours talking about the money they were going to get from this particular hit. Every now and then a girl would come in and ask if they wanted a lap dance. One dancer even told them that it was a one-day special going on, anything to stack the paper. They downed a quick drink before breaking out. They got about a block from Foxy Sista when they saw Rahmel lavishly riding down the Boulevard on his red and black Decanta bike.

They pulled up on the side of Rahmel and said, "Yo, Rah, pull over so I can holler at you."

Rahmel felt an uneasy vibe so he said, "I got to kick it wit you later. I got shit to do." He then sped off.

"I told you so," Rico said. "He knew da street would spit his name out sooner or later, dat's why he bounced like dat."

"Catch up wit him," Dread ordered, now angry. He pulled out his weapon and cocked it back, ready to get down.

Rico sped up, trying to get close enough to Rahmel so his cousin could spray him. Rahmel peeped the Maxima coming at him through his rearview mirror so he started weaving in and out through traffic. Rahmel looked again and noticed the Maxima was way back stuck in traffic. He relaxed a little, but not much, knowing his bike offered no kind of protection. He decided to get with his click to get at Dread and his sneaky ass cousin before they caught him off guard again. He turned off the main road and drove down a side street. He quickly drove down the street almost hitting a little boy on a bike.

"Oh shit!" Rahmel yelled as a bullet whizzed by his head. He rode wit his head down like a Hollywood stuntman. Dread was leaning out his car window yelling.

"Yo, Rah, we just want to talk to you." *Tat, Tat, Tat.* Dread blasted his gun again.

"Yeah, right" Rahmel said to himself. He saw a park, which he drove into. He was going to come out the other entrance and hit the ally. *By da time they drive around the block, I'll be long gone*, Rahmel thought. He looked back a second time and saw Dread and his cousin getting out of their car blasting their guns and running after him like mad men. Rahmel made a sharp turn around the jungle gym and caught one in his left side. He lost control of his bike and slid on the rubber mat. He felt dizzy, but his survival instincts kicked in and he pulled out his .38 revolver and let off all six shots at the running figures. After his gun was empty Rahmel half crawled, half stumbled away. The next thing he knew, he saw the blurry figure of Rico standing over him. Rahmel's last thought was *where da fuck wuz Dread,* right before Rico laced him up in the face and head. Rico then ran back to Dread, who was struggling to get on his feet.

"Yo, cuz, are you all right?" Rico asked Dread, grabbing him from under his arm.

"I'm straight. Motherfuckers can't do me none," Dread weakly said. They reached the car and sped off. Dread was breathing hard trying to put a CD into the CD player.

"Chill out and relax," Rico told Dread. He did as he was told, holding his wounded shoulder. They reached their apartment at record speed. Rico partially carried Dread up the steps and laid him down on the couch. Rico ran to the bathroom and came back with a cold, wet towel and placed it on Dread's bullet wound.

"Yo, cuz, I'm going to Nicole's crib and bring her back here. She's a nurse so she knows all about dis type of shit. I'll be back in ten minutes," Rico stated.

"Before you bounce, light me up a spliff," Dread replied. Rico lit up the Philly, took a puff, and passed it to Dread. Dread was sweating profusely now, trying to smoke.

"I'll be back real quick," Rico told him and ran out the door.

Nicole lived up the block, but she wasn't home. *She must be working a double shift*, Rico reasoned.

"Fuck it, I'm going to have to take him to the hospital," Rico said out loud. He then raced back to the apartment and yelled at Dread, "We're going to head to the hospital where Nicole works at." Dread just looked at him. Rico walked over and saw the blunt still burning from Dread's lips, but his eyes were opened and staring at nothing. Rico knew right then that Dread had went back to the essence. Rico took the blunt.

"I'll finish that for you cuz," he said. "I love you." And then he sat down looking at Dread.

(CHAPTER TWENTY-ONE)

Ice had stashed the drugs in his grandfather's tool shed located in the backyard. He didn't want to take the chance of having that much dope in his apartment. If the police should happen to find that much quantity narcotics in his possession, they would swear to the courts that he was the biggest supplier on that side of town. Ice knew that police had a track record of making things seem worse than they actually were, just to make their case look all the more significant on the so-called war on drugs.

Ice sat back relaxing, watching rap videos and counting his money. The money came up to twenty-six hundred dollars, plus he had the bundles of coke hidden away. Ice poured himself a tall glass of water and started replaying in his mind what had happened in that apartment earlier tonight.

Shit didn't have to go down like the way it did if she hadn't tried to play me out like a chump, Ice thought. *Banging a female's ass out against her will was not his thing, but fuc it. I guess I taught her a valuable lesson. You never know who you dissing in da streets. When you involved in the drug trade everything and anything goes. Dat bitch had to charge it to the game,*" he reasoned. Ice laughed, got undressed, and went to sleep.

Ice awoke to the sound of his phone ringing off the hook. He looked at his watch and it read 7:10 a.m. He picked up the phone, wondering who it was so early in the morning.

"Hello," Ice answered.

"Nathaniel, they killed my baby, they killed my baby," he heard a weeping woman say.

"Mrs. Jackson?" He asked, wondering what was going on.

"Nathaniel, please tell me that you didn't have anything to do with my baby's death. Please tell me."

Fully awake now, Ice said, "Calm down, Mrs. Jackson, and tell me what happened." He still heard her sobbing on the other line. "Mrs. Jackson, what happened to Shareese?" Ice asked, wanting desperately to know what happened.

"Some detectives came by yesterday morning and said that my baby was raped and murdered somewhere in Queens. Nathaniel, those monsters threw her away in the bushes like yesterday's trash."

"What!" Ice couldn't believe his ears. He had just chilled with Shareese a couple of days ago. "Do the police know who did it, or why?" Ice asked, plotting revenge already. There was a slight pause on the other line. Shareese's mother then spoke again.

"Nathaniel, the detectives were asking all kinds of questions about you." Ice didn't respond so she could continue. "They wanted to know the extent of your relationship, what type of person you were, and a whole bunch of other questions. Nathaniel, I told them the last time I spoke to Shareese, she said she was going to visit you. They acted as if you had something to do with Shareese's death."

"Mrs. Jackson, the last time I seen Shareese is when she braided my hair and that was days ago. Last thing she told me was going to see a girlfriend of hers who they supposed to be going into business together. Do you know who she is, Mrs. Jackson?" Ice asked, not liking the way the conversation was going. Shareese's mother was still crying.

Finally she said, "Some white girl in Queens named Trina."

"Mrs. Jackson, I swear to God I'm gonna find out what happened to Shareese," Ice sincerely replied.

"Nathaniel, please tell me you're not involved with what they did to my baby?" Mrs. Jackson asked.

"No ma'am. I swear to Jesus Christ," Ice answered.

"I believe you from my heart, but her brothers and cousins are going crazy over here mentioning your name. I got to go now. I have a lot of people who are going to be stopping by."

She hung up while Ice still held the phone in his hand. He finally put the phone down and quickly dressed without showering. He grabbed his gun, took a quick look around the neighborhood, and drove off in his whip. He went straight to the corner bodega and bought a New York Daily News and the Post along with a fresh pack of Newports. He lit up a Newport and scanned both newspapers carefully. He finally found what he was looking for. There was a small picture of Shareese in her graduation cap and gown next to a small article. The heading read, "Brooklyn woman found slain in Queens." Ice read the article and thought, *dat's some fucked up shit.*

Ice drove back home and started thinking about what Shareesse got herself into for someone to do her so dirty. But Ice was more concerned about how his name got mixed up in things, and why the Jakes were asking so many questions about him. *Well now I am going to have to be more on point*, Ice thought. Or least until he found out what the fuck was going on.

(CHAPTER TWENTY-TWO)

Preme sat in his living room sipping on Bacardi 8 and reading *Sports Illustrated.* He was wondering why he hadn't heard from Half a Dread since the last time he saw him and his cousin. He hoped they didn't do anything stupid like hanging out with some chicken heads and forgetting to update him on the job. Now his girl Mia was missing in action also.

"Where the fuck could she be? I'll handle her ass when I finish up my business with dis so-called gun slinger, Ice," Preme said out loud. Just then his cell phone rang and he turned back around to answer it. He just knew it was Dread calling to tell him that they had this Ice character tied up somewhere half beaten to death waiting for him to show up to finish the show.

"Yeah," Preme answered.

"Where you been at? I've been calling your cell phone for a while and wasn't getting through." A female's voice replied, seeming upset.

"First off, hold the fuck up. Who is dis?" Preme asked, irritated that someone would call him and then start flipping out like this.

"Preme, dis is Trina. I'm on lockdown. Some motherfucker slid some nose candy in my bag when I wasn't looking, and I took the fall," she lied. Preme already knew that Trina wanted him to bail her out. He told himself that if her bail was over a thousand dollars she was on her own. All Trina was to him was a freak white girl with an ill body. There was plenty more where she came from.

"So, did you see the Judge yet?" Preme asked, wanting to end the conversation.

"No, I haven't. But the detectives are talking about hitting me up with a trafficking charge," she quickly replied.

Preme knew right off the bat that she was caught with some weight. *But whose?* Preme thought. Preme also knew that with Trina's drug record, she wasn't getting any bail. He had seen too many cases where the Jakes made a deal with the scared woman to turn state's evidence or set someone up during a phone conversation. *That someone could be me,* Preme thought. He knew Trina's type very well. Use anyone and everyone toward their own benefit. In this specific case, she needed to prove that the dope was someone else's and she just happened to have it on her at the time.

"Preme, you know what? That shit was garbage anyway. Not dat good shit like yours," Trina replied.

"What! I don't know what you're talking about. Don't call me anymore," Preme shouted and then pressed end on his cell phone. "I knew it," Preme said out loud. "Dat bitch must think I'm a new jack or something." He then fixed himself another drink, waiting on Dread's phone call that would never come.

(CHAPTER TWENTY-THREE)

Ice took it easy for most of the day and evening. He needed time to map out what his next move would be. It was only matter of time before the DTs would be pounding on his door. If they couldn't find him, they would always pull the same routine. "Excuse me, so and so, if you happen to see or hear from Ice could you please tell him to call us?" They would say while handing the person their card. If the person were to ask, "Is it serious," they would respond, "no, nothing of the sort. We just want to ask him a couple of questions." If the person they were investigating were foolish enough to call or drop by the station, the script would be flipped on them. The police never really wanted to talk to you, only to process you for whatever they were looking for you for. *I would never fall for da bullshit*, Ice thought.

Ice laid up in his apartment, smoking cigarette after cigarette until it got dark. He threw on his baggy orange and blue New York Knicks jump suit and stuffed his gun in his waistband before carefully heading out the back door. When he was sure everything was cool, he went to the tool shed and scooped out a couple of spoonfuls of coke into a plastic bag.

Ice jumped into his Acura, and soon after he arrived at Jezebel's. He definitely needed to kick it with Jade. With all the different types of niggas that was always flowing through the spot, she had to know at least a couple of guys who would want to buy some coke at a real cheap price. He knew for a fact that Jade would want to get hit off with something. *Fuck it*, Ice thought. *As long as she help me get dis shit off.*

When he arrived at the front door, the bouncers were busy searching customers as they went in. When it was time for Ice to be searched he asked the bouncer closest to him, "How much does it cost to get in dis piece?"

"Ten dollars," came the reply. Ice then pulled out a fifty-dollar bill and told the beefy man to keep the change. Security waved him through, knowing what time it was.

Ice strolled in and noticed the place wasn't as packed as usual. He knew later on it would be so crowded that you would have to stand up with your drink in your hand. He spotted Jade giving some clown a lap dance. As soon as the song was finished Jade covered her breasts with her bikini top, which was pulled to the side. As she began to leave the guy, he grabbed her hand and tried to spit his weak game. Ice could see Jade shaking her head side to side as if to say, "No!" Ice walked by and coughed, which caused her to turn around. Their eyes met and she knew what time it was, "real dough."

Minutes later Ice and Jade were seated at a table by the bar talking.

"What's up?" Jade asked. "How did everything go?"

"You shouldn't even have to ask. You know how I get down," Ice responded. Then a waitress came over and sat down a bottle of Hennessy Reserve with two glasses. Ice smiled as Jade poured both of them double shots.

"So how much you did you come off wit?" Jade asked, eager to have some more quick, easy cash.

"I came off with something, but it wasn't dough," he answered.

"So what did you bag?" Jade asked.

"I came off with some coke. You know I don't fuck around with the drug game, too many snitches."

"So what you gonna do wit it?" She asked while taking a sip of the Hen-rock.

"Dat's why I'm up in here. I know you gotta know somebody who's willing to buy at a mad low price," he said.

Jade looked up at the ceiling and then said, "I know a couple of guys dat might be interested, but they haven't been seen here for a while." Then with money on her mind Jade said, "Hold on, I'll be right back." She disappeared and came back with a thirty–five-year-old dancer who still had the body of a tight twenty-year-old. Her hand revealed her true age when Ice shook it after Jade introduced the two. The stripper, whose stage name was Sparkle, got right to the point.

"I heard you got some product you're trying to get off. Give me a sample and I'll see if it's worth my people's time." Ice pulled out the bag and handed it to her under the table. She concealed the bag and went straight to the bathroom.

When she was gone Ice asked, "So how long you been knowing her? Can we trust her?"

"Dis type of business you can't even trust your own mother," Jade remarked. "You said you want to get da shit off quick. Sparkles knows mad people."

Sparkle soon returned with a huge Kool-Aid smile. "Dis is some bomb ass shit," she stated. She then looked at Ice and asked, "So how much do you have?"

Ice looked at her like, *Who da fuck she think I am? What she thinks I'm a moth-ball who just flew out da closet?*

Sparkle caught the look and tried to ease the tension from her last remark by saying, "Well, if you got more like dis here shit, I got some people of mine who would want to talk to you."

"So how you want to do dis?" Ice asked.

"Well you could get me some bigger samples to let my folks know you fa real, and we could take it from there," Sparkle replied.

"I'm gonna be busy for da next couple of days, so I'm gonna hit Jade off wit something proper to bless you with. When she gets back to me, we could set up da deal," Ice said.

"Dat sounds like a plan," Sparkle replied while shaking his hand. "Well I gotta go stack my paper now," she said as she wiggled off, flirting with a customer as she walked by him.

As soon as Sparkle left, Ice said, "After you get off I'm gonna give you some of dat coke so we can get da wheels in motion.

"Okay, I'm going to try to get off early. In the meanwhile, enjoy yourself while I do my thang."

He chilled for a couple of hours finishing his bottle of Hennessy Reserve and watching all kinds of activities going down that you would normally find in a strip club. He wasn't in the mood for lap dances or phony conversations. His mind was strictly on money and how much he was going to make off his deal. A little while later Jade tapped him on the shoulder and told him let's go.

"About time, these bitches won't let a nigga think for a minute," Ice playfully said as he grabbed her bag. They reached the car and Ice floored his whip, feeling bent from all the liquor. Jade put on her seatbelt, knowing that being intoxicated and driving a fast car never mixed well.

"Slow down," Jade shouted over the music.

"I got dis. I would never do anything to put my girl in danger," Ice replied.

Ice reached his block and pulled right up into his driveway. In his drunken state Ice never noticed the strange Maxima sitting across from his house. Ice got out of the car and told Jade to come on. Jade slowly got out with her expensive high heels hitting the pavement. Then Ice heard a voice say, "Yo money!"

(CHAPTER TWENTY-FOUR)

As soon as Ice heard the words, "Yo, money" in a heavy Island accent, his street experience kicked in. He quickly ran behind Jade, ducking down while pulling out his gun. Jade's first and last thought was, *Ice is always playing around*, right before a bullet from a tech-nine tore through the left side of her neck. Ice quickly sobered up and took aim at the dark figure in a sweat hood. Ice blasted his gun, all three shots missing their target. The mysterious figure shot again as bullets whizzed by Ice's head. Jade wasn't so lucky as two more bullets ripped into her body. Ice held her up by her jacket, but she was slowly falling to the ground. He knew he was about to lose his human shield and the would-be hit man was walking closer and closer while still firing his weapon. Ice's back window of his car blew out along with the passenger side mirror. Ice then heard a voice say, "Drop it, motherfucker!"

Rico turned toward the voice and was instantly cut down by police issued nine-millimeter guns. Bullets turned his chest and stomach area into a mass of bloody pulp. The dead man's trigger finger spasmed, firing off the remaining shots as his body fell in the middle of the street.

"Fuck dat shit," Ice said as he threw Jade off him, her shocked death face hitting the front tire and bouncing onto the ground. Ice scrambled to his car and threw it in reverse, ramming an unmarked police car.

"Freeze!" yelled another voice as he heard bullets hitting his car.

Ice sped off and saw what looked like the whole police force in his rearview mirror. He recklessly drove through the quiet neighborhood at high speeds trying to find the right spot for him to ditch the car and make a run for it on foot. He knew it would only be a matter of time before the police coordinated a plan to trap him in. Ice spotted what he was looking for, an alley that only had one exit. He planned to ditch the Acura in the alley and hit the backyards that he knew so well. He turned the corner at neck breaking speed, losing control of the car and crashing into a corner house. Ice's chest hit the steering wheel, feeling as if someone had hit him with a fifty-pound sledgehammer. When he regained his composure, an army of plain-clothed and uniformed officers were pointing their guns at him.

"Don't move or I'll blow your yellow nigger ass off face of the earth," a red-faced detective yelled. Another cop ordered Ice to place his hand in the air as they slowly approached. He was then roughly snatched out his wrecked car, thrown to the grass, and handcuffed. Other officers were searching the vehicle as another cop held Ice's gun up in the air, smiling as if he held a winning lottery ticket.

All the commotion had caused lights in the quiet Queens neighborhood to flicker on, and curious residents started coming out, standing in doorways for a better view. After being carefully searched, Ice was thrown in the back of a patrol car and whisked away.

The passenger cop turned around and said, "Boy, there are two dead bodies back there, one of which used to be a pretty girl. What you get yourself into?" Ice knew these men were just a couple of nobody uniformed cops trying to get some information so they could have something exciting to talk about in the locker room.

"Well, shit started dis way," Ice stated while the police looked at Ice with amazement. When he knew he had their full attention Ice continued, "we couldn't agree on which corner to pimp your mother on, and dats how da beef jumped off."

The driver laughed and said, "he got you on that one."

"We'll see how many jokes he's got once his pretty ass is sitting up in Sing-Sing," the embarrassed officer spat back. All the men rode the rest of the way in complete silence.

Ice was then led through the back door of the station house and taken to a small room with a large mirror. He knew it was a two-way observation mirror. They told him to sit down and thirty minutes later two detectives came into the room carrying some paperwork. They told the uniformed officer that he could leave. Detective Kowalski and Detective Mathews were the ones investigating Shareese's case, and they were watching Ice's house to pick him up when the gun battle irrupted. Kowalski spoke first.

"I'm Detective Kowalski and this is Detective Mathews." He held his hand out. Ice just looked at him, not moving. "Well, I see you're a man who likes to get straight to business, so let's not waste each other's time," he said. "First of all, we know all about the problems you had with your girlfriend, Shareese Jackson. We also know you raped and murdered her because she knew too much. That guy who was shooting at you tonight, was that one of Shareese's family members out for revenge because of what you did?" Ice just looked at Kowalski and yawned.

"We have reliable sources that would swear under oath that you were the last person to see Shareese alive," Detective Kowalski continued. "We also have a couple of credible witnesses coming down right now as we speak, who saw you dumping the body." By now Kowalski had loosened his tie and was inches away from Ice's face. "Do yourself a favor and tell us in your own words what really happened that day. Did a simple argument get out of hand and you temporarily lost it? We all know how women can get sometimes. You're not a bad kid. Not a spot on your record. I'm sure the D.A. would take into consideration any extenuating circumstances. With the gun charge we could just toss that out. We know you were just defending yourself," Kowalski finally finished.

Ice just looked at Kowalski thinking, *Is dis cracker for real? They think they could pressure me into confessing to murder to make it better on myself before the so-called witnesses get here.* Ice threw back his head and laughed. Detective Mathews, who was black, finally spoke in a heated voice.

"Boy, you think this is a joke? We're not playing games with you. We got a pretty, young girl whose family is planning her funeral because of a scum bag like you. Then we have two more bodies lying in the morgue who happened to be around you at the time of their demise. Ice wanted to say, "yeah, and one of those bodies is in the morgue compliments of the N.Y.P.D.," but he held his tongue. Mathews then took a deep breath and lit up a Marlboro cigarette.

Ice finally broke his silence, "I'm not confessing to shit. I got fucking rights. I'm not saying another word until my lawyer gets here.

"You got the right to life without parole. You got the right to have all your homeboys running up in your pretty stripper girlfriends. Yeah, you got a lot of fucking rights," Kowalski yelled as he slammed the folder down on the table and started pacing the room.

Mathews sat down next to Ice with a worried look on his face and said, "Listen, son." *Oh now I'm a son*, Ice thought. "We have a sworn statement from someone who positively identified you as the perp who killed Shareese Jackson. The jury is going to look at you as an inhuman monster once the D.A. describes in detail and shows pictures of how this young lady who was full of life was tortured and then murdered. The state will play on the sympathy of the jury who has daughters, granddaughters, sisters, and nieces, which is about ninety-eight percent of the general population."

"Then a couple of days later, another young female was killed in your presence," Mathews continued. "Not by your hand though, but nevertheless the D.A. will focus on how you were somehow the cause. The guy you were having the shoot out with, we knew you were just exchanging gunfire in self defense. We could persuade the district attorney to overlook the gun charges if you just tell us exactly what happened with you and your girlfriend." Detective Mathews waited a few seconds for the words to sink in before he continued, "Once you get all of this off your chest, you'll feel a whole lot better and we'll put in our report how remorseful you were."

"Listen here, you Uncle Tom, Oreo cookie motherfucker. I told you before I wanted a lawyer," Ice shouted.

Mathews was momentarily startled. He thought the young guy was buying his "I just want to help you" routine.

"Okay, tough guy, you won't be so smart assed when we match your D.N.A. with what we found on your girlfriend's body. I'm positive that forensics will match up that piece of hardware you were caught with, with a couple of unsolved homicides in your area," Kowalski said with fire in his eyes.

Ice had a confident smile on his face, secretly knowing that his gun was clean and he was no way involved in Shareese's death. *It was only a matter of time before the truth came out*, he thought.

Detective Kowalski banged on the door and a uniformed officer came back into the room. "Get this piece of shit out of my sight before I ram his teeth down his throat," Kowalski yelled. The officer then led the prisoner down the corridor to a small holding cell.

(CHAPTER TWENTY-FIVE)

"Who da fuck he think he is, hanging up on me like dat?" Trina yelled while slamming the phone down.

"What's wrong honey? Your lawyer acting up on you or something?" A prostitute asked, trying to act concerned, but she was really just bored.

"Nah, dat was just some nigga I fuck with now and then," she responded, giving the woman who was all in her business a good look. *Damn*, Trina thought, the dope fiend hooker had tiny red sores around her dry lips, which looked as if she had just ate a powdered doughnut. Trina just wanted to vent her anger on someone so she continued.

"That nigga Supreme has mad money. He just copped a new Range Rover sitting on twenty-fours, and now that he found out dat I'm on lock, he wants to act brand new." By now Trina was walking back and forth and putting on a good show.

"You know Preme?" A voice asked out of nowhere. Trina turned toward the voice and saw an attractive girl with disheveled hair looking as if her world was coming to an end.

"Yeah, I know Preme. Why? Who are you?" She asked in a curious tone of voice.

"If you're talking about Big Preme with da Chinese writing on his neck, den dat's my man. How you know him?" Mia asked. By now the noise in the holding cell had died down and the incarcerated women just knew a fight was brewing. Just then a light bulb went off in Trina's conniving mind.

"Let's go over here and kick it. These nosey bitches have nothing else better to do dan to be all up in mine," Trina replied, loud enough so everyone could hear. Both women walked together to another part of the cramped-up cell and began talking.

"I never knew Preme had a girlfriend," Trina lied. "I only knew of his baby's mother. If I knew he was wit you or anyone else I would never have started fucking with his sneaky ass," she said as innocently as possible. She paused as she looked Mia in the face trying to determine if the fake words were sinking in. "You deserve better dan him. You're pretty and smart. So anyway, what you in here for?" Trina asked, still trying to come up with a plan for her own benefit.

Mia felt that Trina was a goodhearted person who was mislead and deceived by Supreme. She then told the stranger how she and Carlos were up in his apartment when a robber broke in. She went on to say how she was raped and then her friend was killed by the police. To top it off, the detective didn't believe her story, so that's why she was here.

Trina wasn't stupid. She knew Mia was creeping out on Preme and somehow drugs were involved. She didn't care who Mia was fucking. She had found her angle on how to get back at Preme for leaving her in jail.

"You said dis guy raped and beat you? What he look like?" She asked.

"He was tall, light-skinned with mean green eyes. I thought maybe he looked as if he knew me," Mia responded.

"Oh shit! I didn't think nothing of it until now. I was wit Preme and I heard him kicking it wit someone on the phone. I heard him say dat he suspected dat you might be running around on the low-low." By now Mia's mind was paying full attention.

"He was telling somebody on the other end to do a good job on you," Trina continued. "I think Preme set you up to get beaten and raped because of what he thought. Dat phony break-in was just to throw you off. Dat's some fucked up shit to do, after you stood by him," Trina said sounding sympathetic.

When she saw Mia's eyes swelling up with tears, she said to herself, *I should get a fucking academy award.* She told Mia to be strong and do what she got to do. Mia's mind was jumping from one thing to the next like an out-of-control remote control.

The next morning Mia's name was called out and she was escorted out of the cell. As she was leaving, Trina gave her a look as if to say, "You know what you have to do." Hours later Trina was shocked when the guards informed her that she had been bailed out. Throughout the release process, she kept asking everyone whom she came in contact with, who had bailed her out. The answer was always the same, "I don't know."

After getting her personal belongings, she stood outside the precinct thinking the mysterious person was going to drive up any minute with a smile on his or her face. After about ten minutes, she waved down a gypsy cab and headed home. Trina told the driver that she'd be back with his money as she got out a half a block away from her true destination. She made it inside her apartment thinking about her much-needed bath.

"Oh, you scared the shit out of me!" Trina shouted in surprise while holding her hand to her chest. Born was sitting on the sofa sipping out of a small bottle of Hennessey, revealing no type of expression on his face.

"You know I couldn't let my baby get caught up in the mix like that," he said.

"Born, let me explain. When the police rolled up on us like dat, I was caught off guard. Sniffing all dat coke got me tripping for a minute. You know how far back we go," she said, stating her case even though they had known each other only a short while.

"Don't sweat it, it's a small thang to a giant. I know how women can get rattled sometimes, even you," he replied with a smile. Trina relaxed a little as she sat down next to him and took a long sip of his cognac.

"Dis came for you today," Born said as he handed her an official looking document. She took the paper and quickly scanned its contents. *You have seventy-two hours in which to vacate the premises for nonpayment of rent etc., etc.* Trina balled the note up and threw it on the floor.

"You don't have to worry about dat. I got an ill job, where you can make decent dough to get back on your feet," Born said, knowing that by mentioning money Trina's antennas always went up.

"How much you talking about?" Trina asked.

"An easy gee," he responded back as he took out a roll of money and handed it to her.

"Dat's what I'm talking about. What I gotta do for dis much money?"

"I know dis little white guy who's a stock broker," Born said. "He just like to role play with beautiful girls and talk about his problems, plus he usually gives a couple of hundred dollars tip."

"Hell yeah, so when do you want to do dis?" She asked, wanting to get down to business.

"He wants to see you tonight, because he's heading out of town in the morning. If you're not up to it, I'll get someone else," Born stated as he stood up.

"No, I got dis one. Let me get ready real quick." Trina rushed off to the bathroom as Born continued sipping on his drink.

Trina put on a simple dress with pumps and sprayed some White Diamond limited perfume on her pubic hairs. They were soon on the highway in Born's Navigator.

"I got some more liquor in the glove compartment if you want some," he said. She opened the glove compartment and pulled out a bottle of Crown Royal. In her haste Trina didn't notice that the seal was broken.

Midway though the Crown Royal, Trina was feeling good as they pulled into the driveway of an expensive looking house in Yonkers. They walked out to the door where they were met with a security camera peering down at them. Born waved his hand at the camera and a second later, the door cracked opened.

"Come on, let's go. He's just a private person," he said as he took her arm and led her inside the spacious house. They arrived at the well-polished oak door down the hall as Born said, "He's inside. Just smile a lot and listen to everything he says. He usually takes about forty-five minutes. I'll be outside the door reading a magazine or something." He then gave her a passionate kiss as he opened the door for her.

Trina entered the room, which appeared to be a library room of some sort. There was a note on the table that told her to make herself at home. Trina kept thinking that he was scared to show himself because he looked like the Hunch Back of Notre Dame or something. A couple of minutes after settling herself on a plush leather chair, another door opened. A nervous looking little middle-aged white man walked in wearing glasses that seemed to be too big for his face. He had on a Scottish smoking jacket as he approached Trina.

"Hi, I'm sorry to keep you waiting. I had to feed my bird." She looked the pathetic looking male specimen up and down and relaxed. *Oh, I'm going to get the trick off in five minutes*, Trina thought as she stood up smiling.

"So, what you want to do first?" She asked while trying to untie his robe. To her surprise her hand was gently pushed away.

"You have to ask my friend Lynell," the man said in a weak voice. In past situations the guy was always referring to his little pink cock.

Trina got down on her knees in front of his crotch and said, "So Lynell, can we play for a little while?"

"That's not Lynell. Here he is," the man replied as he pulled out a sock that had black buttons for the eyes and some dark red lipstick drawn into a grotesque smile.

"I'm sorry I didn't recognize you," she said as she kissed the sock that was on the man's hand.

"Can you have a drink with me pretty woman?" The sock asked.

"Yes, of course," she answered. He then went over by the bookshelf and brought back an old expensive looking bottle of wine. The guy poured him and Trina drinks as the sock rambled on, on how he would love to be on Trina's foot for a day. Trina smiled, wishing he would get to the point so he could get his freak on. She drank a couple of glasses of wine as Lynell complained on how no one really understood them.

"I shouldn't have mixed my drinks," Trina said out loud as she started feeling very light headed.

Trina woke up thinking for a second that she was back in her own bed. She went to rub her forehead when she realized that her hands were restrained. She looked wildly from side to side and noticed her feet were tied down spread eagle on a lumpy bed just like her hands. The man apparently rolled a foldaway bed into the room while she was unconscious, and placed her on it. When it came to her that she was completely naked and helpless, she started screaming out Born's name.

"Now, now. There, there. Don't you go having no fits. Everything's all right," he said with a smirk. He still had Lynell on his hand, but this time he had his smoking jacket off. It seemed that he had taken Trina's dress and cut it up into a dozen hand puppets complete with the button eyes and the knowing wicked lipstick smile. He had all the puppets on a string fashioned into a dress of his own. He went over to the bed clicking as he walked because he had on Trina's high heels.

"Untie me, you sick motherfucker. I don't care how much money you got, I ain't wit it," Trina spat out, her eyes glowing with anger.

"You said you like us. Why are you talking like that?" The man asked in a whiny voice.

"If you don't let me go right now, I'm gonna have your little ass stomped the fuck out. Den I'm gonna have you locked the fuck up on kidnapping charges," she said in her most serious voice.

"Now we told you before to quiet down. He just wants to get to know you," the sock was speaking now.

"Born, Born, Born. Get in here," Trina was yelling at the top of her lungs now. The man hammer punched Trina three times with his sock hand, knocking the wind out of her. He then reached down and ripped off a chunk of her pubic hair, knocking the breath from her. When Trina started breathing normally again, she heard a strong humming sound coming from beneath her. She decided on a different tactic because she knew she had no wins the other way.

"Okay, listen mister, I didn't mean what I said. I just bugged out when I realized I was tied up. I want to make you and Lynell feel real good, but I need my hands to do that."

Without warning the man snatched off one of Trina's pumps and started beating her about the head and shoulders shouting, "God will forgive him," as the sock mimicked his out of control laughter. While she was momentarily dazed, the man had hooked up some kind of contraption to Trina's nipples. The humming noise was some kind of homemade electrical device connected to a car battery for power. The wires attached to the girl's body served as a powerful current.

"Please mister, just let me go. I'll give you back all your money."

The man had his sock hand inches away from Trina's battered body and said, "We're going make you more in tune with the universe." Before confused Trina could respond, a sharp intense pain shot through her whole body causing her to involuntary twist rapidly on the bed. Her nipples felt as if someone were slowly cooking them in hot grease. The hand with the sock yanked out the remaining hair on Trina's privates and the man's other hand controlled the electrical device, giving it more juice as he saw fit. Trina soon became too weak and exhausted to scream as she blacked out.

She awoke when a cup of cold water splashed against her black and blue face. Born was standing over her, telling her to get up.

"I was calling you, where were you?" She asked in between sobs.

"I didn't hear you, the music must have been too loud," he said while wrapping her up in a stained bed sheet.

"Where is he now?" She asked.

"I don't know, he must have ran out when I busted into the room," Born said. Trina just wanted to leave her torture chamber as soon as possible. They walked outside toward the S.U.V. Once Trina was safely inside the confines of the Navigator and on the highway, she asked Born what he was going to do about what that man did to her.

"Listen, I'm never going to do business with him again, but we have to leave the police out of this. We don't want to have to go through all da bullshit," he said. Trina looked at Born more closely and spotted a hidden devilish grin on his face. She knew right away it was payback from what happened the other night. They rode the rest of the way in complete silence.

(CHAPTER TWENTY-SIX)

"Wake up if you want to eat," a voice yelled into Ice's cell. A police officer was rattling his keys against the bars.

"I'm up, "I'm up," he sleepily replied. He put on his scuffed up Nikes and splashed some cold water on his face to fully wake up. He went over to the bars, where there sat an extra thick cheese sandwich and a lukewarm cup of coffee.

After breakfast he was taken down to central booking in a police van. On his arrival, they fingerprinted and photographed him, and logged his things into property. He then was led to a stuffy, overcrowded holding pen with about forty other men. The holding cell was filled with jailhouse lawyers, bums, drug dealers, D.U.I. suspects, and everyone else whose luck had run out. Ice looked around and noticed that there were two wooden benches attached to the walls opposite each other, which were completely filled up. Most of the men who couldn't find a place to sit were sitting on the floor or stretched out on it. A few were standing up like Ice. The cell was extremely noisy due to the fact that everyone was talking at once, raising their voices so they could be heard. The place had a strange mixed odor of unwashed bodies, vomit, stale piss and the general smell of too many men jammed up in such a tiny area.

"I'm not standing up or sitting on no pissed stained floor," Ice said in a low toned voice. He glanced at all the occupants and spotted a frail looking Spanish boy about seventeen barely sitting on the edge of the bench and just staring at the scenes around him. Ice walked over to him and said, "Yo, I'm mad tired. Can I get dis seat?" Instantly the whole cell became quiet, hoping something jumped off to kill their boredom.

"What?" The kid responded, looking at Ice confused.

"I said I need a seat!" Ice responded.

"What, you going to do fight over a seat?" The Spanish boy asked.

"There ain't going to be no fight. I'm just gonna knock you da fuck out," Ice spat out while moving just a bit closer.

The guy got up and quietly said, "I'm about to go home. You can have the seat."

As Ice was sitting down still watching the guy, he said out loud so everyone could hear, "If you were facing a life sentence, your punk ass still would have raised up." The remark was followed by some laughter and some disappointed whispers. The noise resumed back to normal.

Ice started thinking about how much his bail was going to be. The only thing the police could charge him with was gun possession and evading arrest. Since his gun wasn't dirty, and he didn't have a police record, he should get a low bail. The most he could get was five years probation and have to pay restitution for the property he damaged.

The next day Ice and about twelve other men were shackled together and led to a large police van. It was eight in the morning and the sun was shining brightly with a slight morning breeze. All the prisoners took in the much-needed fresh air on their short walk from the back door to the waiting van. On the way to the courthouse for arraignment, most guys, including Ice, stared out the barred windows lost in their own thoughts. They arrived at the courthouse and were placed in yet another holding cell, which held a few more men. There was nervous chatter among the detainees telling each other that their case was weak. A few times someone tried to strike up a conversation with Ice by asking him what he was in for. His look let them know he didn't want to be bothered.

Guys soon started having their names called out by the guards to appear before the judge. A few never came back, which meant the judge released them, with their promise to appear on the next scheduled court date. Those who came back arrived with various degrees of disappointment showing across their faces.

"Terrance Lendson, Nathaniel Wilson, get ready for court," the officer yelled. Ice and the other guy were led out and placed in a small room with a door that led out to the courtroom. A few minutes went by and the court officer told Ice that he was next. His handcuffs were taken off and he was led into the courtroom. He looked around the packed room and spotted Shareese's mother being held by her brother and some other family members he didn't recognize.

Ice was directed to walk over to a table where his court appointed lawyer was busy shuffling through some papers. His lawyer introduced himself while still flipping through folders. The District Attorney was a hard faced woman in a gray tweed business suit. She spoke first.

"Your honor, the defendant Nathaniel Wilson is charged with possession of a stolen fire arm, attempted murder on two New York City detectives, as well as a civilian. He's also the prime suspect in the horrific murder of a Miss Shareese Jackson. We ask the court to remand the defendant until trial." Ice's lawyer was still fooling around with his papers when he spoke.

"You Honor, my client has no prior criminal record. We ask the court to grant reasonable bail."

The judge, an old black man, looked down at Ice and quickly said, "Request denied. The defendant is to be remanded to the custody of Rikers Island until a trial date has been set." The court officer standing behind Ice then placed handcuffs on him and led him back through the door from which he came. When Ice arrived back to the cell the expression on his face let everyone know not to ask him any questions.

[CHAPTER TWENTY-SEVEN]

Later on that evening Ice and the remaining prisoners who were denied bail or unable to post one were taken to Rikers Island. The next morning the group was processed, given new I.D. cards, and taken to the prison clinic for a thorough medical exam. Some guys bonded, hoping to go to some housing unit together. Ice, and a guy who introduced himself as Rich, were sent to a fifty-bed dorm unit. They were given a small bag containing the necessary toiletries for their new home.

"Yo, Ice, what's the deal?" A voice yelled out showing love. Ice quickly scanned his memory bank and knew the kid as someone he recognized from around the way, but didn't run with. Ice responded back, but still stayed on point just in case the guy might try to rock him asleep for something he might have done in the past. The guy, whose street name was Ill-will, introduced him to some other guys from Queens. In Rikers, guys who came from the same boroughs tended to stick together and form clicks.

After getting all the "do you know so and so?" and "what they got you for?" out of the way, Ice crept away from the cipher to use the phone. *Since the judge denied me bail, I might as well get a good lawyer. Da way dem crackers were talking at the arraignment they looking to hang a brother*, he thought. He needed to call his grandparents so his grandfather could get his money and hire a good lawyer for him.

"Somebody please pick up," Ice said out loud.

"Hello." He recognized the voice as grandmother.

"Hi grandma, dis is Nat."

"Oh child, were you been at? A lot of mess been going on around the block," his grandmother said, sounding stressed and worried. "Some poor girl was killed right in front of our house and another young man right across the street in front of Davidson's house. The police have been around day and night. Me and your grandfather thinking about selling the house and moving down to Florida," she said taking a deep breath.

"Grandma, you know I told you about those crazy Bloods, gang members who were always coming around the neighborhood starting trouble. It probably has something to do with dem. I'm sure dat girl dat got killed wasn't no saint. Anyway, I don't have too much time. Can you please put grandpa on?" He asked.

"Okay, but I want to say bye before you hang up," she added.

His grandfather got on the phone and said, "Hello, Nathaniel? Where are you been at? Were those some friends of yours that got killed the other night?"

"No, I didn't know dem. Right now I'm locked up on Rikers Island because a so-called friend mentioned my name in something dat I had nothing to do wit. You know how these white folks think dat every black man is mixed in something illegal." Ice knew that by throwing that statement in, it would give him a little leeway with his grandparents. His grandfather grew up in the deep south and used to tell him stories on how white people got away with this and that, and on how bad they mistreated black people.

"Grandpa, I need you to go in the basement and get my money I've been saving so I could pay for a lawyer," Ice said.

"I didn't want to tell your grandmother because all the commotion has her worrying enough, but someone broke into your apartment like they were searching for something. Those vandals even put holes in the walls," he stated.

Ice already knew that someone had found his stash, but who? He couldn't ask his grandparents for money, because they were living on a fixed income. He told his grandfather to say bye to his grandmother for him. Ice started calculating his next move. Who could he trust enough to retrieve the hidden coke from the tool shed? Everyone he thought of, he dismissed for the fact that they couldn't be trusted with valuable items. People have a habit of changing up, especially if you were on lockdown. Ice made up his mind that he was just going to have to take a loss.

Easy come, easy go, he thought. His only other alternative was to go with a public defender, which didn't give him a good fighting chance. Most of them were overworked, inexperienced, and just didn't give a damn. The court-appointed attorneys were always quick to tell the defendant to plead guilty whether the person was innocent or not.

Next month Ice went to court, going through the same mundane routine as before. Another court appointed lawyer was assigned to his case. Right away he advised Ice that it was in his best interest if he pleaded out. Just to know where he stood, Ice asked him what the plea deal might be.

"I know the D.A., and since you have a clean record, I could get you a straight fifteen years if you admit to guilt on all the charges," Mr. Goldstein, the attorney, replied.

"Only if your mother takes it first," Ice shot back.

Ice remained on Rikers Island with Ill-will and some other guys from Queens. There was the usual fighting and stabbing among the inmates when their frustrations became too much to bear. Their anger usually boiled over from the one-sided injustices of the courts or problems with their wives and girlfriends who changed on them over a period of time.

Ice went to court about five more times before the D.A. decided to drop the murder charges because of insufficient evidence. Court documents revealed that his gun wasn't used in any other crime. He finally pleaded out to two to four years for illegal possession of a firearm and reckless endangerment. After his plea deal, he was moved to a different building where inmates who had already been sentenced were housed. He was now waiting his turn to be shipped to an upstate prison.

(CHAPTER TWENTY-EIGHT)

Ice was taken out of his cell early one morning to be transported to an upstate prison. It was standard procedure for prison officials to transport inmates without notice for security reasons. He rapidly packed up his little bit of property and was escorted by two C.O.s. They made stops by other housing units to pick up sentenced inmates who were due to make the trip also. All the men were given breakfast and then double checked to make sure their I.D.s matched up with their transport list. They were loaded onto a wire meshed bus with two armed C.O.s plus the driver. The driver made a couple of more stops to other buildings, picking up more sentenced inmates who were scheduled for the trip.

Now the bus was filled to capacity with forty men heading toward their new home. All through the long trip, the prison bus made scheduled stops at other upstate prisons dropping off guys and picking more up. After about six hours Ice made it to his destination, the newest privately owned jail called Cold Mountain. All the prisoners were checked again to verify who they were as they exited the bus. They stood shackled in a couple of rows as a huge red necked C.O., who looked as if he lived on steroids, began shouting the rules of Cold Mountain. While the officer was going through his tirade, four other C.O.s were unlocking the inmates' shackles. Ice noticed some of the guys who he was on Rikers Island with were quiet as church mice during the speech. He often heard them say in a bold voice that when they reached upstate they weren't taking any shit from any C.O. hillbillies. Ice had to laugh to himself as he peeped the guy's true style.

The next thing Ice knew a Correction Officer was up in his face yelling, "What you chuckling at boy? You find this funny? You think I'm funny?" Ice was ready to flip when he noticed two other C.O. coming toward him, so he decided to chill. The C.O. yelled a couple of more things to Ice and directed his rants to the rest of the group.

"You think this is a game, well its not. You think you're tough, there's someone always tougher. You have no friends here at Cold Mountain. I seen guys come in here with their childhood buddies and the buddies were the one's who played lookout while their friends got stabbed and raped. Do not accept any gifts because you will be paying more than you bargained for. Don't loan out any of your property, because you will end up catching another charge trying to get it back. Just mind your business and hopefully you'll make it back home the same way you came in."

The group was then led to the reception area where they each were ordered to strip and take special showers that killed any type of body contamination. Each inmate was given state-issued clothes, one pair of boots, one pair of sneakers, three shirts, three pants, one chino jacket, one winter coat, five T-shirts, socks, and boxer shorts. After lunch they were given knew I.D.'s and taken to their new cells.

Ice's cellmate happened to be the guy who was sitting on the bus next to him on the ride up here. He said his name was Infinite from uptown. Infinite kept hinting that he and Ice should have each other's backs. Ice took his new roommate to be a coward because he was overly friendly, spilling his whole life story.

"Yeah, dat motherfucker asked me to hold his backpack for a minute and the jakes rushed me outta nowhere. How was the fuck was I to know he had a burner and some jumbos stashed at the bottom," the roommate told Ice. Ice kept wishing that he had another cellmate besides this clown ass nigga, who kept trying to force a friendship.

A week later Ice chose plumbing as his trade. He wanted to take college courses, but all the prisons up north canceled those programs. All they offered was GED preparation classes. He had been to the yard every day, but still didn't spot anyone he knew from around the way.

Ice was in the yard doing a couple sets of chin-ups trying to relieve some stress. He had asked his grandmother to send him a package of things he needed so he could be a little more comfortable. They informed him that they were behind in a lot of bills. To ease their mind he told them that he would be all right. To make matters worse, Infinite received a package from his girlfriend containing the new Lebron James sneakers and other items. For the first time Ice felt envious of another guy's possessions.

Ice started thinking how when he first came to this jail, he'd been hearing about some cat that was going by the name of Mother Dear. From what he heard he was a pretty decent boxer until he started fucking around with woolies (weed sprinkled with crack), and then graduated to the crack pipe. *What kind of name iz dat for a nigga on lock down?* Ice thought. From bits and pieces of information he gathered, Mother Dear kept getting hit with extra time for knocking guys out for practically nothing. Ice learned that he was currently in the box for breaking another inmate's jaw in three places over a bet.

Just then Infinite walked over and asked if he could join in on the workout with the chin-up bar. He was rocking his brand new kicks and a Sean John sweatshirt.

"Yo, I'm almost done," Ice replied, hoping he got the message.

"Fuck it I'll finish up wit you," Infinite said. Ice then noticed a group of guys watching them and whispering. They approached just as Ice hopped down from the chin bar.

A tall slinky guy asked Infinite, "Ain't you from uptown?"

"Yeah," he answered back, happy that some crew acknowledged his existence.

"We from uptown too," the guy responded as he looked at his friends. "Let's take a walk around the yard. You might know some of our peoples," he said.

Infinite, still smiling, said, "Ice, I'll catch up wit you later." They all began walking away as Ice continued his workout. Five minutes later Ice saw that the group had Infinite surrounded, with him bending down untying his two day old foot wear. They took his sweatshirt too, and then threw him some old, state-issued sneakers, leaving the scene of the jail robbery laughing.

The whistle blew for recreation to be over as everyone in the yard lined up. Everyone then headed back to their cell. Ice knew he was a bitch from jump street, so there wasn't anything to say on his part.

The next day Ice was on his bunk bed reading a *Jet* magazine when Infinite came into the cell accompanied by a lady C.O. He began putting his belongings into a pillowcase.

"Yo Infinite, what's up?" Ice asked. "Where you going?"

"I got into a little bullshit drama up in the library, so now they want to move me."

Ice knew that he was lying, especially when he saw that he had a swollen eye. He knew that his roommate requested protective custody. After Infinite finished gathering his things he told Ice peace and left. Ice now had a cell to himself, but he knew it wouldn't last because of all the overcrowding. He finished checking out the Beauty of the Week in *Jet*, not giving it a second thought that his cellmate had just got his ass whooped.

(CHAPTER TWENTY-NINE)

Ice was enjoying having the cell all to himself. He didn't have to worry about annoying conversation when he was trying to think or read. He came back from trade school one afternoon and noticed everything in his cell in disarray. His mattress was thrown on the top bunk with the pillows and covers rolled up in a ball on top.

"What da fuck," were the only words he could say. He saw that his new roommate had an abundance of cosmetics and a variety of junk foods. He also saw a couple of sneakers in all right condition in the corner. "Whoever dis nigga is, he gots to go. I'm not going for nobody disrespecting my shit. As soon as he walks in, I'm going to handle my business and do what I got to do," Ice said, talking to himself in an aggravated tone.

Twenty minutes later a guy with an afro walked in his cell with his shirt opened, revealing a pumped up chest. He had his shirt sleeves rolled up showing tree stump arms with jailhouse tattoos. He went straight to the bottom bunk and laid down, ignoring Ice like he didn't even exist. The new guy had Ice outweighed by at least fifty pounds, but still Ice spoke.

"So I see you made yourself at home." The guy remained quiet so Ice said, "You know dat was my shit you threw on the top bunk."

"Yo slim, I'm not in the mood for no shit. I just came out da box doing ninety days. Dis was my old cell before I went in, so I took it back. If you feel like you want to get down for what you think is yours, then let's get busy," the new cellmate replied in a pissed off tone of voice. Ice knew from the way he was acting and talking, he must have a shank on him or at least one close by that he could get to if something were to jump off.

Ice walked out the cell and into the dayroom where everyone was watching *Soul Train*. As usual, all the seats were taken up whenever that particular program was on. It was a well known institutional fact that many men had gotten seriously injured when trying to change the channel when that show was on. Ice was standing up in the back thinking on how to handle his new cellmate when he heard a couple of guys talking about how Mother Dear had just come out the box. He put two and two together and came to the conclusion that his new roommate had to be Mother Dear. *Dat kid ain't making no waves dis way. All he is is big, and he's probably slow*, Ice thought.

Ice and his new cellmate moved around each other for a day and a half without speaking.

"Hey Slim, what you in here for?" The new guy finally spoke. Ice was writing a letter to his sister at the table when he looked up at his roommate and noticed a razor cut on his face, starting by the ear and ending down his neck.

"I'm Ice, not Slim. They bagged me for mad charges that they couldn't prove. Later on I just said fuck it and copped out into a gun case," he answered back.

"What you was a gunslinger out in the world?" He asked.

"You know it," Ice replied with pride. "I caught mad bitch ass niggas sleeping for their dough and shines. Dem niggas turned soft as baby shit once I threw da big ass gat in their face," he said while laughing. "So what do they call you?"

"My peoples call me Mother Dear," he answered with a hidden smirk. Ice knew enough not to push the issue even though he was crazy curious as to why this big dude would have a tag name like that. Mother Dear continued, "I got caught on some bullshit strong-armed case, but kept getting more time added to my sentence for letting dudes know how I get down." Then out of nowhere he asked, "I bet you got a lot of little bitches out there sweating you because of your looks."

"What!" Ice asked, caught off guard by the strange statement.

"You know with you having those green eyes and being light-skinned, you could have anybody you wanted." *Dis nigga been on lock down too long*, Ice thought. He changed the subject asking Mother Dear did he hear about that lady C.O. that got caught smoking crack in the laundry with an inmate she'd been fucking with.

Ice had spoken to someone about buying a shank because for some reason Mother Dear had a very sneaky weird way about him that he didn't trust. He was just waiting for a money order his sister had sent him so he could buy his weapon.

It was two a.m. and Ice was lying on his bunk wide awake because his stomach was rumbling from some bad jail fish he had eaten. He had to take a much-needed shit. He usually waited until the cell was empty before he did his business, but he couldn't hold it any longer, so he quietly hopped down from the top bunk. He hoped his roommate was asleep. As Ice sat down on the steel toilet, he saw Mother Dear under the covers, but he couldn't see his eyes because of the darkness. He then put a towel on his lap for partial privacy. A minute went by and Ice wasn't sure what he was seeing. He could swear he was seeing rapid movements under the blankets as if Mother Dear was jerking off. He became a hundred percent positive when Mother Dear turned his head, looked directly at him, and sickly smiled.

Ice quickly jumped up, pulling up his boxer shorts shouting, "What da fuck!!" Mother Dear snatched the covers off himself with lighting speed, letting Ice know that he was completely nude. Ice saw that he had a crazy look in his eyes as he stood up, so he threw a wild haymaker that missed its intended target, but landed on Mother Dear's collarbone. Mother Dear positioned himself in a boxer's stance and threw a two-piece combination at his opponent. The first blow caught Ice in the ribs, and the second one in the kidneys, causing him to drop to the floor.

Mother Dear then backed up saying, "Come on and get up pretty boy" as he shadow boxed. Ice rose to his feet and threw his own combination, which was easily avoided. Ice then swung a hard kick toward Mother Dear's groin, which was blocked, leaving Ice momentarily a little off balance. That mistake caused him to have five hard body shots rocked to his frame, leaving Ice grasping for air. As he slowly rose to his feet, he was met with a vicious upper cut to the jaw. He saw the room spinning and lost sight of his attacker. Meanwhile Mother Dear had gone behind the sink and retrieved a hidden homemade knife. He then walked over to Ice, kicking him in the face and knocking him out.

A couple minutes later Ice regained consciousness, finding himself in a chokehold lying across the bottom bunk. He felt a sharp instrument pressed tightly against his neck. He tried to break the grip but to no avail. He blacked out once again and when he came to, he felt a hard pressure against his rectum. Ice's reality came crashing down around him when he realized that he was being raped by a man. In his fear he tried to scream out, but he was met with a hard punch to the temple. He awoke feeling as if all his insides were being torn apart. Mother Dear's face was inches away from his. He was breathing heavy and started whispering in Ice's ear.

"You feel soooo good, just like a bitch. Without your gun you just a sissy punk. Yeah, soft as baby shit." Ice tried to struggle with his last remaining strength, but then he felt the jail made dagger sink deeper into his neck. Mother Dear pumped Ice like his long lost sweetheart. Ice barely heard his rapist moan as his whole body relaxed. Ice tried to push himself up as Mother Dear began raining blow after blow into his face. Then he threw Ice back on his top bunk and went back to sleep as if what he had done was the most normal thing in the world.

(CHAPTER THIRTY)

Ice woke up in the prison infirmary wearing an all white prison issued hospital garment. Later on, during that day, the duty nurse informed him that he had a broken nose, a couple of cracked ribs, needed four stitches to his rectum, and had some bruised internal organs. Ice lay in his bed not eating anything in a state of depression.

Bright and early the next morning two prison officials wanted Ice to sign a sworn statement against Tony Neely, aka Mother Dear. After twenty minutes of telling the men that he just wanted to be left alone, they hinted that he had to like it. Why else would he protect the guy who brutalized him? The other man figured it was no big deal, just some jail love that got out of hand.

Ice spent two weeks in the hospital and then was moved to another tier. They moved him in with a faggot who called himself Sassy, and who was doing a bid for credit card fraud. Ice knew the warden purposely put him as a cellmate with a faggot for retaliation of not cooperating with the investigation. Even though Ice got violated as a man against his will, he wasn't turning a snitch by his own hand.

After the incident, Ice spent most of his time staying in his cell reading, and ignoring Sassy and all of his feminine friends. Ice soon began hearing rumors that him and Sassy were doing wicked shit to each other at night. He soon started hearing people call him Ice Cream behind his back and to his face. He planned on stabbing someone so he could be transferred to another facility.

Once in a blue moon Ice would go to the yard and sit by himself. He happened to be sitting on the benches when he spotted Rob from south side. He was talking to another guy over by the weights. Just then Rob noticed him, smiled, and was about to walk over when the guy he was with said something to him. Rob looked at Ice with a shocked look on his face, shaking his head as in disbelief. Both men then started walking toward the opposite side of the yard.

"Oh shit, dat's my man Ice from Queens," Rob said getting ready to walk over to his long time friend.

"You know him?" The other guy asked.

"Yeah, dat's my man. We go way back," Rob answered. "Ice is about as real as they come, why?" Rob asked.

"Up in here we call him Ice Cream. He's Ice Cream for the freaks. Don't fuck wit him." Rob and his friend then walked off.

(CHAPTER THIRTY-ONE)

"So Ice, what you reading today?" Sassy asked in a voice that was husky with a touch of femininity.

"I'm almost finish knocking out dis ill gangster book. Big Al (Al Capone) sure knew how to handle his business. Too bad he had to go out with a rotted head piece because he had a real chance to show the folks of Chicago how it's really done," Ice answered back.

Ice and his cellmate Sassy had grown to have a strange understanding in the six months they had shared living quarters. Sassy, whose government name was Keith, knew Ice had no type of homosexual tendencies whatsoever. He heard Mother Dear stories from other prisons he'd been in, and Ice just caught a bad decision from a psychotic nigga. When Sassy had found out what went down between him and Mother Dear, he automatically assumed like everyone else that Ice could have been a willing participant. If he wasn't then, sooner or later he would slowly be turned out. Sassy, being the person he was, tried to do just that. When his repeated tries, tricks, and outright statement, "I'll suck your dick, who would know," were all rebuffed, he felt a slight twinge of pity for the nickname Cold Mountain residents had tacked on Ice. Ice, being the person he was, didn't want pity, friends, or anything from anyone else, or so they thought. Basically Sassy was the only person who called him Ice instead of Ice Cream. He even went as far as to tell his alike friends to refer to Ice as his street name or nothing at all.

"What you planning on doing when you touch the hood?" Ice asked.

"I'm going to hit base wit my nephew. My sister tells me he has shit on lock in the drug game. I definitely need to get wit him," he replied with glee.

From the pictures that Sassy showed Ice he was doing well in the streets at one time. He had flicks of himself wearing custom made chinchilla furs and blue diamonds, accompanied by some of the most beautiful women Ice had ever seen. Sassy stated that with money and power, the women were always close behind. He said he tried to balance his busy hustle with the girls, but juggling both activities didn't leave him with the time he wanted with the ever-present groupies.

As time went by, he started leaving the important business transactions to his trusted lieutenants so he could party. Sassy said it got to a point when the only time he got in contact with his crew was when he needed the product the expensive women often craved. To no surprise, he started snorting coke along with them for non-stop days of sex and drug use. He revealed to Ice that his new drug habits brought to the surface his deeply buried twisted sexual appetite. He met a stunning two time Filipino beauty contestant winner that also had a strong penchant for coke and abnormal sexual practices. Sassy confessed that she was so ill, that he ate the corn out of her shit one night when he was feeling extremely freaky from the coke high. The expression on Ice's face showed that he didn't want to hear anymore, so he skipped the details and continued.

One night, on a horny coke high, he gave his college Russian girl a big black extra thick strap on dildo and told her to bluntly, "fuck him in his ass, like she hated him." Soon after he became a full fledged dope fiend, with his crew cutting him off because of his reckless ways. The women and his worldly possessions soon followed suit, with him supporting his habit by doing petty burglaries. They hit him with three to nine for his strings of break-ins. Jail became the perfect breeding ground for his unusual sexual fetishes.

"So how many days to the wake up?" Ice asked while flipping through the book and glancing at an old picture of Al Capone.

"Four days to go, and I'm outta here," he answered. Sassy had made his first parole board. Four days later Sassy was walking out of Cold Mountain as Keith, ready to reclaim his former glory. Ice took the bottom bunk wondering who his new cellmate would be and if there would be any problems.

"Whatever happens, happens," Ice said as he continued his jail calisthenics.

(CHAPTER THIRTY-TWO)

Ice was cooling out on his bunk practicing his new hobby, drawing, when a guy walked into his cell carrying a stuffed pillowcase with what appeared to be his belongings.

"So you my new cellee," the stranger stated, not expecting a reply. He threw the pillowcase on the top bed and walked out without saying another word. To Ice the guy was just one of those types of guys who had a chest full of heart when he had his peoples backing him up. Ice finished his drawing after an hour and went to the dayroom to see what was on TV. Everything was as normal as any other day. Some inmates were watching a movie, gambling, or trying to get their turn on one of the phones. Ice sat down in the middle row and threw his feet up on one of the empty chairs.

"Yo, can you move your feet? I wanna rest here." Ice looked up and sure enough it was his new cellmate.

"There's plenty of other seats around," he said while looking directly at the guy.

"So you wanna be a gangster now, is dat it?" The guy asked with a smirk. A group of guys who Ice took to be his friends stood close by waiting for their friend's next move.

"Check it out, Justice, Ice Cream is gonna tell me there's other seats. Can you believe dat shit?" he said while turning around looking at the group of men. Ice then kicked the chair he had his feet on, got up, and moved closer toward the TV. Ice heard the stranger talking.

"You know how I get down," he said as his friends laughed, making him feel like the man.

After the movie, Ice went back to his cell and saw his roommate sitting on his bed looking through his drawings, which Ice had left out in the open. In prison that was a sure sign of total disrespect when you touched someone's stuff or ate their food without asking permission. The guy looked at Ice.

"It' seems dat you got more den one talent up in here, ain't dat right Cream?" He said and then busted out in a laugh.

Ice laughed back with him as he went to one of his books and took something out. Sassy had left him a little present (a half of a scissor sharpened to a fine point with hardened wax and strips of sheets for a handle). Ice walked over to the stranger, still laughing, and stabbed him with such force on the cheek that the weapon went clean through and pierced his tongue.

"Aaahhh," the stranger yelled as he jumped up holding his face. In one swift motion, Ice grabbed him by his collar, stuck his foot out, and pulled him back toward him, knocking him off balance. He then stabbed him twice in the stomach. Meanwhile, the guy was yelling in a high-pitched voice.

"You killing me. Oh my God, you killing me. Somebody please help me, help, help." Ice just laughed as the guy leaped to his feet and stumbled out the cell still screaming like he was still in danger. All the commotion had caused people to appear in front of the cell looking at the spectacle. Ice noticed two of the guy's friends from the dayroom.

"Come on in, if you feel it's real," Ice said to them in a quiet sinister type of voice. The guys looked at Ice as if to say,

"Dat's between you two, we got nothing to do wit dat drama." Ice knew the C.O.s would be arriving any second now from all the bitch screaming, so he slid his shank behind a garbage can a couple of feet away from his cell. He knew that a weapon of this caliber was valuable, so someone was sure to pick it up and stash it for their own.

The C.Os came running just like clockwork and threw him up against the wall, along with about five other guys who happened to be standing around. They were strip searched and told to keep standing with their hands were on the wall. An old pot bellied captain arrived, irritated that the melee had broken up his afternoon nap. He ordered all the men to be taken down to segregation and placed in separate cells. The men were told that they would be questioned later.

Sometime later, the slot in the steel door where the food was placed opened up for a few seconds and then closed again. The next morning Ice was taken out of his cell and placed in a room with a big desk stacked with papers. The sergeant informed him that a one Michael Jones positively identified him as the one who attacked and stabbed him without provocation yesterday afternoon. He asked Ice how did he plead. Ice pleaded not guilty.

Two weeks later he had his institutional hearing with Michael Jones sitting across from him with a bandaged up face pointing like an outside snitch working with the Feds. Ice was found guilty of assault and given one hundred twenty days only because they never found the weapon he used. They took him to S.H.U. (Special Housing Unit) the same day as the jail trial.

(CHAPTER THIRTY-THREE)

"Hello Mr. Wilson. How we doing today? I see you looking a little buff today," the lady C.O. stated as she looked hungrily into the cell. Ice got up from the floor sweating and went to the cell door.

"You know I got to look good for you Miss Mary," he said as he flexed his skinny arm muscles like he was in a Mr. Universe contest.

Miss Mary, as everyone in S.H.U. called her, was in charge of all the happenings in the unit. She was fair, but could flip the script on you in a second if you crossed her. Since day one when Ice arrived, she'd been throwing obvious sexual oriented hints his way. Most inmates in S.H.U. salivated over her, but Ice wasn't locked down long enough to find this short, overweight, eighties-style, Jheri Curl wearing lady attractive. He talked and flirted back with her out of sheer boredom.

"So you checked on dat thing we talked about the other day? You know I've been down here for a month already," he said with an intense look.

"You know I can get in trouble, but you seem like a nice kid," Miss Mary responded while getting a good look at his rippled stomach muscles. Ice forced a mental picture of a nude R&B singer to come to mind, causing his dick to rise slightly. Her eyes were like magnets drawn to his crotch.

"C.O., C.O., I need to speak to you for a minute. It's an emergency," another inmate yelled out. The unexpected shouting caused Ice's spell to be broken.

"Stop fucking screaming on my tour. I'll get there when I get there," Miss Mary yelled. "I'll get back to you sometime tomorrow. Let me go see what this asshole wants," she said as she walked off trying to switch like a music video honey.

Two days later C.O. Miss Mary informed Ice that he would be let out of his cell three times a day after chow to do routine clean up. In S.H.U. all the occupants were allowed one hour of exercise in the small-restricted yard and a ten-minute shower once a week if they followed all the rules and regulations. For an inmate to come out his cell three times a day was more valuable than gold.

Once Ice started his clean-up job, he became popular with the other men passing coded notes, pussy magazines, cosmetics, etc. Every once in a while the correction officer on duty would let him watch a little TV, not because they were being nice, but because they just wanted someone they could make comments to on a basketball game or when someone did something foolish in a horror movie.

It was a normal day after lunch and mostly everyone in the unit was sleeping or just being quiet. Ice was lazily sweeping when he heard a voice say in a low hushed tone, "Excuse me, can you come here for a minute? I need to ask you a question." The voice was coming from the end cell down the hall.

"They must have moved someone in this morning," Ice said to himself. He walked to the cell with the broom in his hand

and looked in the cell saying, "What's up?" The guy had his back toward the door, sitting on the bed like he was scribbling something down.

"Yo, I don't have all day, what you call me for?" Ice asked, wondering why the guy had his back turned away.

The guy suddenly stood up, turned around, and said while smiling, "I thought dat was you. I'd recognize dat cute ass anywhere." Ice recognized the voice as Mother Dear. He stood there just looking at the man who had raped him when he first came to Cold Mountain.

"Come on now, dat's da way you treat me? You act like what we had wasn't even special, like a one night stand or something," Mother Dear said as he approached the front of the cell door. Ice just walked away as he heard laughter bouncing off the bleak gray walls. That night Ice dreamed only of a wide mouth with rows of endless teeth and a mocking laugh that seemed to go on forever.

The next couple of days Ice performed his normal duties with an increasing amount of comments coming from Mother Dear's cell. "I thought we could work past me cheating on you. Come on Ice Cream, give me another chance." He blew kisses and whistled when Ice was close by.

It was Wednesday, and some of the special housing inmates were due to take their quick showers. Regulations stated that under no circumstances should inmates come in contact with one another whatsoever. Ice was no exception. He usually got locked back in his cell when the guys went to the shower, clinic, etc. This particular day, Ice spilled a full bucket of dirty mop water on the floor on purpose. The C.O. on duty saw no harm in letting Ice stay out of his cell this one time, so he told Ice to hurry up while he let an inmate out to take his shower. Ice had looked at the schedule and sure enough, just like clockwork, Mother Dear was let out of his cell. He was strolling down the hallway in his boxers, dollar ninety-nine commissary slippers, and a towel like he was at the mall or somewhere else.

"What's up playboy?" Ice asked. Mother Dear turned his head and received a concoction of one hundred eighty degree boiling water, mixed with baby oil and sugar that Ice had fixed especially for him. The liquid caught its victim flush in the face. The rough particles of the sugar highly irritated the now super sensitive skin causing his victim to automatically grab his face. When Mother Dear reached for his face to wipe away the burning liquid, the baby oil caused him to unknowingly slide his skin off, leaving him looking like he stepped out of cheesy seventies horror flick.

Ice was surprised that Mother Dear didn't scream or try to run to safety. He just stood there in a shock looking at his face in his hands. Soon everyone was screaming, shouting, and banging on their steel doors causing the C.O. to come running. He radioed in for more help and for the prison nurse. By then Ice had quietly crept back to his cell and slid the door closed. At this point he didn't care if he got caught or not, but he wasn't going to make a public announcement either. Mother Dear was whisked off to the clinic, while the cellblock investigator did their watered down investigation. The C.O. on duty at the time of the incident swore on a written statement that everyone was on lockdown during the incident. He knew that if he told them that Ice was out at the time, he would have been severely reprimanded or fired.

"Fuck it, why risk his future on some convict getting what he probably deserved," he reasoned with his wife. Mother Dear also kept his mouth shut for reasons of his own. The final report stated that no assault took place. Mother Dear had spilled hot coffee on himself. The file was stamped "accidental" and closed. What the file didn't explain was how would an inmate come to have a hot steaming cup of coffee in his possession, and why would he want to take it to the shower with him.

Word had reached population that Ice had wilded out on Mother Dear barehanded, and sent him packing. Then the story changed that he had applied some slick boxing moves of his own. Now everyone in Cold Mountain was waiting on round three of Mother Dear vs. Ice.

(CHAPTER THIRTY-FOUR)

"Yeah, dat's what I'm talking about," Ice said out loud. He was holding a piece of paper he had gotten in the mail that he had been waiting for, for over a month. The week crawled at a snail's pace for Ice. No matter what he did, everything seemed to be moving in slow motion.

"Nathaniel Wilson, be ready in one hour for your parole hearing," a solemn faced C.O. yelled into his cell. Ice had been ready for weeks. He had fresh pair of state issued pants, and a shirt neatly folded under his mattress for a jail crease. He dressed, taking his time with each button and looking in the scratched up mirror every couple of minutes. He told himself that he would be denied for the simple fact that he was young and black, and therefore he was considered a danger in white America's eyes. Since his two years of incarceration, he had heard many guys brag on how they just knew they were going to make the board.

"Yeah, I completed mad programs, so dem white folks gotta let me go," one man would say. "I had crazy people write the parole board, even a couple of ministers," another said.

They were so sure they were going home that they started doing and saying things that were premature toward their situation. Most times they would write reckless letters to girlfriends or family members who they thought weren't doing enough for them during their stint. They would curse them out saying, "Fuck you, I don't need you anymore. I'm stepping out on the set real soon." Then when the parole board gave them two more additional years, they would send a heartbreaking apologetic letter stating that they weren't in their right mind at the time due to the stress of prison life.

Other guys would keep their secret that they thought they might be let go, so they borrowed and gambled heavily with no intention of paying back. They just knew they were getting over when they smoked up carton after carton of cigarettes and lost an occasional bet. When they were denied freedom, their whole world came crashing down around them.

Ice told only a handful of people he had a scheduled date to see the board. He was escorted to another part of the jail he had never been in before, and sat down in a row of chairs with five other guys who were there to meet the "Man" also. Three of the nervous looking inmates wore non-prescription eyeglasses in hopes of looking respectable. A guy came out of a room and said to the guy nearest to him that they told him they would let him know in writing of their decision, which everyone knew to be that he had been denied.

Ice's turn came, and he was led into a small room where he sat down facing a long wooden table. There were three men and women who introduced themselves and asked Ice how he was doing today. He replied that he was okay as they all looked at his incarceration file folder.

"So Mr. Wilson, what would be your plans if we decided to let you re-enter society?" A bald man asked.

"I plan on registering for college, and during my spare time, working at a part time job so I can have a little extra pocket money," he answered back.

"Are you planning on contacting and re-establishing friendships with your friends from your neighborhood?" The second man asked with an expressionless face.

"No, I feel hanging out with guys from my old neighborhood wouldn't be beneficial toward my rehabilitation," came Ice's reply. The men took turns asking Ice the standard questions they asked a thousand times. Ice gave the answers they heard a thousand times.

"We see that once you are released you will be staying with a Miss Lana Ming. She wrote a very convincing letter stating that you would be living with her and working in her family's Laundromat. Is that true?" The woman asked.

"Yes ma'am, dat's correct." The group in charge of Ice's freedom discussed in whispers about his future. After what seemed like an eternity, they informed Ice that he was granted parole and was due to be released one week from today. The involuntary smile on his face told the other men waiting the whole story. Ice went back to his cell daydreaming on all the things he had planned for himself.

(CHAPTER THIRTY-FIVE)

"So are you going to stay out of trouble this time?" A C.O. asked as he signaled the C.O. in the gun tower to open the final gate.

"It depends if your sister didn't give up da pussy while I was on lockdown," Ice said as he slowly walked to a waiting bus. The C.O.s face turned beet red as he wished the newly freed inmate failed at freedom once again. Ice walked onto the bus and sat down somewhere in the middle by himself. The bus was half full with ex-convicts from Cold Mountain and some from the surrounding prisons. Most were chattering about how this time around, it was going to be different for them out in the world. Some were talking or dreaming about opening up some kind of legitimate business. Ice knew that if they came in contact with any type of reasonable amount of cash, they would be the first ones to run to the dealer to purchase a car at a flat price.

Ice recognized one guy he saw occasionally in the jail as a straight-laced Muslim, sitting not too far from him talking to another guy. He remembered him as a person who always preached to other inmates in a circle on how you had to set an example for the youth because they are the future. He was often heard in the yard spitting out persuasive rhetoric on how black men had to band together and rid the destructive elements that were perpetrating genocide on the unsuspecting black people across America. Ice halfway liked the guy and thought briefly that he would make a good role model to a lot of kids without father figures to look up to.

"So what's the first thing you going to do when you reach uptown?" The guy asked the Muslim.

"You know Eddie's Rib and Chicken Shack down the block from dat church?" The guy shook his head, as to say yes. "Well I've been feining for weeks now about one of their double decker pork sandwiches on an extra long roll smothered in their secret sauce."

"What you gonna do for money? Are you still gonna open up dat bookstore wit your cousin?" The guy asked.

"Hell No! Ain't no money in no goddamn book store. I've been writing these two chicken heads who wanna help a brother out. I'm going to put dem bitches out on da block slinging dat ass." Both men then laughed so hard it even caused the bus driver to briefly turn around. Ice had heard enough. He blocked everyone's bullshit out and closed his eyes.

Ice went back to the night he was arrested and how the police at the station house had robbed him. Some weather-beaten white faced officer had told Ice he had to take off his Rolex and custom made platinum ring and put it in property. When Ice asked for a receipt, the cop told him that he would be back in a minute with it. After a while, he started asking other officers about his property receipt.

"Who did you give your property to? What's the officer's name?" When Ice couldn't answer any of their questions, he knew for a fact that he got beat.

He then went back to the day he received a letter from his grandparents four months after his incarceration. The letter stated that New York was getting too much for them and they wanted to live in peace and quiet. They had sold the house and had put some money down on some property in a senior citizen gated community.

"Last stop," the bus driver yelled, waking Ice up. Ice snatched up a cab and gave the driver an address in Hollis, Queens. Even though Hollis was only a stone's throw away from his old stomping grounds, he never really liked niggas from that area. He remembered getting chased by them in his early pre-teen days because he used to bag all the pretty girls from the neighborhood. They especially hated him because he was a stranger and his looks made the situation even worse. Later on in life he made it a point to rob guys, especially from that area.

Ice made it to his destination and hopped out, taking a good look around. After two years, things still looked the same. He knocked on the door and a boyish looking Chinese girl answered. She wore a Yankees baseball cap pulled down low, with extra baggy jeans and a fresh pair of classic tan Timberland boots.

"What's up? I'm looking for a Lana Ming," Ice stated.

"You must be Ice. I've been waiting for you. Come on in, and cut out da Lana shit. Call me Lemon," she said in perfect English as she opened the door wider so he could come in. Ice walked in and noticed that the house looked like someone had just moved in and wasn't finished unpacking yet. There were cardboard boxes piled up in every corner.

"Where your bags at?" She asked.

"Dis all I'm holding," he said as he stuck his arm out.

"I'm about to light up, you want some?" Lemon asked while taking out a pre-rolled Philly blunt from behind her ear.

"You know it," came Ice's response. They smoked half the blunt before Ice said, "So where's Kendew?"

"He's finishing up some business outta town. He'll be back in a couple of days," she said.

After they finished the weed, she showed Ice where he would be staying. It was a small room with a worn mattress on an old style metal frame. *It's better than staying at a halfway house with a bunch of crack heads*, he thought to himself. Ice was too excited about being home to sleep, so he broke out to the corner bodega and picked up a couple of forties. Ice knocked out both beers while flipping through some rap magazines. He drifted off to sleep so he could start fresh tomorrow morning.

Ice woke up, took a long hot shower, and prepared himself to see his parole officer, which was standard procedure for all new releasees.

"You are not to associate, call, gather, or engage in any type of activities with persons of a criminal record, or I will violate you. You will report to me when I say, and how often I say, or I will violate you. You are not to use, sell, or posses any illegal narcotics whatsoever, or I will violate you."

Ice wasn't really listening to this man with the gravy stained shirt, who seemed to be enjoying his imaginary power he had over him. All Ice kept hearing was "I will violate you." He hated this man who seemed so intent on sending him back to prison where he just got out of a day ago. After forty-five minutes of rambling, the parole officer stood up and gave Ice his card, telling him to call if he had any problems. He added that he had one week to find a job or he would violate him.

Ice rode down the elevator thinking on how he would love to pistol whip his parole officer for the sheer pleasure of it. He made it back around the way feeling like a bum because he had no shines and all he had was one hundred and six dollars to his name. To make matters worse, all he had was one outfit, which he wore two days in a row now, something he never did in his whole life.

"Excuse me, do I know you from somewhere?" A voice asked out of nowhere, breaking Ice from his thoughts. He turned around and saw a short, pretty, stacked female looking at him like she was trying to remember something.

"I don't know, do you?" he shot back.

"You have a brother maybe?" She asked. Before Ice could respond she shouted, "Oh shit, you're Rob's man." When she saw the puzzled look on his face, she continued, "Remember you and Rob picked me up in your Acura in front of Jezebel's. I'm Spank, what's your name again?"

He then realized this was that dancer that was sweating him on the low low. Damn, she looked even better now than before. "I'm Ice," he said.

"Oh yeah, I almost didn't recognize you without your braids," Spank said while looking Ice up and down, noticing he wasn't rocking any sick jewelry as before. Plus his gear looked a little outdated.

"Yeah, I cut my shit off. I might grow it back though. So what you doing right now? You wanna hang out for a little while?" He asked, knowing he was going to break his jail cherry on this bad bitch.

Spank thought for a minute that maybe Ice was out hustling all night and left his jewelry at home so she said, "Where you parked at?"

"I'm on foot right now, but we could catch a cab somewhere," he stated.

"Oh shit, I forgot that I have to go meet my moms in a little while. I'll catch you another time," Spank said as she started to walk off, waving a weak hand over her shoulder. Ice knew right away that she played him out like a derelict living on the street.

"I'm never going to let another bitch see me like dis again. I'm gonna get mines any way I can," Ice said as he headed back to the house.

(CHAPTER THIRTY-SIX)

Born parked his champagne colored Cadillac sedan and told his boy to hold tight while he checked on something. He walked up to a huge, rundown looking house and stood at the door for a second before someone said, "Who is it?"

"It's me." The door swung open and a linebacker looking type of guy stood in the doorway with a slight smile on his face.

"What's up? I didn't expect to see you so early," he said.

"You know me, I got to stay on top of things," Born stated while giving Bigger some dap as he casually walked in.

Bigger was the ex-college football player turned doorman slash bouncer. By looking at the outside of the house, you would never have guessed that the interior of the house resembled something out of House and Garden urban style. The carpet was three inch thick imported Indonesian gold. In each corner of the spacious living room sat four plush Brazilian sofas with individually hand-stitched designs. Directly in the middle of the floor was a custom-made, solid cherry oak, fully stocked bar complete with multi-colored overhead lights setting off the effect. The walls were covered with one of a kind oil paintings from some of the most sought after, up and coming black artists in the city.

"Where she at?" Born asked.

"She's in the last room," Bigger responded. Born walked down the hall past five rooms until he reached the last one. He went inside and sitting there on a queen size bed was Trina smoking a cigarette, looking worn out.

"So you stacked dat paper last night or what?" He asked in a regular manner.

"Yeah, it was a busy night. I had dis regular customer, some fat Mexican who kept asking me to move in with him," she replied as she put on a fresh pair of panties and bra in front of him.

Once that episode jumped off with Trina and puppet man, he kept a close eye on her, watching her every move. Since that night two years ago when she tried to tell the police the drugs were his in front of his face, even though she was the one getting her party on in a reckless way, Born knew she was out for herself. But he never thought she could get down and dirty with him like that. The only reason he kept her around was because she knew how to toot that ass and get that dough fattening his pockets as well. Soon her coke habit started to get expensive, even for him. Plus he suspected that she started seeing his high paying tricks on the low low.

Early one morning she called him begging for some nose candy so she could start her day off right, or so she said. When he got to her place, he informed her that he wouldn't be getting any product for a week because there was a drought in the city. Trina started saying she couldn't wait that long and that she knew he had something to get her through the day.

"I have a couple of grams of rocks I'm supposed to drop off, but I know you'll never fuck wit it," he slyly stated.

"You right, but just dis one time won't hurt," she said unconvincingly.

Born knew he had her, so he started to walk to the door and said, "Nah, I don't want my baby fucking with crack. Dat's for low life motherfuckers. I say we hold off until next week."

She grabbed his arm and said, "Give me da shit and let me try da bullshit. I wanna see how da other side lives," she added, trying to make the whole situation into a joke.

Born pulled out a small bag filled with assorted shapes and sizes of beige crack rocks, along with a cheap glass crack pipe. Trina almost smoked up half an ounce that day as Born sat back smiling to himself. Soon after when she would meet up with Born he always had a story to tell on how he didn't have any coke at the moment or was about to pick some up later. Trina never questioned as to why he always had crack and a pipe on him. It got to the point where the subject of coke never arose. A month later Born knew that Trina was a full fledged crack fiend, when her appearance started slipping and clothes weren't that important to her anymore.

A couple of months later he had her working out of a whorehouse that he and his brother just recently opened up.

"Dat's why she could sling that pussy for me twenty-four hours a day," Born would joke to his friends, remembering how she once tried to take him down. All the other women Born had working for him were either Honduran or Ecuadorian. Trina was the only white female. So she was considered a hot commodity to the drunken Mexican patrons.

"Born, you been promising me a day off so we could hang out or something," Trina said, trying not to make him angry.

"I told you before, shit is slow because of the new asshole mayor trying to shut everything down," he said.

"I know I must have fucked and sucked about a hundred niggas over the weekend," she said while reaching under the bed and handing him a metal lock box.

The box had a tiny slot where you could drop coins into. When customers first entered the spot they had the option of buying the silver coins, which cost thirty dollars, or buying a gold coin that went for fifty bucks. If you had a gold coin you received a trip around the world. The tricks gave the girls of their choice the valueless metal, so the women never handled any type of actual money. They could make extra money if they persuaded the guys to purchase an overpriced bottle of liquor from the bar to be sent to the room.

Born took the loaded box and knew that Trina was more than telling the truth. "Next week we definitely going to hit da town and show folks how we can party," he said, smiling and revealing princess cut diamond teeth.

"You got something for me so I can relax?" She asked. Without responding, Born threw her a couple vials of crack and headed back out the room.

Born went to each room and collected a box from all the girls promising one thing or another to them. He and Bigger then sat down at the bar making sure all the coins matched up with the money he had. Once he was satisfied, he told Bigger that if his brother were to come by, for him to give him a shout out. Born went to his whip and saw his man laying his game down on some young, pretty Puerto Rican girl trying to recruit her. She was leaning over the passenger side, laughing and blushing that an older man was finding her so irresistible. She handed him her number as Born took a good long look at her taut body and peeled off.

(CHAPTER THIRTY-SEVEN)

"Hello, let me speak to Santos," Ice said.

"Who's dis?" A male voice asked back.

"Dis is Ice. He knows who I am. Put him on."

"Ice from the city?" The voice asked.

"Yeah why?" Ice asked back.

"Santos told me about you, how when shit got thick with the pigs you still wouldn't talk," the guy said.

"So now you know who I am, are you gonna put him on now?" Ice said, tired of playing the game of who's who.

"Right now he's indisposed at the moment. Is there something I can help you wit?" He asked.

"I need some new front tires, but I'm a little low on da cash tip. I'll take whatever right now to get me rolling in da meanwhile," Ice said speaking in codes, not taking any chances.

The guy on the other line told Ice that he had some peoples close by and that he would call ahead and let them know he was coming through. After the phone call Ice wasted no time in getting to the address that was given to him. His money was getting low, and he had no idea when Kendew was getting back. People always had the tendency to say, "only for a couple of days" whenever anyone ever went out of town. He rode the train, and an hour later he arrived in the Brownsville section of Brooklyn. Ice started thinking about a female who he used to deal with, who stayed on that side of town. For some reason he remembered her brother always saying, "Brownsville never ran, never will. Walk slow, so the Guinness don't spill."

He made it to some project where the guys on the corner eyed him suspiciously because of his stranger status. He went up to the fifth floor of the apartment building, if you could call it that, and had to mention Santos's man's name before they let him in. Five minutes later he left with an old .38 police special that had heavy black tape around the handle to keep it together, plus a half a box of bullets. Everything together cost him seventy-five dollars. Now he was definitely feeling washed up with only twenty dollars left to his name. He had to load the gun in the elevator because the seller wouldn't let him do it in the apartment. It was an unwritten rule that if you were selling anyone a firearm, you never sold it to them loaded because they could turn around and rob you with the same gun they just bought. Ice knew the gun he just copped was a piece of shit, but it was a stepping stone. *But to what*, he wondered.

Ice rode a different train heading toward Manhattan. The only person he could think of who had mad dough was Nick Castitine. "Dat cracker always treats me as an ignorant nigga from da hood who he could use for his own benefit and get over on. We'll see who gets over on who today," Ice said to himself with a self-assured wicked smile. The sun was just starting to go down as Ice left the train station and headed toward his destination.

Ice soon arrived at the jewelry store ready to get down for business. The only thing Nick knew about him was his name, which was a nickname at that. Ice was dying to get inside Nick's safe. He had never seen the safe, but he was sure Nick definitely had to have one with all the high priced merchandise he dealt with. When Ice approached the glass door, a white couple was just leaving. Before he could go inside, the door swung shut. Ice threw up his arms as if to say "let me in." A woman whom Ice had never seen before pointed to her watch and shook her head as if to say "sorry." Ice left, wondering what his next move should be.

Ice happened to look up the block and spotted the couple who had just left the jewelry store walking slowly and looking at an object as if they were admiring it. *They must have just bought something and might have some cash left too*, Ice thought. He followed the couple, who were unaware that their quiet evening was about to have a drastic change. They headed to a parking garage with Ice close behind watching the surrounding area very closely. Ice pulled out his house keys, pretending it was a set of car keys just in case someone was watching. The couple went over by a dark corner where a shiny black 740 BMW sat. The couple stood by the car kissing as Ice crept up to them and interrupted their little romantic interlude.

"Okay motherfuckers, I know you all ain't from da hood, but it ain't hard to tell what time it is," he said as he pointed his gun at the terrified man and woman. The woman had on a cashmere low cut sweater and a suede skirt with some expensive looking calf high leather boots. The guy had on regular shirt, slacks, and pair of Gucci loafers. The way they were dressed, and plus they had the crazy ride, he knew they had to be holding.

"Don't say a motherfucking word. I want it all, and if you try to hold back, you'll never make it back to your fancy perfect world," Ice said, dead serious.

"Do as he say, Steve. We don't want no trouble," the woman said as her eyes were fixated on the gun. Steve gave Ice his wallet, watch, car keys, and college class ring.

"Now bitch, your turn," Ice said as he kept a close eye on Steve. Ice knew white boys have the tendency to play hero and try to snatch the gun away. The woman gave Ice everything she had, including her newly purchased diamond tennis bracelet. Ice was about to leave when he looked at the guy's brand new BMW, and the pretty white girl he had with him. Then he thought how when he had his ride, money, and jewelry, how all the girls wanted him. He started to grow angry when he thought how Spank had dismissed him like a nobody.

"Yo, Steve, how long you known her?" Ice asked.

Caught off guard by the unusual question, the guy said, "Excuse me?"

"I said, how long you known her?" Ice repeated himself.

"This is only our second date," Steve answered.

"And you tricking already? Did you get dat pussy yet," Ice asked.

"What?"

"I said did you fuck dis bitch yet? You buying da female diamonds and shit, plus you rolling in something hard. So what's up?" Ice asked, forgetting about sticking to his game plan on getting the money and bouncing.

Steve looked at the woman and said, "No."

"I bet if you were riding da train and working at Wendy's or somewhere, dis type of uppity bitch wouldn't give you a chance, even if you got down on your knees and begged her. Ain't dat right?" Ice asked, not expecting a response. By now the couple started to panic thinking Ice was some kind of demented black man who hated all white people.

"Bitch, get on your motherfucking knees before I peel back your head piece," he ordered. The woman did as she was told and started whimpering while looking at her date for some kind of help. "Now playboy, just relax. I'm not gonna hurt you. As a matter of fact, I'm gonna help you out. Pull dem pants down," he said. Steve did as he was told. "The tighty whities too," Ice ordered, referring to his bikini briefs. The guy stood there naked and ashamed that his date, who he hoped to impress with jewelry, could see him humiliated like this.

"Now bitch, do what you do best and suck his dick," Ice said in a whisper, but his voice seemed like thunder to the shocked couple. When she didn't move, Ice said, "Either you put your lips to work or I leave you here with a tea bag for a face." The crying woman took the small shriveled up pinkish penis in her mouth and started sucking like she hadn't eaten for a week. "Put some feeling into it, like he brought you a matching chain," Ice said while smiling at the spectacle.

Meanwhile, it seemed that Steve had relaxed a whole lot because his eyes were half closed. His dick grew to three times its normal size as he unconsciously grabbed a handful of her blond hair, pushing her head down further for more pressure. Without notice Ice kicked the woman in the chest sending her flying on the ground.

"Okay dat's enough," Ice said. In Steve's mind he was saying, *Damn why couldn't the black bastard just wait until couple of more minutes.* Ice backed away slowly, leaving the woman crying in a ball and her date standing there with his still stone hard dick breathing hard. Ice threw the car keys and wallet into a garbage can after taking the credit cards and money. He jumped back on the subway laughing to himself and playing the scene back in his head.

(CHAPTER THIRTY-EIGHT)

"Bigger, Bigger, I need to speak to you for a minute. It's very important," Trina yelled throughout the house, waking up a few girls who were trying to rest.

Bigger appeared at Trina's doorway and said, "What you want now?"

"I have to go to da doctor. I think it's serious," she stated.

"You know Born said for you to hold tight. If you needed to go somewhere, you supposed to let him know ahead of time," the door man responded.

"I didn't get a chance to tell him because he ran out so quick like da house was on fire or something. I been having female problems for a couple of days now," she answered, trying to gain his sympathy.

"So why didn't you tell someone during dat whole time?" He asked, wondering what was coming next.

"I thought maybe it was da same infection I had before. Usually I would douche and it's over, but dis time I started having a heavy discharge sort of like old cottage cheese or something. If you don't believe me, here take a look," Trina said as she grabbed a wrinkled up paper bag from the nightstand.

"What da fuck you got in there?" Bigger asked.

"It's just a pair of panties I had on all last night. My drawers smelled like someone had dragged dem through sour goat milk. My doctor said if it were to happen again I was to bring him a sample for da lab," she said while holding the bag and walking closer to Bigger.

"Here take a whiff if you think I'm bullshitting," she said with a dead serious face.

"Hell no, get dat infected bag away from me. When you think you'll be back?" He asked, covering his mouth and nose with his jacket.

"Well, da doctor got to spread my legs..."

Before she could finish the details, Bigger said, "Okay, fuck it! Just go and handle your business and make sure you take dat bag wit you."

"Thanks teddy bear, I owe you one," Trina said as she grabbed her jacket and ran out with lighting speed. A half a block away she threw the paper bag in the sewer and laughed to herself thinking on how Bigger is one stupid motherfucker.

Trina stood on a corner in front of a cheap Chinese clothing store smoking a Newport. Twice she ran into the street thinking it was the person she was expecting. *Beep, beep.* Trina ran over to the car and heard, "come on, hurry your ass on," coming from a below average looking Toyota 4Runner. Trina took a quick look, smiled, and jumped in the jeep.

"What took you so long? Some bum ass motherfucker kept circling da block trying to pick me up," Trina said.

"I had to hustle up some gas money. You know how shit flows sometimes."

"You got dat or what?" Supreme asked anxiously, waiting for an answer.

"Yeah, dat nigga only hit me off wit a couple of rocks. Who da fuck he think I am, a fucking crackhead or something?"

She stated, not really taking a look at herself in the mirror lately. The couple cruised the streets smoking the cheap, available drug and lost in their own personal thoughts.

Supreme started remembering on how he had everything, including one of the baddest women the ghetto had ever produced. Mia had called him after she went missing and told him that there was a crisis in her family and she had to be there. He then found out that both of his most-trusted boys/hit men, Rico and Half a Dread, were murdered one day apart from each other. His people on the street were giving him conflicting stories on how things unfolded with the murders. With all the street drama going on around him, he just told Mia to keep in touch and let him know how everything turned out. Preme just naturally assumed that her anguished, sad voice accompanied with silent tears had something to do with family problems. He would have never suspected that the mental turmoil Mia was going through had something to do with him (or so she thought).

Rumors started circulating around the hood that a hit squad was on Preme's ass by someone he did dirt to in the past. The streets also said that a Haitian bloodthirsty gang from Connecticut wanted to move in. It just so happened that most of the unsubstantiated rumors were kicked off by some of his own soldiers, who for a long time wanted Preme out of the way. They knew he didn't have the killer heart for the ruthless drug trade. The only thing he had for himself was a good connect and some sick Jamaicans backing him up and keeping everyone in line when necessary. With Dread and Rico out the picture, they scared Preme into hiding, telling him it was for the best for right now until they found out what was really going down. His trusted lieutenant even went as far as to shoot up a couple of Preme's cars to secure the fact. He convinced Preme to let him deal with his coke connect directly until things died down a little.

Unwillingly, Preme gave up his most sought after connect to his co-conspirators. Just to be on the safe side, they told his connect in a roundabout way that Preme was becoming unstable due to the pressure, and they weren't sure how long he could handle it. The connect took it as if Preme's character was snitchable, something he wanted to avoid at all costs. Preme let his boys run his day-to-day activities, receiving bits and pieces of the happenings from time to time. When he hadn't heard from Mia for over a month, his crew truthfully told him that it was as if she had disappeared. They hinted that maybe she had been snatched up by rival crews adding to his already full-blown paranoid state. Preme had to take the news at face value due to the fact that she left all her belongings at his place.

Preme's lieutenant would drop bundles of money off to him relaying that they still had their people sorting things out. The bundles kept getting smaller and smaller until a couple of his top men told him straight out that it would be in his best interest if he quietly bowed out. Preme knew he had no wins at this point so he spread out with what little money and dignity he had left. Without the vast amount of money coming in now, Preme soon found his resources exhausted, along with his props.

Preme took a long swig on his Old English 40 and said, "When are we gonna get dis bitch ass nigga?"

"Everything's in motion. I just hope his ass is where he's supposed to be, so we can make dis move," Trina replied while crumbling up the empty pack of Newports and throwing it on the floor of the car.

"You sure he's going to be holding? I definitely need to get my hands on some dough. I got dis new connect who got some high grade product dat will make a nigga shit on himself just by looking at it. When I get rolling again, niggas gonna feel Preme's presence again."

Trina leaned back in her seat and rolled her eyes. *Here we go again,* she thought. Every time Preme started talking about money and drugs he went off track rambling on about what he used to have like a mad man stuck in the past.

Trina one day accidentally bumped into Preme walking by a Hess gas station four months ago. She had to look twice to make sure it was the man she once knew. He was pumping gas into a car that couldn't possibly be his (or so she thought). He wasn't flashing any of his head turning jewelry, and his wears looked shabby. Curiosity made her stop to see if it was indeed him. They greeted each other like long lost friends, eventually smoking an eight ball and sexing all night. Preme constantly blabbed on about how he was going to be on top once again. Trina knew that if he did by some slim chance happen to defy the odds, she would want to be there from the jump.

"Preme, you can drop me off on da corner? I gotta get back. I'm gonna call you and let you know da deal," Trina said.

"You know it's you and me baby, nothing gonna stop us now," Preme said, full of enthusiasm as he pulled up to a stop sign. "Call me," he said as he slapped Trina's ass as she got out.

(CHAPTER THIRTY-NINE)

Ice made it back to the house with both arms filled with shopping bags. The white guy he robbed in the city was holding crisp fifties and hundred dollar bills totaling fifteen hundred dollars. It wasn't what he was used to coming off with, but it was a start from someone just arriving home with nothing but his desire to get paid. For all his purchases, he laid out strictly cash because he wasn't familiar with the credit card craze. *Why take a chance of some red cheeked racist sales clerk white woman thinking a young black man couldn't possibly be the true owner of some credit cards, and alert security,* Ice thought. He could picture her smiling that fake sincere smile that she only used toward her black customers, telling him "it will only be a minute sir," while pretending to write up the items and stalling for time until help arrived.

"Yo, Lemon, you here?" Ice called out with only silence answering him back. "She probably out doing her," he said as he went into his room, placing his bag next to his bed.

He took out a bottle of Grey Goose Vodka along with his victim's watch. The watch said "Mozoni collection," on the face with a shiny gold frame. The band appeared to be expensive alligator or crocodile of some sort. The watch was okay, but it wasn't his style. He needed something that the hood rat chicks knew cost a lot. He then took a long hot bath, something he took for granted during his incarceration, while drinking straight out of the Grey Goose bottle. He dressed slowly, savoring the smell of new clothes, and headed out the door to complete his private welcome home party. He stopped by a black owned restaurant that'd been open since he was little, and hungrily ate fried chicken, mixed vegetables, and a large serving of mashed potatoes with homemade gravy.

Out on the sidewalk Ice smoked a cigarette thinking now that he was ready to wild out with some girls. He bagged a few numbers while shopping, but he wanted a big butt freak right now.

"Yeah Jezebel's," he said aloud while smiling. He called a cab and when the cab arrived Ice jumped in the back saying, "Hurry up! A nigga want to see some pussy. It's been a long time," while playfully slapping the driver on the shoulder.

The first thing Ice noticed as he got out was that the old Jezebel's sign was taken down and replaced with a new one that said Jezebel's 2. It had colorfully flashing lights going off and on in sequence. There were about five guys he didn't recognize standing outside talking and joking. A few others were waiting their turn to be searched by the bouncers, who he also didn't know. He nonchalantly walked around the corner and stashed his burner in some bushes, and then went back toward the front.

Ice asked, "So da bitches showing luv or what," when he was getting patted down by one of the men. The bouncer just ignored him and told him it was ten dollars to enter. Ice paid the money while sizing up the guy who had just disrespected him by not even bothering to answer back.

Once inside Ice automatically felt a different vibe about the place. For one, the whole club looked as if it had been completely remodeled. The bar looked as if it was only a couple of months old with a highly glossed finish highlighting the wood. Two female bartenders stood there dressed identically in tight T-shirts and the club logo printed across the front. They were busy expertly mixing drinks in front of a huge wall mirror that held twice the selection of liquor as before. Ice went over and ordered Grey Goose with cranberry juice, sticking to what he had been drinking earlier.

He went over and sat in a chair close by the stage, placing his drink on a small black table. Even the stage was remodeled. Instead of one pole, there were two. All around the stage were assorted colored light bulbs going off and on, giving the dancer an exotic, mysterious appeal. There was a girl on stage who looked like she had spent one too many times at the gym, but otherwise she had a pretty face with a flowing reddish-brown weave.

In the middle of the stripper's routine the DJ quieted the music down and rung a serious of bells. A tall woman appeared on stage from behind a curtain carrying a shiny silver tray. As soon as she placed the tray on the stage floor and the contents were revealed, the crowd cheered and clapped. The tray held dildos, creams, lotions, and other items for the sexual deviants. The second woman handed the first stripper a large, see-through, plastic pink dick, which she gladly accepted into her waiting pussy. As she slowly eased the monstrous toy into her body cavity, the DJ was shouting, "put it all in, put it all in" in a musical sort of way. Then the D.J started singing, "Bring him on stage, bring him on stage," as the woman who brought the apparatuses out minutes earlier selected a nerdy type of guy from the growing audience. She guided him on stage toward the girl who was on her back with the dildo.

"Rub lotion on her, rub lotion on her," the DJ continued. The nervous guy did as he was told, joining the act by rubbing the glittery lotion on the girl's thick and already sweaty thighs. Meanwhile, the second woman slid off the nerdy guy's pants, showing tight boxer shorts with cartoon prints on them that brought the crowd to ear shattering laughter. The stripper performing the show slowly stood up, leaving the nerd in a bending position with his pants still around his ankles. She snatched the dildo out of her vagina and pressed a small button on the side causing a thick white cream to shoot all over his unsuspecting face. Dollar bills started raining on both of them as the DJ shouted over the music, Put your hands together for Safire, Mystic, and Unknown Guest." Someone handed the embarrassed guy a hand towel as he stumbled back down to his chair with fingers still pointing at him.

There was some kind of commotion at the front entrance that drew Ice's attention. A group of four guys were entering with two women who wearing tight fitting outfits. They could easily pass for strippers, or straight-up hookers, depending on who was doing the looking. Most of the guys wore heavy gold jewelry as they were lead to the back of the club toward the newly done V.I.P. section. They laughed and talked out loud beyond normal, throwing a couple of bills at some dancers as they walked though the floor. Ice could have sworn he recognized one of the guys who appeared to be the leader of the pact. But Ice wasn't going to play himself by approaching him and take any chances that he could be mistaken and be dismissed like a groupie or something. It seemed like all of the waitresses were tending to the guys every need, so Ice went to the bar for a drink.

"Yo, shorty, dem bottles of Cristal ain't cold enough. Bring over some new ones, all right," one of the young guys who had just arrived said to one of the bartender women.

"Oh shit, Ice! What da fuck? I didn't see you up in dis piece," the guy who was leading the group said to Ice. Ice looked through the hazy cigarette smoke and knew right away it was his little man Rizz from around the way. It was Rizz all right, except he wasn't that little anymore and from his appearance he definitely wasn't slinging no crack on a rusted BMX bike anymore.

"What's up Rizz? I see you and your peoples doing it up," Ice said, looking at Rizz's dinner plate sized piece with the words "Step it up" spelled out in diamonds on his neck and trying to determine its worth.

"Nah, it ain't nothing, but when did you touch down?" The young guy asked.

"Da other day," came Ice's answer.

"Come on in the back in V.I.P. We got champagne, shrimp da size of bread sticks, and of coarse we got da bitches," Rizz stated while smiling and showing a full bottom row of platinum teeth. To get to the V.I.P. section you had to walk up three carpeted steps where red velvet rope had to be unattached to get in. Ice sat down on the corner of the expensive butter soft leather couch as Rizz sat in the middle of his entourage. The men as well as the girls eyed Ice, wondering who he was. Ice looked back at the group noticing that no one seemed to be over nineteen, except the girls.

"Yo, dis is my man Ice. He just came home, so you know I got to show him a good time," Rizz yelled as the rest of the group seemed uninterested in the tall stranger. The mood was broken by a couple of smiling waitresses bringing chilled buckets of champagne along with larger platters of jumbo shrimp and hot wings.

"Tell da girls they can come now, and bring dat new shorty back wit dem," Rizz said while pouring himself a full glass of Cristal.

Moments later three strippers appeared, wearing various seductive outfits that left little to the imagination. One girl, wearing a Hawaiian matching print set, went straight up to Rizz and started giving him a lap dance while the other two girls started a strip tease for the rest of the group.

"Hold up shorty, what's your name?"Rizz asked the dancer doing the grinding.

"Kansas. What's yours playboy?" She asked, praying he was interested in her even though she lived with her baby's daddy.

"You see my man over there?" Rizz said, pointing to Ice. "Well he's been away and hasn't seen pussy for a while. Ice, how long has it been?" He yelled out as everyone laughed and looked at Ice, who didn't find the humor.

Kansas did her thing with Ice as he thought, *I know dis nigga ain't trying to play me. I'm just bugging. I used to bless his little ass.* The champagne turned into shots of Hennessy as two of Rizz's boys received some quick drunken blowjobs in the darken section of the V.I.P. lounge. The girls that came with the group of men got into the swing of things, dancing and feeding each other champagne soaked grapes. Soon everyone started to light up pre-rolled Philly blunts as they traded insults with each other in a friendly sort way. Ice didn't like Rizz's style or the way Rizz's boys kept on looking at him, like he was beneath them.

"I gotta make moves. I'll check you another time," Ice said, directing his comment to Rizz as his boys looked on.

"Damn kid, I was hoping you was enjoying yourself. But don't worry, next time we'll do it like real motherfuckers ought to," Rizz stated. By now Ice was preparing to leave, thinking that Rizz was acting too much like a wannabe Don, when just a couple of years ago he was buying him four dollar Chinese value dinners.

"Ice, give me a call. I don't want to see you looking like dis. I might have something for you," Rizz said. Ice screwed up his face knowing for sure that Rizz was trying to play him in front of his soft ass crew from what Ice could tell. Rizz, in his arrogant manner, didn't catch the look as he handed him his hustler's business card with a hundred dollar bill folded underneath it. "Don't forget to holler at me, and maybe you can get back where you used to be," Rizz shouted while holding his gold diamond piece up in the air with both hands. Ice heard some slight laughter from Rizz and his crew as he walked away and out of the club.

Ice's first thought when he reached the sidewalk was to get his burner and wait for Rizz and his lame ass crew to come out. But he knew he wasn't prepared for no war with an old .38 that he wasn't sure even shot straight. When the time was right, he was going to see how much of a man Rizz really was. He definitely needed to get with Kendew and get down to some serious business.

"Motherfuckers not going to keep playing me cause I've been away," Ice said to himself as he gripped the taped-up handle of his gun, hoping someone would bump into him right now.

(CHAPTER FORTY)

Mia was sitting down in an average looking house counting a large trash bag filled with money. After a few hours of organizing the cash in neat bundles of fives through hundreds, with rubber bands securing them, she snatched up three stacks of twenties, fifties, and hundreds each. She then placed the money in the bottom of her coach bag and covered it with a matching silk scarf. The money she had just counted wasn't hers yet, but the fifteen thousand that she had taken was a done deal. She smiled a sincere smile, which she rarely did.

Since the day she was brutally raped, and a guy she really liked was murdered in front of her eyes, the nightmarish scenes played at least twice a night in her dreams. To make the ordeal even more unbearable, she found out that Preme had masterminded the whole set up. After she was released from jail because the D.A. saw no reason to hold her, she went to her cousin's house with just the clothes on her back and only half her sanity. She confided to her cousin about what had transpired in the last twenty-four hours over a bottle of Tequila which eased the pain of betrayal momentarily. She decided never to see

Supreme again, leaving behind all the fashionable clothes, jewelry, and money she had stashed away.

Mia had planned to bounce on Preme to Trinidad to be with her young son Isaiah that he knew nothing about. She secretly sent money back home to her sister who was caring for Isaiah (if you could call it that) to pay for their day-to-day living expenses, not to mention the expensive medicine for her son's condition, which had to be purchased on the black market. Mia knew that her older sister was taking the majority of the money and spending it on herself, trying to emulate a successful American lifestyle. She had no choice but to send the money to her sister, even though she knew how it was being recklessly spent, because that was the only family she had.

Her father was a strong-willed political activist who was trying diligently to change the disease and crime-ridden conditions of the ghetto. He uncovered widespread corruption by local officials pocketing money intended for paved streets, medical care, fixing the stopped up sewers, etc. Soon important political figures higher up were starting to listen to this simple ironworker from an impoverished ghetto. He went out early one morning to meet some men to discuss the problems that had been plaguing his community for nearly a decade, but he never returned. When his wife went to the local police station to file a report, they just laughed, saying it was common for a man his age to find a younger woman and run off with her. A week later they found his bloated, decapitated body floating in Black Mill Creek with his work card identifying who he was. Five month's later Mia's mother died a heart broken skeleton of a woman, finally finding peace next to her husband in the town's cemetery.

Mia's cell phone went off, causing her to jump slightly, and breaking her thoughts. "Hello, what's up baby," Mia said. "Oh, I just finished up taking care of dat. It came to ninety-eight thousand dollars."

"Dat's it!" The person on the other end asked.

"Yeah, I counted it twice," she lied. "Dat bucktooth nigga from da hill, I think he's working wit dem niggas you been having drama with, dat's why you been coming up short lately," Mia spat out.

"Yeah okay, I'll check you in a little while. You want me to bring you anything back?" He asked.

"Nah, I'm good. You just make it home safe. I miss you, boo," Mia said in a sexy voice, lying once again. She turned off her cell phone so she could be alone with what she considered her only true friend, an imported bottle of Triple Gold Tequila from Mexico.

(CHAPTER FORTY-ONE)

"Bigger told me you had to go out because you had some sort of female problems. What da fuck was dat all about?" Born asked as he cruised through East New York, Brooklyn in his brand new one month old Cadillac STS whip.

"I don't know if I told you, but I got dis weird customer who all he wants to do is eat my pussy for an hour. I didn't really care because he seemed harmless enough. Den da next day I found some whitish shit on my panties. He must have been licking on some dirty bitch's pussy before he came to see me. So I figure I should handle shit right away," Trina answered, trying to gather sympathy.

"Damn, next time his perverted sick ass come around, cover your cunt wit some glad wrap and charge his ass double," Born shouted as he and his boy who was in the backseat broke out into a laugh at Trina's expense.

The threesome reached their destination, which was a large project building with six other smaller buildings surrounding it.

"Make sure you let me know right away what he says," Born said to his man as he was getting out. Born then rode the side streets heading back to Queens and checking out the view along the way. He pulled up in front of a beauty salon in a mostly white neighborhood. He then told Trina to get what she needed done and he'd pick her up later. When he did scoop up Trina later on, she was sitting by the door reading a magazine. He beeped his horn and she ran out, hopping in his car as the other white women in the shop twisted their faces at the out of place couple, secretly wishing it was them pulling off to do (God knows what) with a black man.

Born left Trina off at an expensive, fashionable boutique while he waited for her, conducting business on his cell phone. Trina emerged from the store carrying two small shopping bags just as Born was telling someone on the other end of his call to handle shit right away. Trina was all smiles as she gracefully glided into the passenger seat. Born looked her over and thought, *Damn, shortie is looking mad good. I should take her to a hotel later on and bone dat fat ass.* He then snapped back to his pimp status, frowning his face knowing that Trina was still a conniving crack whore who just happened to have a thick body and a pretty face that made him crazy money.

"So how I look?" Trina asked, knowing the answer already because the sales lady who was helping her tried to push up on her in a sly way. She had busted into the dressing room, saying, while pretending to blush, "Oh, I'm sorry. I didn't realize you were in this room." Trina was standing there in her panties only, not bothering to cover up. Her first response was to flip on the saleslady, but she had a stolen credit card that Born had given her. If she had wilded out in the store, even though she was in the right, they would definitely ask her for some sort of I.D. Born would have beaten her ass if she came out the store empty handed.

"Do you think I should go with the silver or light blue dress?" Trina asked the lusting lady as she purposely dropped the blue one, bending over to pick it back up and giving the saleslady an X-rated back shot of her ass and puffy pussy mound. The lady just stood there speechless with her mouth open until Trina said that she would just take both of them while giggling. Trina had thrown away everything she had on, including her undergarments, and wore out a silver Valentino dress with a matching handbag. She choose Manolo Blahnik open toed shoes as her footwear. The dress perfectly emphasized her naturally curvy body.

Born drove through a fast food takeout window. He ordered a deluxe burger meal and Trina had a small salad. Halfway through the meal she asked, "Why do I have to be there when you meet him? You know how his ugly ass always gives me da creeps."

"I told you before, baby, I need you there. For some reason he always agrees to whatever I say when you're around. I'm trying to wrap dis deal up as quickly as possible, plus he asked me to bring you along," he said, giving her his best smile.

"Yeah okay, whatever, but I want to get lifted before we get there," Trina stated while rolling her eyes without Born peeping it. After their quick lunch, they drove off toward the meeting.

(CHAPTER FORTY-TWO)

Ice made it back to his temporary place and walked in feeling played, angry, and most of all horny.

"Yo Lemon, you back yet?" he called out.

"Yeah I'm in da kitchen. Come on back," she responded. He walked back and spotted her sitting down cutting up three pancake sized crack rocks in a large plate. Next to the plate was a small, filled-up sugar bowl with what Ice suspected to be cocaine.

Lemon turned her chair toward him and said, "Come on give me a hand. I'm tired as hell." She was wearing a pair of pink panties and a pale pink tank top that showed her flat stomach that had some kind of dragon tattoo breathing fire out of his nostrils. You could only make out half of the artwork because it was done low toward her shaved pubic area. *Shorty definitely holding, all dat baggy shit had me fooled da fuck out,* Ice thought as he pulled up a chair, taking a closer look at all the product sprawled out in front of him.

"What you want me to do?" He innocently asked.

"Just keep cutting dis up like I've been doing," she stated while handing him a fresh straight razor. She got up and opened up a bottom drawer pulling out a weighing scale. A strong feeling stirred up in Ice's groin as she wiggled her apple shaped ass back and forth. If Lemon knew Ice was staring a little too hard, she made no indication, because she just put on her breathing mask and proceeded to measure the coke, like a professional chemist. After a couple of hours, she noticed Ice getting bored, or tired, or maybe both, so she they should take a break.

They both headed back in the living room where she turned on the radio to an all night R&B station. Ice didn't know where she got it from, but she came back with a fifth of Jack Daniels Whiskey.

"Is dis all right with you?" She asked as she flopped down on the couch crossing her legs under herself Indian style.

"I'll take whatever right now," Ice stated as he grabbed the bottle and took a good swig. They just kicked it with each other like they were on a date or something, drinking straight from the bottle. Lemon didn't talk much about her life except that she had a lot of brothers and sisters. Rival Chinese street gangs had murdered two of her brothers six months apart from each other. Her sisters, along with her mother, ran three successful massage parlors out in New Jersey and Connecticut.

Ice just talked about how he was going to do it Big Willie style this time around and not let anyone fuck up his plans. He didn't tell Lemon what happened at Jezebel's, because he didn't want her to think that niggas were always trying to diss him.

"So you got your nut off since you been home or what?" Lemon asked the question, coming out of left field.

Ice didn't want to tell her a straight no, so he just said, "I'm about dat paper first. Da bitches just gonna have to wait," he said as he laughed. Lemon wasn't giving any type of sexual vibe, but the question left the door wide open.

He tried to kiss her neck and she said, "Hold it cowboy! I hope I didn't give you any mixed signals, but I don't fuck around with dudes. No offense to you, but I like a good fur burger every now and den."

"I feel you, but if you ever feel like the real thing, give a nigga a shout out," Ice said with a smile that had seduced many girls in his lifetime.

"I'll tell you what, since you just coming home and I feel your style, I'll give you a little treat," she said as she walked off back ito the kitchen, still driving Ice crazy with her walk. She came back a second later and told Ice to straight up drop his jeans. He did as he was told wondering why she went to the kitchen in the first place.

"Yeah, you just did a bid," Lemon stated while laughing as she looked at Ice's member, which seemed to be frozen solid in time pointing right at her. She immediately dropped to her knees, cupping his sac with her delicate, butter soft hands. She took him in her mouth and Ice automatically felt a cold sensation shooting through his loins. Lemon had gone to the kitchen and scooped up a large portion of butter pecan ice cream and placed it in her mouth. By now both of Lemon hands were on Ice's buttocks making sure he didn't go anywhere so she could give him what he needed. She felt Ice's dick start to throb, and she knew it was about to be a wrap any second now.

She withdrew herself from him, spat a cold pecan on his belly, and said, "Not yet, cowboy. You ain't getting off dat easy," she said as she pinched a secret nerve in his scrotum that her mother had taught her would stop a man's long awaited ejaculation. Lemon continued as Ice held her shiny black hair. Unknowing to Ice, Lemon hands were inching their way toward the middle of his ass. In his conscious mind, he knew where the fingers were heading, but he made no attempt to stop it.

Her middle finger touched the tip of his anus, and Ice opened his eyes to find Lemon looking directly up at him. He felt her velvet finger pushing deeper and deeper into his ass. For some strange, unknown reason he felt his dick thicken and become more blood filled at that particular moment. He wanted to kick her in the face and ask her what the fuck she thought he was, but it was as if someone had injected him with some kind of paralyzing drug. As soon as Lemon's finger reached its limit, Ice let out a deep moan and released a hot stream into the girl's mouth, causing her to gag.

She stood up and spit into an empty soda can. While Ice was pulling up his pants, he felt another presence in the room and looked to the side. Sassy was standing there grinning and said, "I see you made yourself at home."

"Sassy, oh I mean Kendew, what da fuck you doing in da dark?" Ice asked a little embarrassed on what had just happened.

"I just touched down an hour ago. I saw you and Lemon doing your thang, so I just waited until you got yours," Sassy, aka Kendew, said while stepping forward and giving Ice some dap. "So how's everything running?" Kendew asked, directing the question to the girl.

"Shit is cool. I should be finished in about four more hours," she replied as she lit up a Newport.

"I'll help you out. Ice, you look crazy tired, so you get some rest and we can get down to business in da morning," he stated as he took the cigarette out of Lemon's mouth and took a drag, well aware of the fact that just a moment ago she had a mouth full of hot cum.

Ice was tired from drinking all day and night not to mention that he just bust one of his biggest nuts in a while. He drifted off to sleep, thinking what was going through Kendew's mind as he watched him get off. He also wondered if Kendew had told Lemon what happened to him in jail, and that's the reason she decided to play with his ass. The thought that freaked Ice out most of all, is why didn't he stop Lemon when her finger first touched his rectum?

(CHAPTER FORTY-THREE)

"Wooo! You peeped da ass on dat bitch?" Rizz yelled at no one in particular.

"Spin around and let's see what she's talking about," Lakim stated while turning his head, still staring at the girl standing in front of an all night chicken spot. Rizz made as wide, illegal U-turn in his high performance Yukon Denali, not caring that he didn't have a driver's license.

Rizz and his boys had just came back from the strip club and they still were looking for more shit to get into. After they got rid of the girls they were hanging with, they just rode around smoking weed, as young guys with too much time on their hands would do. Rizz pulled up directly in front of the young girl so his partner could have better access.

"Yo, shorty, whatcha doing outside so late by yourself?" He asked, blowing weed smoke into the night air. The girl acted like she didn't even see or hear Lakim's comment. "Why you gonna act like dat? Don't be mad at me, be mad at your man for leaving you stranded like dis in da middle of da night," he added.

For the first time, the girl looked up at the expensive SUV, then at the guy who was trying to holler and said, "For your information, my man didn't leave me stranded. He's on his way."

"Tell her to get in and we'll drop her off," Rizz said, not caring if the girl heard or not.

"Chill I got dis," Lakim whispered as he got out so the girl could fully see his jewelry. "I'm just saying, if I had a dime piece like you, I wouldn't let her be waiting for a second, especially at night, cause a nigga like me might try to holler," Lakim said, causing the girl to blush and loosen up.

"What's your name?" She asked, staring at his shines.

"Lakim, what's yours?"

"I'm Reenay. So do you and your friends always roll up to girls trying to get with dem?" She asked, getting wrapped up in the conversation and forgetting that her boyfriend was on his way.

"Nah, I'm foremost and first about paper, as you can see. It's not every day you run into a female dat has dat star potential like yourself. I told my boy to swing my whip around, because I might never get a chance again," he said, stepping closer to her.

"Dat's your jeep?"

"Yeah, I like to get my smoke on and relax, so I let my right man handle things for a while," Lakim lied, knowing he had her already. "Let me get your math and I'll scoop you up tomorrow night," he said as he pulled out his cell phone to put her number in.

"Reenay, who da fuck you talking to?" A male voice yelled out of nowhere. Both Lakim and Reenay had turned around and saw Reenay's boyfriend standing there fuming at the mouth. He had parked around the corner and crept up on his surprised girlfriend. He was about six feet tall, a solid two twenty, and looked as if he could have been the star wrestler on his college team.

"No, it ain't like that. He was just asking me for directions, dat's all," she said, looking at Lakim hoping that he co-signed for her lie. By now the scene had caught Rizz's attention.

"Oh shit, playboy. It looks like that big motherfucker is gonna tear that ass for fucking around with his bitch," he yelled out while cracking up.

"Come on and get your ass in da car," her boyfriend shouted while grabbing her arm with a beefy hand.

"Yo money, it ain't dat serious. What do you expect when you leave your bitch unattended like dat," Lakim said with a smile, causing Rizz to laugh even harder.

"Who you calling a bitch?" The boyfriend asked in a threatening manner. Rizz had got out and leaned on the Yukon's fender just in case the situation got out of hand. The other two passengers in the backseat were passed out cold from all the heavy drinking and drugs mixed together.

"I'm saying, if you don't want niggas kicking it wit your bitch, I suggest you lock her up in a convent or tell her stop wearing those short ass skirts flashing dat fat ass. I'm just a regular-" Before Lakim could finish his sentence, a hard blow caught him in the temple, sending him flying halfway into the street and on the sidewalk.

"What now, little nigga," the boyfriend yelled in a triumphant voice as he stood over the fallen guy, not worrying about the skinny Rizz.

Reenay started telling her boyfriend, "Let's go, he ain't worth it. Fuck him, he's a nobody."

Rizz had reacted with street time speed pulling out a Glock nine and shooting at the guy. The bullet missed its intended victim, but caused both him and the girl to fall down, trying to avoid death. The couple stood frozen on the sidewalk as Lakim rose to his feet pulling out his own gun. He pointed the gun at the guy's head and pulled the trigger, but the gun jammed.

He was so mad at being knocked to the ground, especially in front of a girl he was trying to impress moments earlier, he just started pistol whipping the shocked guy on the head and face.

The girl started screaming, "Oh my God, Oh my God," over and over as her boyfriend was reduced to a mass of bloody swollen tissue.

Lakim was breathing hard as he turned his rage on the girl saying, "So, I'm a fucking nobody? Bitch, do you know who I am?"

"Shorty da one who caused all da drama in the first place," Rizz said, throwing his two cents in. Lakim stuffed his gun back in his waistband and snatched the girl to her feet.

"Dis is just something for you to remember me by," he said while pulling out an orange plastic box cutter and slicing the terrified girl from her forehead to her jaw. For a couple of seconds Lakim wasn't sure that he cut her until he saw the cut widen and reveal clean, white face meat.

The girl screamed, holding her face as Rizz yelled, "Come on, dat motherfucker in da store on da phone calling the po-po." Both men hopped in the jeep, speeding off just as the owner was coming out of the fast food joint. Later on in life, the embarrassing scar would cause Reenay to depend heavily on drugs to escape her low self-esteem, eventually making her overdose at only twenty-three.

Rizz joked about what happened with Lakim saying, "Dat big nigga would have never caught me sleeping like dat." Rizz dropped everyone off and headed back to his place, tired from partying all night. Rizz entered his house and stumbled to the bedroom, waking his girlfriend up.

"What time iz it?" Mia asked.

"Fuck all da other shit. You put away da money?" He asked, throwing his sneakers in the corner.

"Yeah, like I was telling you on the phone, I think your man is getting over on you. Dis is da third time he came up short in a couple of weeks," she added as she turned on the nightstand light. Mia looked at him, waiting for a response, then said, "You been out fucking wit dem chicken head bitches? Dats why you too tired to fuck me again, huh?"

"You know I was out taking care of business. How do you think you get to push dat Jag," Rizz sleepily shot back.

Mia had met Rizz in a hip-hop store where she was working part time as a sales person. As soon as she spotted Rizz and his hoodlum friends acting uncivilized and pointing out everything they wanted, she knew they were little drug dealers with too much money and not enough sense. She knew Rizz was the head honcho of the pact because of the way the other guys were agreeing with everything he had to say. She went straight over to Rizz, ignoring the other loud guys, and suggested he go to another store because the owners were cheating black people by selling inferior clothing that was rejected by the manufactures for one reason or another.

"Why do you care?" Rizz asked, suspicious that this beautiful woman was taking an interest in him.

"I can see you have a little dough and style, so why waste it on some fucked up shit?" Mia asked.

Mia ended up leaving the store with him and Rizz told his peoples he would hook up with them later on. They went to various urban stores in Brooklyn, Uptown, and Queens, with Mia picking out the majority of the gear she thought looked best on him. When he asked if she wanted anything, she just said no, which shocked Rizz because she was the first girl he knew who had turned down anything free, especially since he was holding a fat knot.

From day one Mia had laid down her plans by not accepting gifts, money, or giving him sex. Every once in a while she would throw salt in the game by telling him you can't trust this or that person and to keep some of his business deals to himself. Rizz showed off his older, model type girlfriend by riding around the hood real slow. After a month, when she finally did have sex with the young drug dealer, she freaked him like he was the emperor of Rome, causing Rizz for the first time to say, "No more!"

Mia looked at Rizz as he slept. She really didn't care that he messed around with other girls because deep down she hated him and all other guys since Preme set her up to get raped. She had to keep playing the role of an envious girlfriend to make the role seem real, but she couldn't overdue it. If she was to overdue it, Rizz might just flip the script and find a new chick, no matter how bad she looked. Every chance Mia got, she would dip into his stash, saving up the money so she could buy that land in Trinidad to be with her son.

"American guys are so fucking dumb," Mia thought as she drifted off to sleep, adding up the money she had stolen tonight with what she already had.

(CHAPTER FORTY-FOUR)

"Come on playboy, it's time to get da fuck up," Kendew yelled into Ice's room in a playful manner.

"What time is it?" Ice asked, looking around the room wondering where he was for a moment.

"It's about dat time for a nigga to get paid," Kendew answered back. Kendew stood in the doorway wearing a leather vest, some black jeans that Ice thought could have been a little bigger, and a pair of expensive looking ostrich skin boots.

Ice jumped in the shower and threw on some of his brand new gear. While folding away his clothes from last night, a folded piece of paper fell out from his jeans. He curiously opened it up and saw the name Kansas on it with her number also. *Oh, shorty must have slipped it in my pocket giving me dat lap dance. I'm definitely gonna give her a shout out,* Ice thought. He walked in the living room and spotted Kendew and Lemon smoking a Philly blunt.

"Yo, you want some of dis?" Kendew asked, holding the blunt up for Ice to take a hit. Ice sniffed the air and knew it was more than just weed they were getting off on.

"Nah, I'm good. I got a crazy hangover from last night. Maybe later," he lied. Twenty minutes later, all three of them were walking out the door. Lemon still looked the same as when Ice had first met her, wearing a baggy jeans outfit that hid her small, compact body, a baseball hat, and a different pair of Timberland boots. *Shorty all right, but I need to know more about her game,* Ice thought as they headed towards Kendew's car that was parked out front. They all jumped in a custom painted lime green Audi TT limited edition car, with Ice taking the front seat.

"So how you been handling yourself since you hit da streets?" Kendew asked.

"I've been doing what I got to," Ice answered nonchalantly.

"Yeah, I saw all da new clothes dis morning, and I peeped dem credit cards. I knew it wouldn't be long before you caught some motherfucker sleeping," he stated while smiling.

"Yeah it wasn't much. Just to get a brother a head start."

"What you holding right now?" Kendew asked as he dipped through the side streets driving a little too fast. Ice pulled out the old .38, causing Kendew to break out into a deep laugh.

"It's not da gat, it's da nigga behind da gat dat really counts," Ice shot back, a little embarrassed that he had took out the weapon with the taped up handle.

"Don't sweat it. Lemon, pass dat thing up front," he stated when he saw the look on Ice's face.

She handed the driver a gun, which he then passed to Ice saying, "Dis is a little coming home present." Ice took the gun smiling. It was a gleaming silver .45 automatic with a double pearl handled grip. Ice took the clip out, saw that it was loaded, and placed it back. He examined the gun for a couple of minutes before saying thanks.

The trio pulled up in front of a house, which Ice knew to be a crack and dope spot. Even though it was daytime, there was a steady stream of all sorts of characters coming and going, trying to beat one another for the almighty dollar. The house was huge with boarded up windows, and it had that chipped paint, weather beaten type of look about it. The surrounding area didn't fare much better with the three feet high dry weeds barely covering the scattered debris and garbage. That house alone lowered the property value by at least twenty percent for its unlucky neighbors.

"Dis is one of my spots. My cousin put me on to it. I had it for about two months and already I turned it into a gold mine. With the product I'm handling, motherfuckers practically abandoned da other spot around da corner. Da only time dope fiends hit their house is when we run out or they take my shit and smoke over there," Kendew said, stating the facts.

"Word!" Ice said.

"And you know dem niggas be getting salty now dat I'm digging into those pockets," he said while pulling out his cell phone and dialing a number. "I'm out in front," Kendew said before hanging up his phone.

A moment later a couple of guys came out from around the back of the house and approached the car. Kendew got out and talked to the men for ten minutes before he gave Lemon a signal for her to come out. Lemon then jumped out the Audi, grabbed a backpack, and handed it to one of the guys who appeared to be the older of the two. Kendew then motioned for Ice to come out. He pulled Ice away from the group so the others couldn't hear.

"Check it out, I'm gonna leave you here for a while-"

Before Kendew could finish, Ice said, "Hold up, I'm not finna sling no crack rocks, especially hand to hand on no spot I know nothing about."

"Chill, chill, playboy. It ain't even about dat. These dudes I got working for me ain't handling their business like they supposed to. Dem other niggas around the corner got them shook and dats starting to effect my paper. I need someone like you, a real outlaw who gets down for his. I just want you to watch the spot for a little while and see how things run. Right now I'm trying to work something out with dis other spot across town."

"So what time you talking about swinging back around?" Ice asked.

"Sometime dis evening," he responded, handing Ice another cell phone. "I'm trying to bring dis spot up to at least one hundred gees a week, with you getting twenty-five percent of da profits," Kendew said, knowing that the only thing Ice understood was gun language and money figures.

Kendew then introduced Ice to the two men, and then whispered that he had a surprise for Ice later on. Ice wished for a second that it would be another round with Lemon, and then he asked himself why he kept thinking about that particular sexual episode.

(CHAPTER FORTY-FIVE)

"You straight now?" Born asked Trina as they sat in the car in the parking lot next to Jezebel's.

"Yeah, let's see how much dough dis nigga really talking about," she said.

"Just keep your motherfucking mouth shut and maybe you might learn sumtin for a change," Born said, knowing how Trina often ran off at the lip getting out of pocket when she was high.

"I'm just saying, I hope he ain't wasting your time, because you always tell me if it ain't about business, it ain't about nothing," she stated in a low voice, trying to win him back over.

"Come on, let's get going," Born said as he hit the unlock switch and then proceeded to get out.

They walked around the front and told the bouncer that they were here to see Black Sam. Jezebel's wasn't quite open yet because it was still early in the evening. The only other person in the place was an elderly man sweeping the floors and wiping down the tables.

"Sam, they're here," the bouncer stated while knocking on the office door located way in the back of the club.

"Send them on in, and get back to da front," a deep voice shouted from behind the door.

Born and Trina walked in the room and saw Black Sam sitting behind a huge oak desk in an executive style black leather swivel chair. Standing next to him with her hand on his shoulder was the blondest, bluest-eyed white woman, who looked as if she came straight off the boat from Norway. She looked even skinnier standing next to Sam with her slender frame.

"Born, I'm glad you could make it. You too Trina," Sam said, standing up and shaking Born's hand.

The name Black Sam fit the man perfectly for he was that shade of black that the older white people referred to as "deep south blackness." His lips were his most prominent feature, being that they were hot dog thickness and blackish blue in color. He was wearing a lavender three-piece suit and a pair of green Solomon Brothers gators, which were hand signed.

"Have a seat. What can I get you?" He asked.

"Get me a Hennessy straight up," Born said.

"I'll have mine with a splash of coke," Trina threw in as they both sat down.

"Sasha, can you get dem what they want," he said. Sasha hit a button on the wall and a small mini bar slowly slid into view.

When she was bringing them their drinks Sam said, "Oh excuse, me dis is Sasha. She's from Russia. You know how I like Russian girls," he said, the only one in the room laughing.

Sasha nodded, and Trina rolled her eyes back at her. Trina always hated that specific type of white girl that went with black men. When their conservative friends or family would question their relationship about the black guy they were fucking, they would be quick to say, "What are you crazy? What the fuck would I want with a no good nigger," saying nigger in the most vilest way possible.

When Trina was taking a sip of her drink, she noticed Sam trying to glimpse under her skirt, causing her to quickly cross her legs. Sam didn't care that Trina caught him looking, he'd been wanting her since the first day he ever saw her. He practically promised her the world if she would be with him. Sam had a deep-rooted passion of hate against all black women. Growing up during his school years they teased him relentlessly about his prominent African looks and most of all his skin complexion. They tagged what they thought was the most insulting name on him, (Black Sam). The name stuck to him like his skin color, with the white suburban teachers sometimes calling him that thinking it was just a normal ghetto thing.

Black Sam often day dreamed on how he was going to strike it rich one way or another, plotting on all the people, especially black girls, who made his existence a living torture. His warped dream finally became a reality when he was compensated for a permanent injury on a construction site. He saw the perfect chance for his subconscious revenge when he was offered the opportunity to buy out a strip club called Jezebel's, located in the heart of the black community with his settlement money. He elatedly jumped at the chance. He then used the remaining money to lavishly renovate the club, knowing that it would lure the most beautiful dancers away from the other surrounding strip clubs.

Once the newly redone Jezebel's was up and running again, he placed several ads soliciting new dancers. Black Sam became cruel and callous during the interview process, asking the most obscene and humiliating questions possible. "Do you douche regularly? You know you will be fined fifty dollars if you come to work with a foul odor? You have an all right face and body, but you going to have to do something about dem yellow stained teeth if you want to work here."

The more desperate girls, who were just trying to make a living, he subjected them to outrageous perverted sex acts all in the name of adult entertainment. The prettier the woman, the more Black Sam debased and belittled them, somehow linking these girls to his so-called traumatic childhood. When he finally could have his pick of women, even the lightest red-boned half white black girls still turned his stomach. He chose to deal with pure white girls to boost his already shattered self-esteem.

"So what you wanna do about da whole situation?" Born asked Sam.

"Dem young niggas be rolling up in here ordering mad champagne and shit, racking up thousands of dollars and not paying. Now they talking about extorting my business, those young punks," Sam said while lighting up a Cuban cigar and trying to look more businesslike, even though he really didn't like them.

"Well, when I come up in here, dem young cats gonna know they dealing wit a real motherfucker. I'll fuck around and rob their asses," Born said with a laugh, not caring if he offended Sam or not.

Sam was just a big pussy who liked to play the role of a big shot. He found out how shook he was off of the young guys through one of his girls, and he came up with the plan to become part owner of Jezebel's. Once he got his foot firmly in the door, he planned to use the strip club as a recruitment base for his real source of money. Meanwhile, Trina being the person that she was, was secretly scanning the office thinking of all the places that Sam could hide a safe. She had heard from street talk that he always kept mad dough somewhere in the club at a specific times of the month.

Just then there was a heavy knock on the door, causing everyone in the office to turn around. "Who is it?" Sam asked.

"There's two guys here to see you," the bouncer answered. Before Sam could respond the door swung open and two guys stepped in.

"What's up, Sam? It seems dat we interrupted some kind of party," Lakim stated, looking at both of the women. Sam then waved his hand as if to tell his doorman that it was all right for him to leave. "Can a nigga live too?" Lakim asked, looking over at the mini bar.

"Go right ahead," Sam replied.

Born quickly put two and two together and knew that these had to be some of the young guys that was fucking with Sam. He noticed how nervous Sam started acting as soon as they entered the room. Lakim went over to the bar and grabbed a whole bottle of Hypnotic while looking suspiciously at Born, who eyed him back. Lakim went back over by his boy and they both started drinking out of the bottle. Born was waiting to see how Sam would play out his hand.

"I wanted to speak with you, because I wanted to let you know that I'm taking on a new business partner," Black Sam stated.

Now Born knew what Sam was up to. He had planned for the guys to come down so that he could mention that he was getting a new partner as if to say, "Shits gonna stop or you'll have to deal with him now."

"So what da fuck that got to do wit me?" Lakim asked, screwing up his face.

"I'm just saying dat my soon-to-be new partner over here is going to be handling all the money aspects of Jezebel's, and I'm going to be dealing wit some new ventures I'm working on," Sam said, looking over at Born and lying through his teeth.

Dat scary black motherfucker. He knew we haven't come to any type of agreement yet concerning da club, and now he's trying to put everything on me so I could deal wit these guys, Born thought, glaring at Sam who looked away.

"Well, it doesn't matter who owns what, we still gotta get paid," Lakim shouted.

"I know you ain't directing your comment to him," Trina said, pointing at Born.

"Bitch, I suggest you mind your fucking business before you get your white ass tossed da fuck up," Lakim responded back, getting on point. His boy just laughed, taking another sip out the bottle.

"Hold up, she's wit me. If you disrespect her, you basically saying fuck me too." Born said, standing up now.

"You don't want it," the guy said to Born.

"Yo, niggas don't know who they fucking wit," Trina said as she went over and stood next to Born.

Before anybody could say or do anything, the guy swung the Hypnotic bottle at Born's head. Born stepped back a millisecond before the bottle would have hit him, and instead it swished by his temple, hitting Trina dead in the face. As Born moved back, he pulled out a razor blade and cut at the guy's face. The razor found its mark, splitting open one of the guys eyeballs like an overripe grape. He fell back screaming and holding his damaged eye as Lakim pulled out his gun. Born rushed him, grabbing his gun arm as they both crashed into the wall and fell onto the floor.

Lakim knew he was no match against the older and stronger man who was on the verge of wrestling the weapon away from him. Lakim reached his head up and tried to bite Born's ear off, but Born turned his head and Lakim caught a mouthful of fleshly cheek. Just then Trina was getting up. Still dazed, she saw blood pouring out Born's face. She ran over and starting kicking Lakim in the face, a few kicks catching Born. One blow caught Lakim on the nose, causing his eyes to water and giving Born the final edge he needed. He snatched the gun away, hitting Lakim on the head a couple of times and knocking him out.

Trina heard the other guy moaning on the floor and she turned her anger on him for hitting her with the liquor bottle. She spotted the razor that Born had dropped and scooped it up. She stood over the guy and started viciously slicing at his face yelling, "So how does dis feel? Huh, bitch ass nigga," as he tried unsuccessfully to block her savage attack with his arms. When Born saw a piece of pinky fly across the room, he ran over and bear hugged Trina saying, "Dat's enough."

During all the drama Black Sam stood statue-like in his chair, unable to move while his Russian girlfriend hid under the desk.

"Boss is everything all right in there?" The bouncer asked through the door. Sam acted as if he were still in shock, so Born ran over and whispered, "tell him everything's cool, and that he could have the rest of da night off wit pay." Sam did as he was told.

The bouncer left saying, "Thanks." Born then grabbed some napkins, putting it to his face and thinking of the best way to clean up the unexpected mess.

(CHAPTER FORTY-SIX)

"Dem fiends can't get enough," Mack said after finishing serving a customer a bag of dope.

The package that contained the drug had a stamped, ghost white picture of Judge Dorothy Woodburn wearing a Dracula style cape with fangs. In the drug underworld she was considered one of the most despised and hated of all the judges in Queens. She routinely gave out the maximum sentences in drug related cases, hardly ever taking a plea agreement. It was rumored that she had a dollar bet with her husband, who was also a criminal judge, about who could give out a million years before they retired.

Ice had to admit that since he'd been in the spot, customers had been flowing through like they were giving away government cheese or something. Mack was from the old school. He'd been around the block more than once surviving on street instincts alone. He had a habit of calling the customer a variety of names: Rock Star, dope head, proof smoker. If you saw him, you could hardly tell the difference of who was who.

Mack wore a no name black sweat hoodie with the pants that seemed as if it they had been in quite few wars. His partner who helped run the spot was Flip, who always kept a shotgun at his side. Ice took him to be a control freak because he observed Flip more than once prodding and poking customers, and yelling for them to get in line to wait their turn, even when it wasn't that crowded.

"Where you from?" Mack asked Ice while counting a stack of twenties.

"I rest in the Heights, but I do my thing wherever da dough is at," he answered.

Ice and Mack kicked it mostly about how things ran throughout the house. Mack and Flip made a little extra money on the side by renting out rooms for fiends who wanted to get their smoke on, while enjoying their high in private. The cell phone that Kendew gave Ice went off.

"Yo Ice, what's up? How's everything?" Kendew asked.

"Everythings, everything. So, what's da deal?" Ice asked, wanting to talk more about the money he was supposed to be getting.

"I'm caught up in some serious shit. You know how it is when you gotta do shit your motherfucking self. If you want, I can have Lemon come get you and you can rock da whip for a while," he said.

"Yeah I can work wit dat," Ice responded. Kendew gave him Lemon's digits and told him to hold down da fort. When Ice was putting the cell phone back in his pocket, he touched Kansas's number and decided to give her a shout out. He went outside in the back yard and sat down on an old plastic school chair as he dialed the number. The phone rang five times before a voice picked up.

"Hello, who dis?" Kansas asked.

"Dis is da guy who you slipped da number to," he said, trying to see if she did her little trick a lot.

"Ice, what's up?" She was saying something, but Ice couldn't make it out because of the loud music in the background. He knew she must have been at the strip club. A couple of seconds later the music was drowned out a little, but not much. She told Ice that she was in the bathroom and couldn't talk long. They both agreed to meet up at the twenty-four hour restaurant on Queens Boulevard when she got off of work.

Ice went back in the house and heard Mack saying, "Who da fuck does he think he is? I'm about to set shit off up in here." Ice walked in the room and saw that Mack was talking to himself while holding a little .25 automatic.

"What's da problem? Where's Flip?" Ice asked, touching his own gat and preparing for drama.

"He broke out to get some Chinese food. There's some nigga in the next room bugging da fuck out, talking about some different shit," Mack yelled, waving his gun around.

These niggas are soft. He's just talking about it, instead of being about it, Ice thought. Mack showed Ice where the room was, and when he approached he heard a strangely familiar voice saying, "Hell no! I bought two sacks for you, and now that you sniffed up everything, you wanna break out now!"

Then Ice heard a woman's voice yelling equally as loud, "Listen here nigga, I don't owe you a goddamn thing. You copped dem bags of dope thinking I was gonna get twisted and den give you some ass."

"What's da problem up in here? You two gonna have to take your drama down da street," Ice said as he entered the room. A man had his back toward the door talking to a woman sitting on a shabby bed. The man turned around to face Ice and both men stared at each other as to say, "what da fuck you doing up in here."

"Nathaniel Wilson, what a surprise seeing you up in here. I guess you're back to your old ways." It was Ice's parole officer, Mr. Spencer, standing there with a shitty grin on his face.

"You know I could violate you for the rest of your sentence for just being here," he said.

Ice's first response was to put two in Mr. Spencer's head, especially when he heard the words "violate you" again. No way was he going back to jail for being in the wrong place at the wrong time by someone who shouldn't have been here in the first place. To make matters worse, he didn't even have a chance to bang out a bitch yet.

"So what you going to do now?" Ice asked, ready to start blasting if the wrong answer came out of his mouth.

"The dope your boy gave us was tainted. Hit me off with some real shit, and we'll be straight," he answered. Without saying a word Ice went back to the other room and came back with four sacks.

"So, we cool?" Ice asked.

"For now," his parole officer replied as he took the product and closed the door.

Ice knew that Mr. Spencer had him in a fucked up position, and he was going to use that against him. Sooner or later he was going to try to extort as much dope, maybe even cash, from him as possible. Ice knew he was in a no win situation. Later on he heard the mattress spring creaking and realized Mr. Spencer and the dope fiend came to a mutual understanding now that she had more drugs in her system. As the couple was leaving Mr. Spencer said, "I guess I'll be seeing you around, Nathaniel," and laughed like he had hit the jackpot.

Ice was thinking about what to do, when he realized he had forgotten to call Lemon. A little while later she pulled up in an artic white Ford Explorer with another female. Ice dropped the couple off at the house as he jumped behind the wheel to meet up with Kansas. She was waiting out front of the restaurant smiling when she saw him hop out the jeep.

"What's up, stranger? I see you right on time," Kansas said. When she noticed the stressed out look on his face, she asked was everything all right.

"I'm cool," he answered as they walked inside. The place was packed with everyone trying to get their eat on from doing whatever they were doing all night. They sat at a booth over by the window.

"Who you rode up here with?" Ice asked.

"Some friends of mine from da club," she said, pointing to a group of friends sitting at the other end of the restaurant. There were three females laughing and joking around about their different experiences they had at Jezebel's. One girl was counting her money saying, "Yeah, in a minute. I'll be able to have enough duckets to put down on that Mustang I test drove last month. Thank you trick ass motherfuckers," she said as all the girls broke out laughing.

Their meal finally came. Ice dug into his steak and eggs, realizing how hungry he really was.

"So why you slip me your number, when you had your choice of ballers to fuck wit?" He asked in between mouthfuls of food.

"Dem guys are some fronting ass niggas who act like it can't happen. I peeped the way you broke out and knew that they weren't on your level," she said, cutting up her Pancakes Special. Halfway through the meal Kansas's cell phone went off.

"I'm about to come home. I know it's closed, but me and some girlfriends decided to get something to eat. No. Okay. You want me to bring something back?" She asked before hanging up.

Neither one of them mentioned the call, knowing that Ice knew it was her boyfriend checking up on her. After they finished eating, Kansas went over to her friends and let them know Ice was going to drop her off.

"You know I gotta be home soon," she stated as soon as they both jumped into the Explorer. Ten minutes later Ice stopped at an isolated dead end street, and talked for about two minutes. He soon had Kansas in the backseat with her skirt pulled up around her waist, doggy style and blowing her guts out while thinking of a fat, ugly woman so he could last longer. It was no use. He had been away too long, and he filled the condom up with a quickness.

"I didn't want it to seem as if I was sweating you, but when they mentioned your name in da club that's when I thought I recognized you," she said with a smile.

"Oh yeah, from where?" Ice asked.

"I peeped you a couple of years ago when you had dem long cute ass braids and you was riding around doing your thang. My sisters used to say they always wanted to get wit you, but I guess I beat dem to it," she said, punching him in the side. "Anyway, I wanted to tell you dat, dat nigga in da club-"

"Who?" Ice asked before she could finish.

"Rizz! He was bragging on how he bought some of his jewelry wit your money when you left."

"What you talking about?" Ice asked, turning the music down.

"I ain't trying to start no beef, but I remember my sister telling me that Rizz's sister told her how he bagged some coke from you a while back. Da way he put it, he had you shitting bricks you were so shook."

"Get da fuck outta here!" Ice said.

"Word up, but my sister knew your rep from da streets and said dat if Rizz did come off you, he must have sneak thieved you. I just thought I should put you on point on how he was trying to assassinate your character," she said. "Oh, you can drop me off at da corner," Kansas said while grabbing her bag.

After Kansas left, Ice started calculating and knew Rizz probably watched him stash the drugs in his grandfather's tool shed a while back when he got knocked on the gun charge. Rizz must have gone back and stolen the coke.

"So dat's how da little fucker blew up off of my shit, and now he's trying to kick dirt on my name," Ice said out loud, driving fast as hell. "Dat bitch ass little nigga has got to go. Niggas gonna know I ain't nothing to fuck wit," he added, thinking about how he was going to have Rizz on his knees begging for his life.

(CHAPTER FORTY-SEVEN)

"Everybody slow da fuck up and relax," Born shouted with authority.

Black Sam's office was in total chaos with everyone trying to talk at the same time.

"Sam, get your scared ass up and make sure nobody else is in da club. And while you're there, bring back something from da storeroom so we can tie these niggas up," Born said while holding the two unconscious guys at gun point. Sam shakily rose to his feet, not believing what had just happened.

"You can come out now," Trina said to the woman who was still under the desk as she walked over by the door for some ice for her swollen face. Sam nervously walked by the two men on the floor as if they were going to reach up and grab his legs.

"Hurry da fuck up!" Born said when Sam had the door opened looking out. By now Sasha the Russian girl was up and looking around as if to say, "I don't belong with you type of people." Trina caught the look.

"I got to go! Whatever is going on between you is you all's business," Sasha replied with a slight Eastern Russian accent.

"Oh, when everything's peaches and cream and da money is flowing, it's all good. But as soon as shit gets thick you wanna bounce," Trina said, telling the truth and looking the shaken woman dead in the eyes.

"Chill out shorty. She's right. You're not going anywhere but over by dat bar and fix me a drink," Born stated.

By now Lakim was starting to come to and started weakly rubbing his lumped up head and face.

"Okay, you just stay sitting down in da corner and everything's gonna be all right," Born said, pointing the gun at Lakim's forehead. "Trina, get your ass over here and drag dis other nigga over by him," Born said, not taking his eyes off his captive. Just then Sam opened the door slowly, carrying some extension cords and some clean white hand towels. "Put dat shit down and help her move him in dis corner," Born said, directing his comment to Sam, whose eyes grew even wider when he saw all the blood slowly spreading on the floor.

"Wake up, nigga," Trina said, kicking the young guy in the ribs, still mad that he had hit her. Trina kicked him again, getting more blood on her expensive shoes. "I think he's dead," Sam said looking over at Born. That's when Trina looked more closely and noticed that she had cut a main artery in his neck from her rampage.

"You think you're gonna get away with sending my man back to the essence," Lakim yelled with revenge in his eyes as if he was preparing for a lunge attack on Born.

"Fuck dat other nigga and help me tie dis one up 'fore I send him where his boy is," Born said as if he had read Lakim's mind.

"Oh my God, you killed him. You murdered him for no reason. You all are a bunch of wild animals," Sasha screamed as soon as Sam mentioned that there was a dead man in the room.

"Bitch, who da fuck you calling animal," Trina shouted, quickly walking over to Sam's girlfriend. This was the opening Trina had been waiting for when she first laid eyes on this type of white girl.

When she was in middle school Trina recalled her aunt telling her how her mother had sent a guy to prison for twenty years. Her mother, who was a spitting image of Trina, was secretly going across the railroad tracks to the black section of town and fucking the local black weed dealer every Friday night. She confided to her best friend one evening when she was pressed on why Trina's mother couldn't go bowling with her friend. Her friend, being jealous and equally curious about Trina's mother's taboo lover, told as many people as she could at school Monday morning. Word soon reached her boyfriend, who quickly told Trina's racist grandparents out of revenge. Trina's grandfather, who was an active member of the White Citizens Council, promptly had the black guy arrested and charged with rape, sexual battery, kidnapping, and contributing to the delinquency of a minor, even though he was younger than her. From the time of his arrest up unil his sentencing only a month passed. Growing up in her small town, Trina heard similar stories and vowed never to be like those hypocrite white girls.

"You hear me talking to you? Who you calling animal?" Trina asked now, standing inches away from Sasha. Before the woman could respond, Trina punched in her nose, drawing blood, and she grabbed a handful of blond hair. Trina started banging the woman's head on the bar yelling, "So who's an animal? So who's an animal?"

"Sam, Sam please help me. Sam, get her off me," Sasha screamed hysterically.

Sam had started to walk over to the fight, if you chose to call it that, when Born said, "Slow your fat ass up and finish tying up dis nigga's hands." Sam did as he was told and when he was finished he ran over to his girlfriend. Trina was sitting on the beaten girl's back breathing hard.

"She's all yours," Trina said, getting up and walking past Sam, her look saying and what you gonna do about it?

"So what's da plan?" Trina asked Born, hoping they made money somehow on what had just transpired, forgetting that she had just killed someone.

"Yeah, you know how I get down. First off, Sam you calm your bitch down 'fore I put my ally cat on her ass again," Born said, winking at Trina who wanted another taste of the crying woman. "Tell Trina what you pushing and give her the keys so she can bring the car around da back exit," Born ordered Sam as he got on his cell phone, trying to clean up the mess Sam had caused.

"Yo, Bigger, what up? Dis is Born. I want you to tell all the girls except da sisters and the new chick dat they can have da night off. No nigga! Just listen! I got some special company over in a little while and I need you to fix up da suite," he said, talking in code.

Born hung up and then called his man he had dropped off earlier.

"Terrance, I need you over at Jezebel's ASAP. Fuck everything else. Dat shit can wait. Yeah, you know da strip club I pointed out to you last week. Peace, I'm out."

Trina walked back in saying, "I pulled da car around like you told me to. What now?"

"We just maintain until da troops get here," Born answered, still eyeballing Lakim, who promptly returned the stare.

(CHAPTER FORTY-EIGHT)

Mia cruised down the street blasting "More money, More Problems" on a mixed CD in her pecan colored Jag. "Dat song is bullshit. Dat's for motherfuckers who don't know how to handle their dough. Fuck dat, give me all da money," she said, hitting the button and starting a new song.

She finally reached her destination, which was a modest two-story family brick house. She had rented the upstairs apartment on the low-low, paying rent four months in advance. Nobody knew of her little hideaway, especially not Rizz, even thought it was his money that financed the rent and furnished the well-kept apartment. Mia came here to relax, be by herself, and get away from all the bullshit associated with being the girlfriend of a loud-mouthed drug dealer.

As soon as Mia entered the apartment in the quiet Queens' neighborhood, she went straight to the kitchen and fixed herself a strong drink. She then turned on the CD player, keeping her music vibe going. Halfway through her Tequila, she went back to the kitchen and opened the double doors beneath the sink. She took out all the cleaning supplies that you would normally find in any home. She pulled back the wooden boards revealing three large rattraps, one which held a dead rat that had its neck broken with an eyeball hanging from the socket by a thin string.

"I'm going to have to put another one in his place. Dis one is starting to rot too much," Mia said as she moved it to the side and grabbed a plastic bag that was hidden under the dirt. She took the bag with her to the bedroom and dumped its contents onto the bed. Stacks of hundreds, fifties, and twenties poured out into a nice sizable pile. Mia then took out the money she had hidden in her coach bag and placed it with the rest of her ill-gotten gains. She then pulled out a small calculator and added up her small fortune that came to four hundred eighteen thousand dollars. Mia seemed to have an inhuman, permanent smile on her face as she ran her fingers through the pile. She started to laugh like a mad woman as she poured herself another drink. She then placed the drink on the nightstand and lay down on top of the currency.

Mia momentarily dozed off when her cell phone went off, shaking her back to the present.

"Hello," she answered, not recognizing the number.

"It's me. You still coming?" A male voice asked.

"You know I'll be there. The question is will you be there on time? You know I ain't had a real nigga in a long time, especially one dat keeps things as interesting as you."

"Whatever," he said with a laugh. He gave Mia the necessary information before hanging up.

Mia had a couple more shots of liquor while saying to herself, "Man, I'm gonna need dis shit for what I go through every time I see his ass."

Mia jumped in her ride, driving slow and in no hurry to get where she was going. Twenty minutes later she was riding the elevator in the Marriott Hotel over by JFK airport. She breathed deeply and knocked on the door. The door swung open with Kendew standing there in a gold silk robe that was open, letting the world know that he had a thing for animal gray bikini briefs with a false elephant trunk dangling from the crotch area. To make the scene even more bizarre was that Kendew had the words "Tarzan" expertly shaved out of each of his hairy thighs. *Dis nigga definitely losing it*, Mia thought with a fake smile.

"Come on in 'fore you catch a cold," he said when he saw that Mia was wearing a short, tight skirt showing off her new tattoo of the Goddess Venus.

When Mia stepped in, Kendew tried to kiss her on the mouth, which caused her to turn her head and say in a nice tone, "Hold up. The door ain't even closed yet. Fix me a drink and let me kick off my shoes."

"Yes ma'am," Kendew said sarcastically. It was true that Mia didn't want to take the chance of anyone seeing them together, but the thing that disturbed her the most was the man's persistently chronic bad breath. *If someone had liquor on his breath, at least you knew what it was, but with stink breath, it could be endless possibilities*, Mia thought every time she came in contact with him. One time she went as far as to crumble a handful of peppermint certs in his drink when he wasn't looking during one of their episodes.

Mia sat on the bed desperately waiting for her drink. Kendew arrived carrying a bottle of Hennessy and two Brandy glasses, while swinging his elephant trunk as he walked. Mia acted if she wanted to consume the whole bottle of Hennessy before Kendew told her to slow down before she passed out. Secretly she wished that would happen so he would finish his business, wake her up, and she could be out. At that moment she thought of herself in the hospital about to undergo surgery. The physician would give her a good dose of anesthesia and when she would wake up, her ordeal would be over. That's the analogy she used in comparing her interactions with Kendew, the liquor being the anesthesia.

"Come on, you know how da nigga always be stressing you when you out of his sight," he said while caressing one of her firm breasts.

"You know how it is. He's your goddamn nephew. Anyway, are you still going to help me with the down payment on dat property in Florida I was kicking it wit you about?" Mia asked, trying to take care of money matters first.

"Of course, baby. You know I wouldn't let you down. I should have the rest of it later on tonight or in da morning. Yeah, it's best you get away from dat nigga. Plus, I got people down in dat part of town where I can expand my business and come check you," Kendew replied, not knowing that he was being sold a dream.

"Yeah, you can holler at me anytime you want. I don't know why you just don't move in with me," she said, throwing the last part in to make it sound good. "You know, how much you got on you?" She asked.

"Only twenty-five thousand," Kendew threw out. That's all Mia wanted to hear, that he had the dough on him. She then closed her eyes and let Kendew roughly undress her and then climb on top of her as she faked moaning pleasures.

She remembered when Rizz first took her with him to go see his uncle Kendew, who he had put down with the drug trade. She knew right off the bat that his uncle was weird, not to mention that she suspected that he had a little sugar in his tank by his feminine mannerisms. Mia noticed that he had a natural knack for the dope game, quickly raking in mad cheddar from what she could tell. Every time Rizz was out of earshot, Kendew would throw little dirt-on-someone's-name comments directed at Rizz.

"My young nephew doesn't really know how to get money. Shit, if I had a bad female like you, I wouldn't let her be around my boys all da time."

When Mia started seeing Kendew with all different types of pretty woman, she then knew for sure he was spending that paper on them. She then started throwing sly comments back at him.

"Damn, I don't know why I'm always horny. I must need some sort of medication? I don't know why he couldn't buy me dat simple dress. It's not like he can't afford it or something." And that's how things got started with Kendew and herself. Mia made sure he threw some of that cash her way, making excuse after excuse on why she needed more and more of what seemed like an endless supply.

"Grab my ass, grab my ass," Kendew started shouting, bringing Mia back to the present. She did as she was told, digging her fingernails into his hairy butt cheeks. "Now smack it, baby. Smack it hard like a good bitch," he started saying now. Mia complied, praying that he was almost through. "Yes, dat's it. Oh God, don't stop. Fuck me harder, harder." Mia started moaning, hoping that her words of ecstasy would make him cum quick like his fast relative. It must have worked because Kendew released his load into Mia's hot money trap.

"Now for the Boston Crème pie," he said as he got off of Mia. *What da hell dis fool talking about now*, she wondered. Kendew quickly crawled between the woman's legs and started trying to suck up his own semen out of Mia's vagina. He went at his unnatural act for twenty minutes before getting up.

"I got to take a shower," she said while grabbing all of her belongings.

"I'll just chill here and knock off da rest of dis here bottle," he stated, smiling and revealing a couple of Mia's pubic hairs stuck in between his teeth. She looked at him thinking, *Dat's why girls start fucking around wit bitches.*

Mia took an extra hot steaming shower, wishing now that she had downed the whole bottle. After the long shower, Mia called her hairdresser and told her to call her back on her cell phone in exactly five minutes. She came out the bathroom and saw Kendew still naked, lying spread out without a care in the world.

"Damn, you look good. I think I want another go at it, especially like that Boston Crème pie," she said, thinking that God was going to strike her down with lightning with such a bold lie.

"I knew you would like it," he said with a smile and traces of cum still on his chin and lips.

Mia's cell phone went off, and she answered it saying, "Hello? Oh no. I'm at da department store. I should be there in about forty minutes. Bye. Dat was Rizz," she said to Kendew. "I gotta bounce. Let me get dat," she said. Kendew reached in his pants' pocket and handed her a roll of money. "Call me in a couple of days," Mia said as she walked out the door, planning to soak in a hot bath for at least two hours.

(CHAPTER FORTY-NINE)

"You can't put nothing else on?" Ice asked Kendew, tired of what he was hearing.

"What's da matter, you don't like Prince?" He asked, turning the music up louder.

"What you need to do is throw on dat new Terror Squad CD," Ice shot back, receiving no answer. *Well at least he's dressed half normal today,* Ice thought, noticing Kendew wearing a top-notch custom-made Fendi sweat suit. A little while later Kendew was pulling his Audi up in the driveway of the dope house.

"Every now and den I got to chill up in da spot to see if niggas are running shit right," Kendew stated while getting out, being aware of his surroundings. Just then an old car with rims, and extra-dark tinted windows, drove by slowly, stopping in front of the house. They stopped for a couple of seconds in the middle of the street before pulling off.

"Yo, dat's da same whip I peeped da other day when I was outside having a smoke," Ice said, wondering who they were.

"I think dat's dem boys from da other spot. They don't want it. They just trying to front cause you're a new face. Anyway, fuck'em," Kendew said, waving at Ice to come on inside.

Once inside, both men noticed about twelve customers, men and women, waiting their turn to get served. Ice saw that some of them had a variety of stolen electronic equipment, hoping to exchange it for the powerful drug they often craved. One man with a scruffy beard with specks of gray in it was carrying an armload of prime steaks that he had lifted from his daughter's chest freezer, not caring that she had five children to feed.

"I come here all da time, you know me. I'll bring da rest of da money right back," a sickly-looking woman was saying, trying to plead her case. Mack had to laugh. He wished he had a bag of dope every time he heard someone say, "I'll bring da money right back," or "I'll pay you when I get my check dis week." He would be the number one kingpin in New York.

"I don't know you, and even if I did, dis ain't no motherfucking credit bureau," Mack responded as Flip nudged the lady out the door with the butt of his gun. The lady went back toward the line and started talking to another girl who had an almost brand new DVD player, trying to convince her that she had some money and that they should go half on what she had.

"What's up, let me holler at you for a minute," Kendew said, talking to Mack. "Ice, you and Flip hold shit down for a minute," Kendew added as he walked through another door with Mack.

Kendew went into the adjoining room and started painstakingly counting money and adding up how much coke and crack was left, plus what was needed for the weekend rush. Ice let Flip handle the customers while he took out his new .45 Gat and kept the line flowing smoothly.

An hour and a half later Ice was smoking a Newport when a fiend entered the room begging for credit. She had on a black London Fog trench coat and a pair of cheap high heels, tapping nervously on the wooden floor.

"Look at me. I'm not like the rest of these people. I work everyday. It's just dat I need a small favor until tomorrow," she stated in a dry voice.

"Bitch, I don't care if you work for da White House, you gots to raise up. You holding up da line," Flip said, getting bored with everybody's excuses. Kendew had just come out the other room and had witnessed most of the conversation.

"Hold up, how much money you got?" Kendew asked, looking the woman up and down.

"I don't have any at da moment, but I was telling your friend here, (with her putting an emphasis on friend) dat I will be back tomorrow wit da money. I'm not a crackhead, I just need something to take da stress off," she said, knowing her chances were getting better of walking away with a hit.

"Oh, I know you. I've seen you around here before," Kendew said, lying through his teeth.

"Yeah, dat's right," she added.

"Flip, give me a couple of nice sized rocks and a fifty dollar bag. I want to talk her about something," Kendew ordered. By now Ice's attention was on overdrive. Everyone in the room knew exactly what Kendew had in mind when he said, "talk to," but what made Ice curious about is why he would want this fiend when he could have any number of bad bitches with the dough he had.

Ice took a closer look at the woman and realized that she wasn't a woman at all. He spotted tiny razor bumps on his chin that were covered by her poorly done makeup job. Ice went to the hands and noticed that her hands were almost the same size as his own. He was about to say something to Kendew, but changed his mind, figuring Kendew knew what time it was way before he did.

"I'll be in da room by da bathroom. Don't disturb me unless it's something you can't take care of," Kendew stated as he and his new friend walked out the door and down the hall. Ice was thinking, *Dis nigga ain't in jail no more, so why is he getting down like dat.* The rest of the men continued business as usual, stacking that paper.

Half of the night had passed and the customers had slowed down to one or two every now and then. Everyone in the room was each drinking their own forty-ounce when Mr. Spencer walked in.

"What you need," Mack asked.

"What I need is to speak to Nathaniel," he replied back.

"Who?" Mack asked.

"He's talking about me," Ice said.

"Let me talk to you out in the hall," his parole officer said, walking back out the room.

Mack recognized him as the man who was giving them a hard time the night before.

"So what now," Ice said once he was out the room.

"I'm a fair man. You know I could have come by your house and took you back to prison if I wanted." Ice had his arms folded across his chest, just waiting for what he knew was coming. "All I'm saying is that you give me five thousand a week and a couple of bags every now and then when I bring a lady friend by," Mr. Spencer said.

"Five thousand of what?" Ice asked, not believing what he was hearing. He thought the most he would ask for was a little coke. This man was trying to get gangster on him.

"Come on, Nathaniel. I've known about this house for a while. I see how much money flows through here," he said while raising his voice.

"Dis ain't my shit, and if it was, what makes you think I would hit you wit dat much dough?" Ice asked.

"Okay, if that's the way you want it, I'm violating you right now for being in the vicinity of a known drug location, not to mention associating with felons. I'll think of some more stuff later on. Now turn around and place your hands around your back," Mr. Spencer said.

"I ain't doing shit. You gonna have to call in a whole squad to come and take me down, you pussy."

Mr. Spencer's face transformed into a mask of pure anger as he grabbed Ice by the wrist, trying to twist his arm behind his back. Flip came out and hit Mr. Spencer in the back with his shotgun as the crack heads scrambled out the way. The blow glanced off Mr. Spencer's shoulder bone as the parole officer rushed the smaller man, grabbing at the 12 gauge shotgun.

Ice was thinking, *should I just blast Mr. Spencer and then get out of town*, when Kendew came running down the hall after hearing all the commotion. He already had his own gun out, thinking it was guys from around the corner trying to set shit off. Ice could tell that Kendew was high as he raised his Glock unsteadily and took aim at the two struggling men. At the same instant as Kendew fired a way off shot, a shocked Mack appeared in the doorway saying, "What da fuck," right before a hollow point bullet caught him just above the bridge of his nose, stopping his sentence and every other one after that forever.

"Okay, you got it," Mr. Spencer said, letting go of the shotgun and raising his hands up. Kendew put the gun under his chin as Flip went to see if Mack was all right. "Wait, wait, I'm a parole officer. If you kill me, it would be just like killing a cop," he said, closing his eyes and thinking he would never see his children again. Tell him Nathaniel, tell him who I am," he added.

"You're trying to take my spot nigga, huh, answer me or half of your face will be up in da ceiling," Kendew yelled, still thinking it was one of his drug rivals. With his free hand Kendew grabbed the man's testicles and squeezed with his extra strength coke high. Ice's parole officer's face showed a look of shock and then uncontested pure agony as his whole nervous system started shutting down. He fell to his knees, unable to even scream as Kendew tried to physically separate the man's most vital organ from his body. Even when Flip started yelling that Mack was dead, Kendew's mind was still on his sadistic job of trying to kill this man in the most horrendous way possible. Kendew's cell phone suddenly went off, causing him to release the man and allowing him to breathe again.

"Ice, hold dis motherfucker down," he said as he answered the phone. "What! I'll be right there," Kendew yelled into the phone. "Ice, take care of dis piece of shit and I'll get with you later," Kendew said, not even bothering to look over at Mack as he unevenly walked out the house still saying, "Motherfuckers trying to take what's mine. It's on and popping." Ice looked at the man still crumbled up on the floor, thinking what his next move should be.

(CHAPTER FIFTY)

"It's about time, what took you so long?" Born asked in an irritated tone. Terrance had just walked in Sam's office with the expression of "what da hell!" plastered across his face.

"The cab driver acted like he didn't know where da fuck he was going," he answered back, having no idea he was going to be mixed up in some sort of homicide.

"Now dis is what everybody's going to do. Tee, you and Black Sam and the white chick are gonna roll in Sam's car to get rid of dis here nigga who's starting to stink up da place. You know where to go," Born said.

"Why do I have to go? I just want to go home and forget about everything," Sasha whined.

"Bitch, I'm just about tired of you mouth. Speak one more time without being spoken to and my man here is going to be dumping two bodies, understand?" Born said in a low voice, but with a thunderous effect. Sam told her to hush up as he tried to console the frightened woman.

"And Tee, don't let either one of them out of your sight. When you finish taking care of shit, come back here and wait for me," he said.

When the group was waiting on Born's partner, they had wrapped the body up in plastic and then in some unused carpet. Everyone helped clean up the blood except Born, who kept constant watch over Lakim, who was starting to get scared now, wondering what Born had in store for him. Sam and Terrence carried the body out to the car, throwing it in the trunk as Trina looked out for passersby, and to make sure Sasha didn't try to run away. Once they were safely in the car, the group slowly pulled off with Sam driving, and Sasha and Terrance in the back.

"They're gone," Trina stated as her high was starting to wear off.

"Get up nigga, we going for a ride," Born ordered, nudging Lakim with his own gun.

Trina drove while the men sat in the backseat with Born pointing the weapon at the man's kidneys. The group soon reached Born's whorehouse and made sure everything was okay before entering. Soon they had Lakim handcuffed to a radiator in the basement as Born pulled up a chair to talk to his kidnapped victim.

"Your boys wanted to play, so now you're playing with a top notch nigga. From what I hear, your little crew rolling. We gonna see how much dough they cough up to get your skinny ass back," he stated as he laughed in Lakim's face.

Lakim breathed a sigh of relief, knowing that they weren't planning on murdering him just yet. His mind was rapidly thinking of a way out or at least how to escape.

"Listen closely. If you fuck dis up, you gonna go back to your peoples looking like the elephant man. You know what I mean?" Born asked. Lakim shook his head up and down. "You gonna call your boy Rizz and tell him dat dem niggas you been having beef wit snatched you up. We want one hundred thousand dollars in a duffel bag. Oh yeah, and tell 'em to throw in a couple of those bricks of dat good shit. They are to make da drop in the back of People of Peace Baptist church at 3 o'clock sharp. If anything jumps off, expect to have maggots crawling out your ass by morning. Now repeat everything I said," Born demanded.

Lakim did as he was told and then repeated the same thing to Rizz after Born dialed the number.

"You did good," Born said, lightly tapping Lakim's cheek while smiling. "I feel like celebrating."

"How about letting me have a little something since I've been through so much today?" Trina asked.

"Why not, you held your own. I didn't know you could chop up a motherfucker like dat," he said as he pulled out a hundred dollar bag of coke. Born smoked a couple of cigarettes as Trina did her thing.

"I'll be right back," Born said as he went upstairs. He told Bigger to clear out the remaining three girls and get ready to leave with him. He then went back downstairs and gave Trina a cordless phone saying, "I'm about to leave, but Bigger is gonna be upstairs watching out," he lied. "Don't go upstairs for any reason. Even if da house is on fire, throw a cup of water on it. Second, do not answer da phone. When I call I will let the phone ring once and then I will call you back. Dat's how you will know it's me. I'll be back shortly. Just stay put. Got it?" He asked.

"Okay, okay, I'm not stupid," Trina said. Born double checked Lakim's handcuffs and then let Trina see him put the only key in his pocket.

Twenty minutes after Born had left, Trina went upstairs to see what she could get from the bar. "I know he didn't leave Bigger up here," Trina said to herself when she saw that the upstairs house was completely empty. She found a bottle of special Hennessy Reserve, some cups, and ice. She headed back down to the basement, turning on the radio before relaxing.

"Excuse me, what's your name again?" Lakim asked.

"Trina, why?" She responded.

"I was just wondering if I could have a drink? What could it hurt?" He said. Trina fixed a double shot as he said, "Thank you," trying to throw on the charm.

Ten minutes later Lakim asked, "What you think your boyfriend's gonna do when he gets da money from my peoples?"

"What da fuck you talking about?" She asked.

"I'm saying he's not going to take a chance bouncing wit you with dat loot, especially since you're going to be wanted for murder real soon."

"Who's gonna tell who did what in dat office? Not you. You might be joining your punk ass friend like he said," Trina spat out.

"You forgot about dat white bitch dat you pounded on. First chance she gets, she's going to holler at every cop in Queens and make sure you get blamed. If your boyfriend was to get caught up for some reason all he'd have to say is dat he didn't lay a finger on the victim, it was all your doing."

"If you know so much, how come you tied da fuck up?" Trina asked, walking and standing over him. Lakim braced himself, expecting a kick from the angry woman who was obviously sky high.

"I'm just saying dat your boyfriend thinks dat he's so smart, but he's not. He didn't even check my pockets. Go ahead and look," he said, knowing that she would.

Trina searched both pockets and found knots of money in them. Her eyes grew wide when she started counting bill after bill of hundreds of the Big Head Franklins.

"So what? Dis means we got a little more of your dough, so what," Trina said, still thinking about what he said about the white girl who she knew would definitely snitch on her first chance she got.

"I'm gonna keep it real wit you, your boyfriend ain't gonna make it back. If he did get dat money, do you think dat he's gonna actually take da chance to come back here and scoop you up? I've seen the way he talks to you. He's all about himself." By now Trina was drinking straight out the bottle absorbing everything that Lakim was telling her.

"So I should just leave and say fuck him and da money?" She asked.

"I think you should look out for yourself for a change. You let me go, and I can personally take you to a hundred thousand dollars of my own, and a brick or two," he said, watching the look on Trina's face and knowing her greed would be her eventual downfall.

"How do I even know you holding dat much?" She asked.

"Listen, paper comes and goes. I can easily make dat back in a week. Why lie and risk my life over it? I know you bout it, bout it. I peeped da way you got down earlier on," he stated, gassing her up.

Just then an idea popped into Trina's head as she picked up the phone and began dialing a number. "Supreme, what's up? Dis is Trina. No, fuck dat other small time shit, I'm talking about major figures. I need you to get over here right away." Trina hung up, anxiously waiting for Preme's arrival. Lakim was hoping that the guy Trina had just called was as dumb and greedy as she was.

CHAPTER FIFTY-ONE

Ice was busy clearing out the house with the remaining crack heads, telling everybody that shop was closed for the rest of the night. After a few grumblings and "I ain't coming back here no more," the house was finally empty. Flip was outraged that a stray bullet had caught his partner, so he started stomping on Mr. Spencer's head saying, "I'm gonna kill you motherfucker!"

"Yo, let's take him out to da back and decide how we wanna handle dis," Ice said. They both roughly snatched the man to his feet with him pleading that it was all a big misunderstanding. The battered man was half dragged toward the back of the house where tall trees concealed the men's movements. Flip had taken Mr. Spencer's state issued snub nose .38 revolver off of him and held his beloved sawed-off shotgun in the other hand.

"Get on your knees," Flip ordered as he kicked the man in the face, who was already half bending down holding his stomach.

"Nathaniel, I didn't mean nothing by what I said. You know I wouldn't do that," he said through swollen eyes.

"Shut da fuck up, you trick ass nigger. You call me Nathaniel one more time, I'm gonna have my man pound on you some more," Ice said.

"I'm so sorry, what do you want me to call you?"

"Ice, nigga," he said.

"Okay, Ice. I didn't mean no harm. Please just let me go and I could take care of that guy in the house so nobody will know you was involved," the parole office stated.

"You're talking too much," Flip yelled as he swung the shotgun, hitting the man over the eye and creating a deep gash causing blood to flow freely.

"Oh, dear God. I didn't mean no harm. Please, tell him Nathaniel, I mean Ice. I can fix everything up," he begged.

"Fuck all dis shit, this dude history," Flip said while cocking a shell into the shotgun's chamber.

Mr. Spencer crawled over to Flip grabbing onto his legs and screaming, "Please don't kill me. I'm sorry. I'll never come back here again. Nathaniel, please don't let him kill me."

"Shut up, you pig," Flip said as he tried to kick the man off of him, who held on for dear life.

Flip was trying to aim the weapon at the man's head when all of a sudden Mr. Spencer grabbed both of Flip's pant legs, pushing him backward with his head. It took a second for it to register to Ice what was going on as he took aim at the man's exposed back. Flip had one of his legs slightly raised ready to kick him again when he was thrown off balance. A split second later Flip fell full force backward, the back of his head hitting the solid brick back door stoop. Ice heard a sickening crunch upon impact as he took a wild shot that obviously missed its mark as Mr. Spencer desperately scrambled to his feet. With amazing speed, Mr. Spencer was halfway over the backyard fence when Ice took another shot. He heard a scream as the fleeing man fell over the other side of the fence and kept running.

Ice could hear Mr. Spencer shouting, "Help me! Help me!" at the top of his lungs, causing dogs to bark and neighbors' lights to flicker on. Ice went back over to Flip and knew right away that he was deceased by the frozen look of surprise on his face. Ice couldn't see any blood yet, but he wasn't waiting to find out as he took off down the block. He slowed his pace to a steady walk, fearing somebody might describe him as the man they had seen running away.

Ten blocks away Ice stopped by a twenty-four hour window and bought a double deuce of old English to relax his nerves. Street crime wasn't a big thing to him, but Mr. Spencer knew his full government name, where he lived, among other important things. There was a slim chance that he wouldn't say anything, because there would be too many questions for him to answer that would definitely raise suspicion on his part.

Ice flagged down a gypsy cab, jumping in and trying to get away from the area as quickly as possible, thinking police were going to start popping up any minute. *I should have stuck to sticking niggers up. Fucking around in da drug game you come in contact with too many shady people*, he thought while riding in the back of the cab, guzzling his malt liquor. He half expected to see the DTs at the house when he pulled up, but all he saw was Kendew's car.

Ice walked in the house breathing regular now and saw Kendew puffing on a woolie, (crack and weed mixed) sitting on the sofa messing around with some guns.

"Ice, I was just about to call you. We gotta handle some shit tonight," he said, putting the clip back into the Glock.

"What's up?" Ice asked.

"Niggers snatched up one of my nephew's close peoples. We think it's dem boys from Stone Hedge's Houses. They talking about they want a hundred thousand plus a couple of bricks."

"Word," Ice said.

"Yeah, they gonna get something all right, but it's not gonna be what they expecting," Kendew replied with a chuckle. "So what's up with the spot?" He asked Ice.

The way Kendew was asking the question it was as if everything was normal, like nothing jumped off with Mr. Spencer and Mack taking one to the head. *Dat nigga must have been so high dat he forgot or something,* Ice thought, so he said, "Everything all right." *Dis nigga a loose cannon,* Ice thought to himself. *Soon as I touch dat bitch ass nigga Rizz, I'm outta here doing my own thing,"* Ice mumbled to himself.

Soon both men heard a car's horn beep twice as they looked out the window. A tinted Yukon Denali had just pulled up.

"Dat's my nephew I've been telling you about who put me on when I first touched da streets," Kendew said.

CHAPTER FIFTY-TWO

"What we heading to Jezebel's for?" Bigger asked, looking as if he was lost in space.

"Dat black motherfucker got me mixed up in his bullshit, now I'm gonna play my hand like a royal flush," Born stated.

"What you mean?" He asked.

"Bigger, just drive and stop bothering me with silly ass questions."

They arrived at Jezebel's and Born said to his driver to park around in the V.I.P. section. They went inside the club and it was just beginning to fill up with dancers and customers alike. On their way to the office, Born noticed Honey, a flawless, light brown, overdeveloped bartender, whom he briefly kicked his game on. She was eighteen and slightly dimwitted, just the way Born liked his girls starting out. He planned to mold her to suit his needs, gradually schooling her on how to make the most money from her feminine assets. She smiled when she saw Born as he came over, giving her a friendly hug.

"What's up, shorty? I see you still keeping it tight," he replied, looking slowly over her five feet, four inch frame.

She blushed and said, "Thank you. Are we still going out to dinner like you promised?" Honey asked, staring at the sparkling three-carat blue diamond dangling from Born's ear.

"Of course, I'm just waiting on my tailor to finish making these one-of-a-kind dresses for you. I got him putting together three so you can pick out one before we go to dinner," he said, knowing she would believe his lie.

"For real, but you don't even know my measurements," she responded back.

"Come on, shorty, you know me better den dat. Since da first day I peeped you, I've known exactly what your size was. It's some sort of gift I have with pretty girls. So far I haven't been wrong yet. Anyway, I gotta go take care of some business with your boss. I'll holler at you a little later on," he said, giving her a peck on the forehead.

"Come on, enough with dat," Born told Bigger, who was busy drooling at the girl on stage swinging from the pole.

"It's me," Born said after knocking on Sam's office door. Terrance cracked it open to make sure it was him as he let them in. Black Sam was sitting in his chair in a sweat soaked shirt with Sasha looking distraught as ever.

"You took care of dat?" Born asked Terrance.

"Yeah, his ass is just a memory right now."

"Cool, now I can get down to some serious business," he stated, looking over at Sam who was wondering what was coming next. Born pulled up a chair and told Sam he wanted to look over the legal documents they discussed a week ago.

"I don't have dem right now. My lawyer's still adding da finishing touches. I'll get dem to you first thing in da morning," Sam stated, knowing he had already planned to leave town the first chance he got.

"What you think, I got a flower pot for a head or something? I suggest you produce dem papers or I'm gonna have my man over here have you eating your breakfast through a straw," Born replied, leaning over dangerously close to Sam.

"No, I meant da lawyers are drawing up some new papers," he said.

"Can I go to da bathroom? I've been holding it for two hours now," Sasha whined.

"What da fuck you talking about?" Born asked.

"Yeah, she's been crying about going all night," Terrance added.

Meanwhile Sam had moved the carpet from beneath his desk and took out some documents that were hidden in his floor safe. At this point he didn't care who knew where his safe was. Things had gotten way out of hand in the last four hours. Born took the papers and quickly scanned them, finding exactly what he was looking for.

"Now you see da section where it says dat I've got ten percent interest in Jezebel's? We gonna change dat to sixty percent of da holdings," Born stated, pushing the papers across the table.

"What! Dat would mean dat you would have more ownership den me. Why are doing dis to me? I just can't do it," Black Sam replied, gathering a little heart.

Born just looked at the man and said, "Bigger." Bigger slipped on some brass knuckles as he walked over to where the men were conducting business, still smiling as he slapped Sam across the face with an open palm. Sam fell back in his chair, grabbing his bruised cheek and looking over at Born as if to say, "Why?"

"I gotta go pee," Sasha said, wanting to get out of the room as quickly as possible.

"Okay, here's what we gonna do," Born said. "Terrance, you take her to da bathroom and don't let her out your sight. Bigger, I'm going to finish kicking it with my soon-to-be new recruit. I want you to get Sam over here to sign those papers any way you can," Born stated as he showed Bigger all the places the man was supposed to sign to make the transaction legal. Born, Terrance, and Sasha left the room, leaving a smiling Bigger alone with the frightened Sam.

"Honey, let me holler at you for a minute," Born said to her.

"I have a break in thirty minutes. Can you wait until den?" She asked while pouring a customer a drink.

"I'm kinda stressed for time. Tell your coworker you wanna take your break right now," he said, not taking no for an answer.

Honey did as she was told, and thinking he was going to cut her off or something, she said, "Is everything all right?"

"Everything's cool. We can kick it in my ride. You know I hate trying to talk over dis loud ass music," he said while grabbing her hand and leading her outside to where his car was parked.

"Hurry da fuck up," Terrance said to Sasha as she went into the bathroom. *Dat bitch must be taking a shit,* Terrance said to himself as he noticed ten minutes had passed since she first went in.

"Why you sweating the women's bathroom like dat?" A female voice asked out of nowhere.

"What did you say?" He asked, turning around to face a dark-skinned stripper with her hands on her hips.

"Da way you posted up by da girls' bathroom, you acting like you trying to get a free peep of a bitch trying to have some privacy. We don't get down like dat up in here," she said.

"Bitch, mind your motherfucking business. What you need to do is get your black ass back on stage and make dat money instead of being all up in mines," he spat back.

"Nigger, you don't know me like dat. I'll have you thrown out and stomped da fuck out," she replied back, pointing a finger in his face.

Terrance grabbed her by the throat, choking the stunned woman and saying, "Bitch, who da fuck you think you trying to raise up on like dat!" He applied more pressure to the girl's neck as she tried to break his grip. The struggling woman's eyes started to water and she was on the verge of passing out when Terrence spotted Sasha heading toward the front door.

"Dat fucking sneaky, white bitch must have slipped out when I had my back turned," he said as he threw the dancer against the wall and started after Sam's girlfriend, who had just went out the door.

"So are you going to sign dem papers or what?" Bigger asked, rubbing the brass knuckles.

"Why ain't Sasha and your friend back yet? What is he doing to her?" Sam asked, more concerned with his trophy piece girlfriend's safety than his own.

"What you need to do is stop worrying about shorty and sign dem papers before Born get back," Bigger said, wanting to have Sam sign before Born gpt back so he could be impressed.

"I'm not doing shit until Sasha gets back!" Sam said, standing up now.

For the first time Bigger realized that Black Sam was about the same height as him, outweighing him by probably about forty pounds. Bigger struck out lightning fast, catching Sam in the jaw and loosening all of the man's bottom row teeth. Sam fell face first on his desk, spraying the papers with blood.

"Now, hot shot, you still wanna talk da good shit or what," Bigger said, walking around the desk and grabbing the man by the collar. "Nigger, you hear me talking to you?" He asked as he punched Sam in the spine, causing him to howl like a wounded animal.

In an instant Sam had grabbed a large letter opener and plunged it into Bigger's shoulder. Sam raised the weapon to strike again as Bigger raised his hand in a defensive position. The letter opener turned dagger went straight through Bigger's hand, causing Bigger to rush toward his attacker. Both men fell to the floor as Sam kept saying, "All I wanted was to see Sasha." Bigger was a little quicker and in better shape than his opponent, so he turned him around bear hugging him, putting more pressure on his already damaged spine. Sam yelled out in extreme pain as he plunged both of his thick thumbs into the Bigger's delicate eye sockets.

"When I catch you, I'm gonna beat your motherfucking skinny ass," Terrence shouted after the fleeing Sasha.

The terrified woman broke a heel, and before she could regain her balance Terrance had her by the hair dragging her on the sidewalk. People passing by just assumed it was a lover's quarrel and knew better than to intervene, especially living in New York City. Terrance was just about to backhand the screaming woman when an unmarked police car pulled up and the officer asked, "What the hell is going on here?"

As soon as they saw the pure white woman being viciously brutalized in their eyes, they quickly jumped out with guns drawn, ordering Terrance to lay face down on the concrete. One undercover police officer was handcuffing their soon-to-be prisoner, while the other one was calling for backup. Sasha was shouting that she was kidnapped, they killed a couple of people, and they were probably murdering her boyfriend right now as they speak. Sasha was still pointing in the direction of the club when the police put her in the car for her to show them exactly what she was hyperventilating about.

"Nah, shorty, I'm not asking you to be a hooker, Born said. "I have way too much respect for you. Da only thing you gonna be selling to these trick ass motherfuckers is conversation. You might have to get undressed every now and den to get dem to dig deeper into their pockets, but dat's it," Born said, spitting out his game.

"Dat's it?" Honey innocently asked.

"Yeah, I'm gonna be there every step of da way making sure things run smoothly with my baby," he said, looking into her big brown eyes.

"What da fuck is going on?" Born asked, getting out of his car and seeing what seemed like the whole police force declaring war on Jezebel's. Born heard a female voice say, "Dats him, too," right before he was tackled to the ground and unmercifully beaten with billy clubs and steel flashlights. From the beating he took, Born's short term memory would be affected, causing him to sometimes forget to put on socks, brush his teeth, among other mundane things.

Everybody in the club scrambled out the way as the N.Y.P.D. entered the nightspot, knocking over tables and pushing people to the side. Various narcotics were thrown under the tables or kicked to the side. The police kicked down the door to Black Sam's office and stood shocked at what they saw. Bigger was leaning against the wall with both eyes torn from his sockets, holding a crumpled up piece of paper in his bloody hands. Black Sam was laying face up with what appeared to be a letter opener grotesquely protruding from his neck.

(CHAPTER FIFTY-THREE)

"So you're da nigga talking dat good shit, huh?" Supreme asked, standing over Lakim smiling.

"Like I was telling shorty here, I got da money back at my place," he said.

"How much you talking about?"

"One hundred thousand and change, not to mention some good coke," Lakim threw in, knowing Preme was an obvious smoker by the looks of his shabby wears.

"If you're gonna make a move, it better be now, cause dat nigger supposed to be back any minute," Trina replied, knowing it would be a death sentence for her if Born was to come back.

"Fuck him, I got something for his punk ass!" Preme spat out, waving a gun around. "And as for you, if you try any clown shit, think about dis big ass gat tearing into dat big head of yours," Preme added.

Preme and Trina searched the basement for something to pry loose the radiator that was secured on some old wood planks. They successfully found a rusted pipe which they put to use right away. With the money and drugs being the motivation, they quickly freed their hostage.

"Let's go. We don't have all night," Preme stated as he pushed Lakim up the stairs with Trina trailing closely behind. On the way out the door Trina grabbed a couple of bottles of Cristal champagne. They all got in Preme's 4Runner and took off toward Lakim's house.

Back at Kendew's placc, Rizz got out of the passenger side and walked up to the door opening it.

"Dis is my nephew Rizz," Kendew said.

"Me and Ice go way back, ain't dat right playboy?" Rizz said in a mocking tone of voice.

Ice asked, "What's up," but his eyes held a totally different meaning behind them.

"Okay, you got da money?" Kendew asked Rizz.

"Yeah, but we got to stop by Lakim's crib and pick up another brick. All I had was one left," he answered.

"It's not like they gonna get a chance to use it, anyway. Who you rolling wit?" Kendew asked.

"I got Mia pushing my shit. I didn't want to take a chance with me not having a license an all.

"Let's get going. Ice, you ride with me," Kendew said, taking the bag filled with cash from his nephew.

Everyone then went outside and proceeded to head to Lakim's house to get the rest of the drugs. Kendew was saying something to Ice, but he couldn't hear a word because he was lost deep in thought of what he had just found out. Rizz and Kendew had built up a lucrative drug empire from the drugs Rizz had stolen from him a while back. He knew that the coke that Rizz first started off with was long gone, but it had given Rizz the foundation for power and a steady clientele. *Basically all dis shit belongs to me*, Ice reasoned, staring at Rizz's brand new SUV with the expensive glossy finish that was driving ahead of them.

"Oh shit, ain't da Lakim crossing da street?" Rizz shouted to Mia. Mia was looking, but all she was concerned with was the man who was following closely behind him.

"Supreme!" Mia yelled as all her pent up rage and pain transferred to her gas foot and she accelerated toward the three people crossing the street.

Mia gunned her four thousand pound steel weapon toward Preme. The vehicle's driver's side fender slightly hit Preme and Lakim, sending them flying onto their backs. Trina jumped on the sidewalk yelling for Supreme to get up as Mia made a U-turn to finish off her job. Preme had just enough time to shakily rise to his feet as the jeep started heading toward him again. He let off two shots blasting through the windshield as the jeep hit him full force in the body, crushing major vital organs. Preme died moments later choking on his own blood, never knowing the fact that his former girlfriend was the cause of his ultimate demise.

Mia had also unknowingly run over Lakim's legs, breaking every bone beyond repair, and causing them to be amputated later on that night. Meanwhile Trina scurried away into the darkness as Mia sped off knowing that she had finally fulfilled her fantasy.

"What da fuck did dat bitch just do?" Kendew asked, not expecting an answer.

Ice didn't care what just went down. He was thinking about the bag filled with money that really belonged to him. Rizz most likely told his uncle how he got started, and here was Kendew trying to play him by putting him in some crack house. Ice pulled out the gun that Kendew had given to him as a present and emptied the whole clip into the man's chest and head. As blood and brain matter sprayed the interior of the luxury car, Ice then pushed Kendew out the door and slid over to the driver's side, peeling off down the street. Ice patted the bag, smiling and ready to hop on I-95 to bounce out of New York forever. He hadn't decided just yet where he wanted to go, but he knew he had to break out.

"Damn, I left my I.D. back at da house," Ice said out loud as he turned the corner and headed back in the direction of Kendew's house.

"Mia, Mia, take me to a hospital now," Rizz was saying. He had taken two bullets to the chest when Preme had shot through the windshield. Mia looked over at Rizz and thought, *Dis nigga a gonna.*

"Hold up baby, I'm on my way. Just hold tight," Mia said.

"Hurry up, drive faster," he added. Moments later Mia pulled up next to her Jaguar that was parked where she had left it earlier.

Mia jumped out as Rizz said, "What you doing, where you going? I need to get to a doctor!"

"Fuck you nigga. You on your own," she spat out as she slammed the door shut. She quickly got behind the wheel of her car and screeched off, laughing to herself.

(CHAPTER FIFTY-FOUR)

Mia drove to her secret apartment and snatched up all her cash that she had tucked away. She had been planning for months for this day when it would be a good time for her to leave. *What better time than when Rizz just got blasted. He's probably dead now just like Preme*, she thought. She was just about to jump on the highway when she remembered that she left an extra twenty-five thousand in her other purse that Kendew had given her. The purse was at Rizz's house, so she started heading back to get the money.

A little while later Mia was cautiously opening the door to the darkened apartment. She closed the door and flicked on the living room lights. Mia lost her breath when she saw Rizz sitting in a chair pointing a gun straight at her. Unknowing to Mia, Rizz was wearing a bulletproof vest. The gunshots only knocked the wind out of him, causing minor, deep bruising.

"What's da matter?" Rizz asked, looking intently at his supposed to be wifey.

"Baby, I know what you thinking. I didn't leave you. I was just changing cars just in case somebody gave the police a description of the whip. I was just looking out for you," she said, trying to see if her lie had any effect on him.

"What about when you said fuck me, I'm on my own. Huh? Answer dat," he said in a quiet voice.

"No, no, you must have misunderstood me. You know I would never flip on you like dat. You done too much for me. You know I love you," she said, walking toward him.

"Nah bitch, all you love is dat dough I've been blessing you wit. You know what, you not even worth a bullet," he said, getting up and turning his back toward her.

Mia whispered, "Thank God," as Rizz turned back around and shot her in the head, causing her two-thousand-dollar weave to slightly come apart.

"I lied, bitch!" He said, looking down at Mia who was flopping around like a fish out of water. He knelt down, putting the gun to her heart, and ended her suffering that had been going on long before he even met her.

Back at Kendew's, Ice ran inside the house and found his prison I.D. card on the table.

"Fuck all da clothes, I'll cop some new ones," Ice said while running out back to Kendew's Audi TT.

Ice had his hand on the car's door, ready to get in, when a bullet ripped into his shoulder, causing him to crash into the side of the car. Ice didn't know who shot him, but his instincts caused him to jump into the car and try to drive off. He was expecting more gunfire when he slid behind the wheel, but none came.

He drove maybe ten feet when his back windshield blew out, causing him to crash into several parked cars. Ice hopped out with the bag of money when he found himself being surrounded by uniformed officers telling him to "Drop it!" Ice weakly raised his hands in surrender. A couple of tazer guns on full power electrified his whole body. Ice slumped to the pavement still clutching the money as the police rushed over and pounced on him. They retrieved the bag and handcuffed him as he lay damn near bleeding to death in the middle of the street. The last thing Ice heard was the strangely familiar voice of his parole officer Mr. Spencer saying, "Boy, this time you're going away forever," as he slipped into unconsciousness.

About the Author

Dejon was born in California, but raised in Queens, NY, where he started writing short stories for various school newspapers. Dejon is in the process of producing a documentary film, which is titled *Rules Of Engagement For The Inner City*. Currently, he is working on two more novels, *Ice Cold Vengence* (the sequel to *Ice Cream For Freaks*) and *My Skin is My Sin*.

PREVIEW
My Skin Is My Sin
by DEJON

"**D**amn baby, why don't you lift up dat short skirt so I can see dat fine yellow pussy of yours?" Mr. Frost asked in a low but horny voice.

"I don't know, what if someone wuz to come and catch us? I wouldn't want you to get in trouble and lose your job over me," Moet replied, shyly batting perfectly shaped almond eyes.

Mr. Eddie Frost was a short, stocky, dwarf type of man with prominent features that resembled a full-grown pug dog. What caused Mr. Frost's heart to race a just a little bit faster and his blood to rise a degree or two higher, was a young pretty teenage girl who just beginning to explore the curious world of sex. Him being the assistant principle of the local high school was the perfect breeding ground for his warped, twisted, insatiable sexual desires that his highly illegal overseas videotapes failed to provide.

"Don't worry, sweetheart, nobody never comes back here this time of day." He looked around as he lightly grabbed Moet's small waist with his thick fingers.

"Okay, I guess you're right, plus nobody would think dat we would ever be doing anything. Let me get it hard first," Moet stated, feeling a little more relaxed now as delicate fingers reached for the cheap pants suit zipper.

"Yeah dat's a very good idea, put it in your sweet mouth so it can be good and ready for your tight cunt," Mr. Frost said in hoarse whisper as he laid his hands on Moet's shoulder, guiding the bashful Moet to the stage floor so a heavy curtain could conceal their illicit act.

Nah I don't want to cum in this bitch's mouth, I got to have a piece of that soft tail Mr. Frost thought as be he pumped Moet's wet mouth as her full lips did their thing.

What Mr. Eddie Frost was totally unaware of was that Moet was really a twenty-year-old transvestite who happened to be HIV positive, and worked the Red Light District deceiving middle-aged lusting men who often got more than they bargained for. On a few occasions, some of Moet's tricks would find out his true gender during the middle of the sex act, but were too far-gone to put an end to it. After the customer would cum heavily, they would most of the time cry, screaming that they weren't gay and that this is the first time something like this has ever happened. Moet would console the whimpering, sometimes-confused men while handing them his business card, which they eagerly took.

"Yeah, motherfucker, I know you like dis," Moet spat out, his voice now taking on a more manly tone.

Mr. Frost barely had time to open his eyes when a group of females rushed the shocked man, tackling him to the hardwood floor. Before the Assistant Principle could regain his balance, Moet threw him in a dope fiend chokehold as the girls took off his pants and underwear.

"What the fuck is going on? Do you all know who I am?" Mr. Frost asked as he looked at the five females who were wearing low baseball caps and bandannas to mask their identities.

"Yeah nigga, we know who the fuck you are. You a piece of shit pervert who like to prey on young high school girls," one girl said as she stood over their victim.

"Since he likes young pussy so much let's give him a little taste," a wide-shouldered girl said while laughing as she stuffed a super absorbent period-drenched maxi pad in his mouth and tied it firmly in place with a pair of dirty, stained, pink panties.

The Assistant Principle tried in vain to struggle free as the other girls held his arms and legs down while Moet, with the strength of a bear, held his vise like grip around his neck.

"Now let's get da real party started," a short, brown skin girl replied while pulling out a couple of cartons of large white eggs.

"Oh shit, dis nigga dick done went and got soft. Somebody get it hard again," someone called out.

"I'm not touching his nasty ass," another said with disgust.

"Fuck it! I'll do it. Hold his arm," a teenage girl shouted out.

Soon she was milking Mr. Frost's organ to its full four inches with lightening speed. A couple of seconds later, when the dick was standing straight in the air, each girl took turns smashing egg after egg on the head of the man's sensitive exposed penis. The sharp eggshells tore into his skin like his privates parts had been dragged through crushed glass.

"Let's go," the girls said as Moet punched the semiconscious man a couple times in the face.

"And we putting in the video tape on da Internet of you freaking off wit a dude," a red bone female spat out with a sly smirk as she held a tiny camcorder.

Before Pumpkin left the scene, she cruelly stomped on the man's tender genitals with her Timberland boots, thinking on how a man she trusted groped her in his office on the pretext of her so-called failing grades. The last thing the Assistant Principle heard before he fully passed out was his ex-students giggling as they fled the scene.

Later on that night, all the girls were at one of their friend's house celebrating that they finally made it through high school. After the group finished cracking up on how they finally got Mr. Frost back from all those years of chills-run-down-your-back stares and "I'm sorry" when he brushed up against you a little too long, they begin discussing their future plans.

"I'm going to move out of mom's house to an ill apartment," one girl said.

"My man wants me to move with him to D.C. where his connect is, so he won't have to travel so far," another female said while taking a sip of E&J Brandy.

"I'm going to enroll in some college where they give out all kinds of grants and loans so I can get me a hooked up ride," Fatima said, even though she dropped out of school three months earlier.

Pumpkin just sat there smoking, not responding because she had no idea what she planned to do now that she was out of school.

Soon after, about six guys arrived at the secret, illegal party bringing with them drinks, weed, and pussy on their minds. Couples soon paired up, going off to different parts in the house.

"So Pumpkin, what you planning on doing now that you squeezed your way through school?" Junior asked, playfully.

"I wish I had your skills, so they could give me a full ass scholarship," she replied back.

Junior was the school's basketball's star who had just accepted a scholarship to Georgetown University. He was six feet 2 inches, brown skin who loved his mother and basketball more than anything in the world. Most of the girls from the hood wanted to get with him, but his rigorous schedule of practicing and studying made it hard to get hold of him. He and Pumpkin met a year ago when they played a friendly game of basketball at the local playground in the dark.

Pumpkin and Junior talked for a while about everything from music videos to how he wasn't going to let any college girls trap him off. It was a well-known fact that he was destined for the NBA. Junior walked her home as they promised to keep in touch with each other no matter what.

"Pumpkin you home?" a voice called out. Pumpkin groggily awoke from her sleep and looked at her watch.

"Damn, it's 4:30," she said to herself. "I'm in my room," she answered back, recognizing her aunt's voice.

Her aunt appeared at her door holding an envelope. "You have some mail," she stated while handing her the letter.

Pumpkin looked at the handwriting and knew right away it was from her grandmother who was living in Muddy Waters, Mississippi. She quickly tore open the letter. Her grandmother was telling her how proud she was of her for graduating from school, especially since all she's been through the last couple of months. She told her how she hopes she attends college like her cousin, and that she's doing fine despite her arthritis. The second page was wrapped around a crisp hundred-dollar bill. In the corner of the envelope were a thin, gold chain and a locket that said, "Best Granddaughter."

Pumpkin put on the chain and read the letter several times before putting it under her mattress. She loved her grandmother so much. This was the only gift anybody gave her. She couldn't blame them. Everybody was going through one problem or another. Pumpkin had a big day planned for tomorrow. She ate some fried chicken, watched a couple of movies, and went back to sleep.

****

Weeks later after Mr. Eddie Frost's ordeal, he developed a painful urinary tract infection, causing his balls to balloon to three times their normal size. When his wife finally convinced him to go the hospital, x-rays revealed that he had a few jagged pieces of eggshells lodged firmly in his urethra. The next day a specialist in urology would operate, splitting Mr. Frost's penis down the middle like a polish sausage and roughly plucking out the shells with a pair of surgical tweezers. Later on after his wounds healed, Mr. Frost would get a reasonable erection maybe twenty times a year if he was lucky.

STREET FICTION FROM

Q-BORO
BOOKS

STREETS OF NEW YORK, V. 1
14.95
ISBN 0975306618

After the mother of his child is brutally murdered, Promise takes on the tasks and responsibility of trying to raise his three-year old daughter by himself. Alone and in the tough position of being a single dad, Promise is forced to choose between being loyal to his crew with their life of crime and being true to his daughter.

BRAZEN
14.95
ISBN 0975306650

Hidden behind the blue wall of silence are the drugs, murders and blood money. This gritty urban tale pulls you into the depths of police corruption in the drug-infested ghettos of New York City. Entangled within is an extramarital sexual escapade that turns violently tragic for everyone involved.

KING OF SPADES
14.95
ISBN 0975306642

Kiniesha Gayle's novel is a gripping tale of one man's struggle to break away from his sordid past, and a mysterious woman's search for justice which lands everyone in her path on deadly ground. Will Chin remain the King of Spades or will he fall prey to the Queen of Hearts?

MONEY POWER RESPECT
14.95
ISBN 0975306677

My theory in life is, "the more money you hold, the more respect you get." As a man, I should've learned from my mistakes and done right with my life. But the thing is, I got the devil, disguised as my best friend Kinko, addressing me in one ear, and then I got my family and my girl preaching to me in the next ear.

MORE STREET FICTION FROM

Q-BORO BOOKS

ICE CREAM FOR FREAKS
14.95
ISBN 0975306693

In the tradition of cult literary icon Donald Goines, Ice Cream For Freaks is written with a realness that accurately depicts the bleak conditions of the story's urban backdrop. Ice, has a reputation of being a brutal and daring stick-up kid, but when he lands in an upstate New York prison, both his reputation and his manhood come into question after an unforgettable and terrorizing encounter in his cell with a prison homo thug.

IT'S ON AND POPPIN'
14.95
ISBN 0977624757

Dee Dee is as sassy, and cute as they come, but she has two overprotective brothers who have clout in the Memphis streets.

The game is dominated by thugs until Dee Dee hits the scene. This action-packed, grimey street classic shows how Dee Dee gets it poppin' in the Memphis streets.

GHETTO HEAVEN
14.95
ISBN 0975306642

Toni is young and sexy with an abusive gangster boyfriend. She struggles as a Brooklyn stripper. Eventually she befriends a rich pretty boy from Long Island. When he meets Toni, their lives change, as they teach each other how to live and grow, and school each other about the opposite worlds they live in and come from.

PAPER CHASERS
14.95
ISBN 097762479X

The east coast version of Boyz-N-The-Hood, Paper Chasers is the Essence Magazine best seller set in Queens, New York during the summer of 1991, a time when the crack epidemic was wreaking havoc on just about every major city in America. It follows the lives of The Fourth Crew, a close-knit group of young hustlers hailing from middle-class homes and a middle-class neighborhood, ultimately proving that the repercussions of the fast money lifestyle is not limited to the projects and the ghetto.

GROWN & SEXY FICTION FROM

Q-BORO BOOKS

WEDNESDAY'S WOES
14.95
ISBN 097695432X

" Wednesday's Child is full of woe. " Zoe Knight certainly wouldn't argue with that. She's got more woes than the law should allow. With an ex-husband that she despises and can no longer trust, a rebellious teenage son with a hoochie-in-training girlfriend, the death of a loved one, and sisters who have lost their minds, can anything else go wrong?

MY WOMAN, HIS WIFE
$14.95
ISBN 0975306626

For most couples, inviting someone into their bedroom is totally out of the question. Any normal woman would flip if her man even thought about trying a threesome with another woman. Jasmine is that woman, and more. It's not until her husband James pressures her into having a threesome that their once "happy" lives get turned into nothing but drama.

THE LAST TEMPTATION
$14.95
ISBN 0975306685

Traci Johnson leading the way has found the new man of her dreams and they are anxious to move their relationship to the next level. But unbeknownst to Jordan, someone else is planning Traci's next move -- her irresistible ex-boyfriend, Solomon Jackson, who thugged his way back into her heart.

THE AFTERMATH - JANUARY 2006
$14.95
ISBN 0977624749

If you thought having a threesome could wreak havoc on a relationship, Monica from My Woman His Wife is back to show you why even the mere thought of a ménage a trios with your spouse and an outsider should never enter your imagination.

CHILLS AND THRILLS FROM

Q-BORO
B O O K S

DEMON HUNTER - *DEMON HUNTER SERIES BOOK ONE*
14.95
ISBN 0976954303

Demon Hunter is the epic tale of Elijah Garland, a young man who has come to the decision that his life was never meant to be. Convinced that love and happiness will only be found in death, he ends his life. But when he awakens 3 days later, framed for murder, he finds out that his life has only just begun and that there was a reason for all of the tragic events in his life. He learns that there is a single being directly responsible for all of his misery- a misery designed to strengthen his soul for the ultimate goal of his true reason for being.

SACRIFICE - *DEMON HUNTER SERIES BOOK TWO*
$14.95
COMING IN 2006

Gabriel's gift has not come without a price. The love Elijah has found in Ebonee Lane will be paid for in blood. The dire duties now placed upon Elijah's shoulders as a Protector of the Faithful will lead him to make a choice. He knows that evil seeks him out at every turn, and more importantly, he knows that Ebonee Lane and their newfound love can only be a hindrance to his cause.

OBSESSION 101
14.95
ISBN 0976954311

Someone raped California university professor Rashawn Ams.

Left pregnant and refusing to report the attack to the police, Rashawn finds herself confused about what she should do next, so she does the only thing she thinks she can do: she hides the rape from her friends and family, and flees town to give birth to her son and repair her life after confiding in her psychiatrist. Later, when the man she believes raped her is killed, she is relieved and feels that she can return to her life, her town, her classroom.

After her return the university, she finds herself the target of an intrusive secret admirer, bringing back frightening memories of the attack.

Three important men are bound by lust, greed, and an obsessive appetite for one woman. The problem is, one of these men is a killer.

MORE SIZZLING FICTION FROM

Q-BORO
BOOKS

ORDER FORM

Q-Boro Books
165-41A Baisley Blvd., Ste. 4 Mall # 1
Jamaica, NY 11434
718-977-0885

Ship to:_____

Registration #(if applicable):_____

Street Address:_____

City:_____State:_____Zip:_____

Phone:

ISBN	Title	Price Each	Qty	Total
		$14.95		
		$14.95		
		$14.95		
		$14.95		
		$14.95		
		$14.95		
		$14.95		
		$14.95		
		$14.95		
		$14.95		
		$14.95		
			Subtotal:	
			Shipping:	
			Total:	

Make check or money order payable to:

Q-Boro Books
165-41A Baisley Blvd., Ste. 4 Mall # 1
Jamaica, NY 11434

LOOK FOR MORE HOT TITLES FROM

Q-BORO
BOOKS

TALK TO THE HAND - JANUARY 2006
14.95
ISBN 0977624765

Nedra Harris, a twenty-three year old business executive, has experienced her share of heartache in her quest to find a soul mate. Just when she's about to give up on love, she runs into Simeon Mathews, a gentleman she met in college years earlier. She remember s his warm smile and charming nature, but soon finds out that Simeon possesses a dark side that will eventually make her life a living hell.

SOMEONE ELSE'S PUDDIN' - DECEMBER 2005
14.95
ISBN 0977624706

While hairstylist Melody Pullman has no problem keeping clients in her chair, she can't keep her bills paid once her crack-addicted husband Big Steve steps through a revolving door leading in and out of prison. She soon finds what seems to be a sexual and financial solution when she becomes involved with her long-time client's husband, Larry.

DETROIT SLIM/ TIME OUT - MARCH 2006
$14.95

In Detroit Slim, Frazier puts the reader in the driver's seat with a "Choose-Your-Own-Adventure" saga about a club heist gone wrong. The ending and progression of the story changes depending on the path the reader chooses.

WALK LIKE A MAN
14.95
ISBN 0977624781

Attention Writers:

Writers looking to get their books published can view our submission guidelines by visiting our website at:
www.QBOROBOOKS.com

Or by mailing us at:
Q-Boro Books
Attn: Submissions
165-41A Baisley Blvd., Suite 4. Mall #1
Jamaica, New York 11434

or email to: candace@qborobooks.com

*** **By submitting your work to Q-Boro Books, you agree to hold Q-Boro Books harmless and not liable for publishing similar works as yours that we may already be considering or may consider in the future.** ***

Submission Guidelines:

1. Please ONLY submit the first three chapters of the manuscript. All chapters should be double spaced and legible.
2. Include a summary of what the story is about and also include what it is that you intend for the reader to gain after they have read your story. (Please limit this to one single spaced page)
3. Include a self addressed stamped envelope if you would like to receive a letter of receipt.
4. Submissions / manuscripts will not be returned.
5. Do not contact us for status updates. If we are interested in receiving your full manuscript, we will contact you.

Due to the heavy volume of submissions, if these requirements are not followed, we will not be able to process your submission.

Q-BORO
BOOKS

Q BORO BOOKS
PRESENTS

It's On and Poppin

AL HATTER

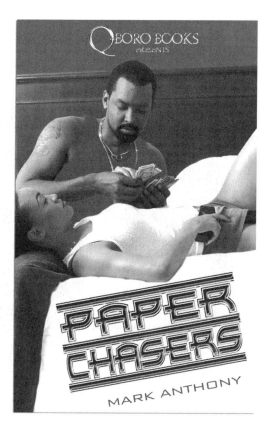

COMING SOON FROM

JANUARY 2006

COMING SOON FROM